SISTINE HERESY

Acclaim for *Sistine Heresy*

"Justine Saracen's *Sistine Heresy* is a well-written and surprisingly poignant romp through Renaissance Rome in the age of Michelangelo. Saracen blends fact with fantasy in writing a homoerotic history of corrupt clerics, lascivious artists, and heretical humanists. Saracen's Michelangelo is a theological rebel whose art must eventually trump his service to the Church while his homosexual longings climax in a complementary conquest. *Sistine Heresy*'s cast includes a beautiful castrato who sings and loves purely and a Borgia donna who meets her match in a female artist who cross-dresses to assist in painting the Chapel.

The Heresy title is appropriate as the book poses serious theological questions. The struggle between flesh and soul (in both aesthetic and sexual realms) recalls Browning's artists and makes explicit the erotic tension of Pater's Renaissance. A corrupt Church of philandering, power-hungry prelates is a usual suspect. Yet Saracen's characters are vivid and moving in their devotion: to iconoclastic love of God and forbidden love of man (and woman). The novel entertains and titillates while it challenges, warning of the mortal dangers of trespass in any theocracy (past or present) that polices same-sex desire."

— Professor Frederick Roden, University of Connecticut
Author, *Same-Sex Desire in Victorian Religious Culture*
Editor, *Catholic Figures, Queer Narratives*

Praise for *The 100th Generation*

"…the lesbian equivalent of Indiana Jones…Saracen has sprinkled cliffhangers throughout this tale…If you enjoy the History Channel presentations about ancient Egypt, you will love this book. If you haven't ever indulged, it will be a wonderful introduction to the land of the Pharaohs. If you're a *Raiders of the Lost Ark*–type adventure fan, you'll love reading a woman in the hero's role."

— *Just About Write*

By the Author

The 100th Generation

Vulture's Kiss

SISTINE HERESY

by
Justine Saracen

2009

SISTINE HERESY

ISBN 10: 1-60282-051-1
ISBN 13: 978-1-60282-051-7

This Trade Paperback Original Is Published By
Bold Strokes Books, Inc.
P.O. Box 249
Valley Falls, NY 12185

First Edition: February 2009

Credits
Editors: Jennifer Knight and Shelley Thrasher
Production Design: Stacia Seaman
Cover Design By Sheri (graphicartist2020@hotmail.com)

Acknowledgments

Thanks, above all, to Angelique Corthals, who made me actually visit the Sistine Chapel, gave me a dozen gorgeous books on the Italian Renaissance, and offered ingenious plot suggestions. Heartfelt thanks also to Derek Ragin, whose seraphic singing (though he is in full possession of his manhood) inspired the character of the castrato Domenico.

For being there during the long gestation of this work, thanks first and foremost to Thomas Keith, who not only commented, but foisted me on his acquaintances. Thanks also to other early draft readers: Inge Horwood, Doris Kaufman, and Elizabeth Mandel, whose reactions guided me.

On the publication end, I want to applaud Jennifer Knight, consummate plot surgeon, who put the pieces in all the right places. A glass of wine also for my religious "experts" Ruth Sternglantz for Judaism and "Storm" for Catholicism.

Finally, I want to thank Shelley Thrasher and Stacia Seaman for heroic intervention and long night hours when we had a last-minute time crunch.

As for research, though I focused on no one source for Michelangelo, I do wish to acknowledge Michael Mallett's scholarly study *The Borgias*.

Last of all, I would like to thank Sheri for her "collaboration" with Michelangelo for a fantastic cover, and Radclyffe and Jennifer, for taking the plunge into LGBT with this novel, letting me reclaim the splendid period called the Italian Renaissance on behalf of queers and dissenters of all kinds.

Dedication

To Giordano Bruno (1548–1600), who,
for declaring that the earth orbited the sun,
and rejecting Church mysteries for mysteries of his own,
was burned alive at the stake.

Dramatis Personae (in order of appearance)

Adriana Borgia (fictional)	Wife of Juan Borgia, Mistress of Cesare Borgia
Rodrigo Borgia (1431–1503) *Pope Alexander VI* (1492–1503)	Last Borgia Pope, considered the epitome of corruption in the papacy
Lucrezia Borgia (1480–1514)	Daughter of Pope Alexander VI. After being widowed twice, married Alfonso d'Este and became Duchess of Ferrara
Domenico Raggi (fictional)	Castrato in the Sistine Choir
Cesare Borgia (1476–1507)	Son of Pope Alexander VI, head of Papal army during his reign
Donato Bramante (1444–1514)	Architect and painter. Designed the original plan for St. Peter's Basilica
Raphaela Bramante (fictional)	Daughter of Donato, modeled after historical painter Artemesia Gentileschi
Gian Pietro Carafa (1476–1559) *Pope Paul IV* (1555)	Clerical reformer and extreme ascetic who established the Roman Inquisition
Michelangelo Buonarroti (1475–1564)	Sculptor, painter, architect
King Ferdinand of Aragon, Queen Isabella of Castille (1451–1504)	Initiators of the Spanish Inquisition and expulsion of the Jews and Moors
Silvio Piccolomini (fictional)	The Piccolomini were a prominent humanist Roman family

Giuliano della Rovere (1443–1513) **Pope Julius II** (1503)	Began reconstruction of St. Peter's Basilica, financed by sale of indulgences ("time off" from purgatory)
Marsilio Ficino (1433–1499)	Florentine scholar and major architect of humanist ideas
Giovanni de' Medici (1475–1521) **Pope Leo X**	Son of Lorenzo the Magnificent of Florence
Baldassare Salomano (fictional)	Jews expelled from Spain in 1492 were accepted in Rome by Alexander VI
Paris de Grassis (1450–1528)	Papal Master of Ceremonies during reign of Julius II
Giuliano da Sangallo (1445–1516)	Florentine architect and sculptor
Martin Luther (1483–1546)	Triggered the Reformation with his 95 theses condemning the sale of indulgences
Leonardo da Vinci (1452–1519)	Florentine engineer, architect, inventor, painter

PROLOGUE
AUGUST 1503

The Vicar of God was dead. Rodrigo Borgia, Pope Alexander VI had succumbed, whether to plague or poison, no one knew, but his already decomposing body lay in the Sistine Chapel. A coach rumbled toward the Vatican carrying Adriana Borgia, widow to one of his sons and mistress to another, unsure of what awaited her.

It was the *sede vacante*, the precarious time of the empty throne. The power plays were underway and soon the vendettas would begin. Adriana was already planning escape.

Ruin could come from anywhere now, though she was not sure who was the greater menace, rivals or reformers. Political rivals, like the della Roveres or the Farnese, would cheerfully cut her throat to advance themselves, but they changed with every new alliance. They could be threatened, seduced, bought off. But the reformers, Dominicans mostly, by their very zeal for piety, could not be corrupted, and therein lay their danger.

She had thrown in her lot with corruption and, for all her regrets, she could not meet the terms of the purists. She was, in every aspect of her murderous, adulterous life, what they detested. All she could do was flee them. Even now, with the Borgia forces suddenly defeated, the wolves circled. She had only enough time to find Lucrezia and perhaps to say good-bye to sweet Domenico.

At the Piazza San Pietro a crowd was gathered and her fear grew. But the mass of onlookers was focused on something at its center.

Perplexed, Adriana threaded her way forward and the crowd opened up for her. One or two recognized her and she heard her name whispered.

Then she saw the penitent. He half knelt, half hung from a chain fastened to the top of a wooden stake. His back was crisscrossed with gashes, and blood oozed in thin sheets down to his waist and into his breeches.

At her shoulder she heard a grunt of approval. From a pilgrim, to judge from his broad-brimmed hat and pouch. His emaciated frame suggested he was a devout one.

"Why do they do this today?" she asked him. "Of all days, during His Holiness's funeral?"

The pilgrim slouched on his staff. "You'll have to ask the Dominicans about that." He looked toward the two monks who stood at the front of the crowd. "They're the ones in charge of the sodomite. And God reward them for it." His eyes shone as another lash fell on the mangled back and the penitent twitched soundlessly. The crowd murmured approval.

"Sodomy? Is that the charge?"

"That's what they said. And when they're done flogging him, they'll do his friend." The pilgrim tilted his head toward a second prisoner shackled at the foot of a guard. "Serves 'em right." He sucked air through brown teeth.

The two Dominicans had caught sight of Adriana and approached. White-robed and tonsured, they seemed colorless against the motley of the onlookers. The taller one spoke.

"Lady Borgia, it is best you leave. You have no place here now and we cannot vouch for your safety." The sound of another whiplash underscored his remark.

"It was my intention to attend His Holiness's funeral, not an execution."

"Then please see to it that you do so, Lady, lest you draw attention to yourself." He tilted his head almost imperceptibly in the mockery of a bow.

She held her ground. "Who ordered this?" She gestured toward the sweating soldier who let fall another lash. "On the day of the Pope's mass."

The Dominican looked down at her with half-closed eyes. "Cardinal Carafa, meting God's punishment on this day as any other."

"But these are boys of Alexander's court. I recognize them."

"Pope Alexander is dead. The sodomites no longer enjoy his protection. Now, if you please." He extended his arm toward an alley between the onlookers, indicating the direction she should go. The sleeve of his white robe, she noted, was flecked with blood.

She returned the mocking head-tilt. Ignoring the direction in which he pointed, she walked along the front of the crowd, toward the second prisoner.

The other penitent, more boy than man, crouched in terror. She had seen him in the halls of the Vatican, one of the dozens of pages and servants she was apt to pass on any day. He whispered, "Madama, please." An urge to take him by the arm, to rescue one of the first victims of the new political order, almost overcame her misgivings. But she knew it was impossible; she herself was in jeopardy. Seizing handfuls of her skirt, she fled through the crowd up the steps to the Vatican.

❖

Kyrie, Kyrie Eleison.

Adriana hurried into the Sistine Chapel only half hearing the choir begin the Greek prayer for mercy. Fourteen voices wove in silken polyphony until a single bright sound, plangent and compelling, rose above the others.

Christe Eleison, Allelujah.

The chapel was full for the requiem mass. A marble screen divided the chapel in two, separating the Cardinals who sat along the walls on the far side from the nobility of Rome standing in rows behind it. The doors at the center of the screen were ajar and Adriana looked through the opening. There it was, at the forefront. Mercifully shrouded and with its head toward the altar, the corpse of Pope Alexander VI lay on its catafalque.

Still breathless, she looked around in the somber crowd for Lucrezia and wondered if she dared to walk farther in. No. Unwise to draw attention to herself.

In that instant the odor of rotten meat assailed her and she held her handkerchief to her mouth. They had told her that the Pope's body had corrupted quickly, had blackened even before he could be washed, but no one mentioned the smell. Trying not to breathe deeply, she leaned forward, peering through the crowd.

"Lucrezia, finally!" Adriana whispered, and made her way along the rows to her sister-in-law. Slender and blond, Lucrezia stood rigid, holding a missal to her chest. Adriana touched her arm. "We've got to go, dear. The Dominicans are in the square flogging Alexander's servants, and Cesare is waiting for us at Sant' Angelo."

Lucrezia was sullen. "Why doesn't he come? Alexander was his father too."

"Shhh. You know why. There are too many here with a score to settle."

"I'll miss him, you know," Pope Alexander's daughter murmured. She regarded Adriana through red-rimmed eyes, as though trying to discern whether her sister-in-law also mourned. Adriana knew she was beyond reproach, at least in dress. There had been no time to make mourning clothes, but in the short period as everything seemed to come apart at the papal court, her maid had simply taken her darkest blue gown and sewn a strip of black ribbon on it, from bodice to hem. With her black hair drawn back into a knot, Adriana looked bereaved, even if she was not.

"Do you suppose they murdered him?" Lucrezia's glance took in the lords of Rome on the near side of the screen before shifting to the somber clerics on the far side. "I think they did. Half the people in this chapel are murderers."

Adriana's face warmed at the word "murdered," and the putrid air of the chapel stirred an awful memory. She closed her eyes for a moment, forcing it away.

"Yes, there are murderers everywhere."

Lucrezia held her missal to her chin, like a child in prayer. "Is there one pure soul left in this awful city?"

"Agnus Dei qui tollit peccatum mundi," a single high voice sang, crystalline, over their heads.

"Yes, of course there is. Up there." Adriana looked toward the choir loft at the castrato who gave forth a thrilling sound in a voice that was neither male nor female.

"Domenico? Is that it, then?" Lucrezia chuckled bitterly. "Is castration the way to make men pious?"

"Shhh," Adriana cautioned, touching Lucrezia's arm.

Across the aisle, two people turned around and stared at them. The man, wide-shouldered and magisterial, looked away again; the tall young woman at his side did not.

Adriana held the stranger's glance, defiant and then curious. "Who are they?" she asked under her voice.

"Those two?" Lucrezia's tone was indifferent. "The architect Donato Bramante. And that's his daughter Raphaela. A painter."

The young woman still stared. The full lips were slightly open as if she were about to speak. Then, unexpectedly, her mouth curled up faintly on one side as if in greeting.

Adriana stared back, puzzled, irritated at having to pry Lucrezia away from her mourning when they should have already been out of the city, when every minute they stayed endangered them.

Movement drew her eyes away from the woman. A more ominous figure—by his white robe, another Dominican—came through the doorway of the screen. A jolt of fear shook her. Gian Pietro Carafa.

The Cardinal's bony asceticism seemed a reproach to the entire Vatican, but his cold inquisitor's glare, Adriana knew, was directed at the two of them.

"It's time to go, Lucrezia. Now." She took hold of her sister-in-law's arm and drew her along the row to the aisle and toward the wide double doors that led out of the chapel.

Two Swiss Guardsmen stepped in front of them with crossed pikes. Adriana glanced back at Carafa. He came toward them with the leisurely pace of a man certain of his captives. The choir continued to sing the mass while the rest of the congregation looked elsewhere, indifferent now to the fallen Borgia women. Only Raphaela Bramante still watched. As Adriana met her gaze again, the young woman's eyes darted toward the eastern wall to a space beneath the choir loft.

The small door under the loft was nearly invisible, covered with the same painted drapery as the wall. "The service entrance," Adriana whispered, urging Lucrezia toward the narrow door.

They passed unhindered into a corridor and hurried toward a second door at the far end of the passageway. A voice called out behind them.

"Signora Borgia! Stop!"

Adriana threw herself against the heavy wood, and as the door opened onto freedom, they broke into a run.

I

1506—GOD'S WARRIOR

Pope Julius II felt the hint of sexual excitement as the dust settled and he could look down onto the field of slaughter at Perugia. He shifted in the saddle as a gust of wind ruffled his papal robe and cooled his armor beneath it. He lifted off his battle helmet and handed it down to his squire, letting the troops around him see the face of God's general, the victorious Vicar of Christ.

Someone handed up a chalice of watered wine, and he took a long drink, savoring both the liquid and the moment. He had defeated the upstart despots of Perugia and Bologna and reunited the Romagna under papal authority.

As battles went, it had been brief and not very costly. All things considered, the triumph had been easier than achieving the papal throne. That had cost him a fortune, not to mention ten long years of bitter exile while the Borgias controlled Rome. When Alexander, the pig, had finally died, Julius had called on every ally and resource. To his fury, one of the other Cardinals was chosen. Yet, within the month, the hand of God conveniently intervened, ending that reign too, and Julius finally ascended.

He took the throne with the forcefulness of a man whose hour was overdue. He did not even bother to choose a saint's name, merely changing his own "Giuliano" to its Latin form. If the pious among the Curia did not care for that, they dared not show it.

Now, the three rivals to his authority, Venice, France, and Cesare Borgia, were all neutralized. Cesare Borgia, under order of arrest, was on the run with his whore, Adriana. Venice had been made to surrender Cesena and Forli. The French—well, they were a constant thorn, but at that very moment, Julius had legates in the German court discussing an alliance against them. It was a chess game, but Julius was far across the chessboard.

Yet he hated political maneuvering, having to form alliances with men he detested. It was so much more satisfying to ride before an army and achieve visible victory on the battlefield. Men could betray him, alliances could be broken, but a sword rendered an enemy permanently dead, and a vanquished town stayed vanquished.

His victory deserved commemorating. He ran several scenes through his mind's eye. A fresco of the battle, perhaps, with himself in full papal armor overseeing the field? No, there would be many battles, and such a specific event would lack timelessness and the aura of sanctity. He wanted to be remembered for centuries.

What subject then? How could he insinuate himself into a sacred thematic and still be recognized? Perhaps a portrayal of himself as Peter with the apostles around him. Possibly. But where was there space in the Papal Palace where men would see it?

It came to him like a revelation. The Sistine Chapel. It needed repair anyhow, and the current star-studded blue ceiling had never pleased him. Why not a fresco? Why not several frescoes, that would forever be associated with his papacy?

Yes. The chapel ceiling. The twelve apostles. Himself as Saint Peter in the center panel. Being touched by God. Julius liked this idea.

Who could he trust to paint it? Botticelli and Roselli were too old and feeble for something of that scope, and on a ceiling no less. Perugino might do it. Well, Bramante, his personal architect, would have some suggestions.

Julius was exceedingly cheerful now. Colors ran through his head. Colors for the ceiling. Colors for the painted papal vestments.

He gazed out over a line of Swiss infantrymen with their pikes. Handsome lads, tall and light-haired. Their drab field dress did not do them justice. A victorious papal army deserved display. He imagined them more flamboyant, in multicolored stripes perhaps, with artfully slashed sleeves and leggings. The pikes, of course, would stay.

II

AUGUST 1508—RETURN OF THE PENITENT

Five years after fleeing the funeral of Alexander VI, Adriana crept again into the Sistine Chapel during the mass.

She felt the passage of time like a weight on her chest, those five tumultuous years, four of them with Cesare in Spain, celebrating with him in victory, comforting him in defeat, feigning indifference to his infidelities. Then, abruptly, he was gone, killed in a meaningless battle. She returned to her father's house in Seville, to a man she scarcely knew. Though the conniving Don Pedro Falcon had married her off to the Borgias for his own advantage in the first place, he allowed her back and she had enjoyed the privileges and protections of being Adriana Falcon-Serra for scarcely half a year when the Inquisition struck. Some quarrel her father had involved himself in at court had ended in denunciation, and within months, everything—lands, businesses, titles, and finally his life—were forfeited.

The Inquisition sent a reign of terror through the country. Not only were the converts at risk; even her father, a landed *hildago* of good reputation, could fall victim. It could only have been royal greed that caused the Holy Office to arrest a feeble old widower and seize the lucrative farms of the Falcon family. Whatever the reason, before he could stand trial, Don Falcon died in prison.

Though Adriana was for the moment free of suspicion herself, Spain had become a purgatory. The auto-da-fé in Seville brought that home to her. If the spectacle of men being burned alive was Spain's testament to the True Faith, Adriana preferred the profane dangers of Rome.

She fled Spain for the Roman countryside, cowering in the one parcel of Cesare's land the new Pope had not seized, and she tried to lead a quiet life. She had been married at fifteen, widowed and the mistress of the second-most powerful man in Rome at eighteen, and at twenty-three she committed murder. She had burned through life so furiously that, for a while at least, she felt she had reached its logical end.

But after the fear ebbed and she learned calm in the Roman countryside, she felt the stirrings of nature again and remembered she was only twenty-nine.

Driven by loneliness and nostalgia she ventured timidly into Rome again. She needed to find old friends, and Domenico Raggi was surely one of them.

She peered out from behind the wooden pillar toward the choir loft and found him instantly. Taller than all the others, the castrato stood at the far end, caught in the harsh white beam that shone through the clerestory windows. In the milky, dust-filled light, his eyes were shadowed as he sang, until he turned his face upward and was bathed in incandescence. Gentle Domenico. His pure voice was as unchanged as the Greek and Latin words he sang.

No, the mass had not changed, but everything else had. The chapel itself was a jumble of wooden platforms and ladders. Even the ceiling was different. The star-scattered heaven she remembered was scraped bare. As I am now, she thought. Bare…raw…waiting.

She saw the rough hand before it touched her, and she flinched. Too late. Forcefully it seized her and yanked her backward toward the door. Alarmed, she struggled to wrench her arm away, but the grip only tightened and she staggered after her captor. For a brief panicking moment, she saw him in profile. His hair was cut short like that of a menial, and an obviously broken nose flattened his face to a sort of pugnaciousness. Finally, as he pulled her through the doorway into the great hall, he let her go.

"Michelangelo!"

"Shhh." He pressed a finger to his lips and pointed toward a marble bench on the far side of the great hall. They sat down together, dwarfed by the vast fresco that rose behind them.

"You scared me half to death. I thought I was being arrested."

"Forgive me. I had just gone to fetch this." He held up a mallet. "I couldn't believe my eyes when I saw you. If you had gone farther into the chapel I might have lost you in the crowd." He took her long fingers in his muscled hands. "I'm sorry I was so rough."

"I wouldn't have gone in. I don't want to be seen in this city yet."

"Why not? You're as beautiful as ever, and that little gray spot right there gives you just the right maturity." He raised a finger toward the side of her head where a narrow swath of black hair had lightened. "You still make every man who looks at you commit a sin."

She laughed softly and pushed his hand away. "And you still don't know how to talk to a woman."

She studied him in return, noting how haggard he looked. The five years had not aged him so much as washed him out, like his clothing. He wore a simple belted smock that had once been blue and, below it, colorless leggings tucked into sooty well-worn boots. He was indistinguishable from any other workman.

"You know I only meant to say you hadn't changed," he said. "When did you return from Spain?"

"A few months ago. But this is the first time I've ventured into Rome."

"And you never contacted me?" His voice held both feigned and genuine injury. She had forgotten how quick he was to take offense.

"I haven't contacted anyone, actually. I fled with Cesare and Lucrezia in the first place because Rome was no longer safe for us. The Dominican reformers had descended on the Vatican, and if they didn't bring some charge or other against us, there were plenty of others who would have cheerfully cut our throats."

"Everyone knows there's no love lost between this Pope and the Borgias. You were courageous to come back."

"Courageous? It was just the opposite. After Cesare was killed, I went back to my father in Seville. But a few months later, he was arrested by the Inquisition. He was ailing anyhow, and he died in prison. Of course the Crown seized his lands, which may have been the whole reason for the arrest. It seemed safer to return here after all. I thought that if Julius arrested me, he would remember he owes me a favor."

Michelangelo seemed amused. "A favor? When did the mighty Pope Julius ever need you?"

"Not me. He needed Cesare, for his papal election. The two were old enemies and had no real channels to talk. But when it looked like Pius II would die, the Cardinals started politicking again. Julius desperately needed Cesare to influence the Spanish Cardinals to throw the vote toward him. It must have galled him to actually need Borgia assistance, and to need it so badly that he had to send messengers all the way to Spain to get it. In any case, I was the one he needed to whisper in Cesare's ear."

"What was Julius's offer?"

"Just that he would leave Borgia lands untouched in exchange for Cesare's convincing the Spanish Cardinals to support him. I did my part but it was hardly necessary. Cesare was too weak to have openly opposed him anyhow, and he agreed."

"So, what did *you* get out of it?"

"As it turns out, nothing. After Julius was chosen, the old animosities began again. Within months Cesare was on the run and most of his lands were seized after all. All but the little villa near Tivoli where I live now. As for me, I might be able to call that favor in one day, but after five years and Cesare's death, I don't think it has much currency."

Michelangelo stared into middle distance. He had set the mallet down and folded his sinewy arms across his chest. His hands were scarred, she noted, marked by myriad abrasions, chisel nicks, and sores from the acid wash that polished his statues.

"And what of you, Michelo? What have you been up to?"

"I finally finished a statue, in Florence. More difficult than I expected, on a used block of marble, already deeply cut. But it turned out all right. The Hebrew David. You should take a look at it."

"I will, when I'm next in Florence. How long have you been back in Rome?"

"Three years. I was supposed to begin designs for Julius's tomb. But there were endless problems." He scratched something dark and gritty on his shirtsleeve. His forearms were knotty with musculature. "We couldn't agree on anything. And now the whole thing has been set aside for the chapel ceiling. Infuriating."

The chapel doors suddenly opened and people poured into the Sala Regia. Adriana pulled the hood of her cloak over her head to avoid being recognized. Courtiers, noblemen, and Cardinals passed by in velvet and satin. Some were familiar: Paris de Grassis, Cardinal Riario, Annio Piccolomini looking frail, the Orsini. None of them were her friends. Most went down the great staircase out into the August heat. Others, who currently held favor and influence, went into the papal rooms. Rooms to which she once had free access.

Finally, only the Swiss Guardsman stood at the door of the chapel. In the vast high-ceilinged stateroom of the palace, she and Michelangelo were alone again, and their voices echoed slightly.

She resumed their conversation. "What will you paint?"

"Paint?" He snorted. "Julius wants apostles with himself in their midst. But I am so bitter these days, only one scene comes to mind." He made a sweeping gesture with his arm. "The Deluge. To wash it all away."

"Why so choleric, Michelo? I don't remember you this way."

"Choleric? I have good reason. I was summoned to Rome to work on the Pope's tomb. I spent months preparing sketches. Then he lost interest. Like that." He snapped his fingers. Specks of sawdust flew off the fingertips.

"Suddenly the new basilica was all he cared about. I was at his side, having just been unemployed by him. I ought to have been given the basilica project. But Bramante got it." There was bitterness in his voice.

Adriana was suddenly attentive. "Bramante? The architect? The one with the daughter who is an artist?"

He scratched at the flecks of plaster that had caught in his beard. "The great Donato Bramante would not care to be known merely as someone's father. But, yes. The daughter's an artist too."

Adriana remembered eyes like lanterns guiding her toward escape. "Is she any good?"

"You can see for yourself. In the Palazzo Piccolomini. Bramante did some work on the courtyard, and part of the arrangement was for her to paint some panels in the library. We can visit them if you like."

"Piccolomini. I know that family. The son Silvio flirted wildly with me when I arrived as a new bride from Spain."

"He may again. He is still unmarried, you know. You should visit him and find out." He toyed with a piece of marble, which he had pulled from his pocket, twirling it between thumb and index finger.

"I don't know, Michelo." She touched his forearm, causing him to drop the object he was holding. It rolled toward her foot and fell flat.

She picked it up and peered at a marble disk, its diameter only slightly smaller than her palm, carved with the haloed face of a woman.

"Very nice. I wouldn't have thought miniature work to be your style." She turned the disk over as he had and saw the identical face on the back. A snake curled around the head in place of the halo. "What does it mean?"

"Woman, seductress and saint. Something I never finished, on a chip left from the 'David.' You're right, miniature work doesn't suit me. You can have it if you like."

"Seduction and redemption? Oh, dear. You do lay a lot at the door of women, Michelo. Could you fix it so I can wear it?" She looked up at him playfully, but her eyes lit on something behind him and she felt the blood leave her face.

With a puzzled frown, Michelangelo looked over his shoulder.

A cleric stood in the chapel doorway. His black cloak hung loosely over a gaunt frame, and when he turned his head toward them he showed the harshly sculpted face of an ascetic.

"Who's that?" Michelangelo asked. "I recall that face."

"Gian Pietro Carafa, the Dominican who hounded us from Rome five years ago. We thought we were free of him, but then he showed up in Spain with Torquemada. And now, like a specter, he haunts me again here."

"Torquemada? I've heard of him. A Dominican doing the gruesome work of their Most Catholic Majesties."

Adriana's mouth went dry. "Yes, gruesome is right. The *Domini canes,* people call them, the hounds of God. Where they go, there is the Inquisition. If you have secrets, guard them well or they'll tear them from you. We should get out of here."

Gian Pietro Carafa appeared again in the chapel doorway, another priest at his side. The muscles around Michelangelo's mouth tightened.

"All men have secrets. But there are still places in Rome where one can speak freely." He stood up. "Give me the medallion. I'll drill a hole in it for you."

She passed the piece of marble back to him and he dropped it into his pocket.

"Come with me to the Piccolomini. They're people like us."

"Perhaps. But today I want to visit Domenico Raggi. You know, the singer at the mass. The choir will be at lunch now."

"The castrato?" His face lit up perceptibly. He rubbed powder off his mallet, avoiding her eyes. "Ah, that's right. Your protégé."

"Come downstairs with me. I'll introduce you." Adriana pulled her shawl around her shoulders and looked back once behind her as they walked. The gaunt cleric watched but made no move toward her.

"I'm supposed to be working, but you've tempted me away from my duty, Adriana."

"Don't blame me for your sins, Michelo," she said lightly as she walked ahead of him.

"Sin? Is that what you are leading me to?" he murmured, and tapped the mallet softly against his leg.

III

Domenico Raggi sat apart from the other choristers in their ruffled collars and black soutanes. Not that the boys and men shunned him. But there seemed to always be a separation between whole men and himself, a nervousness in the conversation when he was there. He sensed both their admiration and their disgust, even when they welcomed him.

He let his gaze wander idly over the chapel staff hurrying through their meals. It stopped at two figures, a bearded man and a dark, attractive woman, lingering just inside the doorway. He stared for a moment, perplexed, then recognition dawned. Without taking his eyes from the woman, he stumbled over benches to the doorway and seized her hand.

"Lady Adriana." His voice was tight with emotion, his Italian still colored by a Spanish accent. "Is it really you?"

Adriana embraced him unreservedly. "Domenico. Agnellino," she said into his shoulder. "You've grown so tall."

He had the long frame typical of the castrato but, unlike others of his ilk, he was not plump. Indeed, in the five years since he had seen her, he had grown lean. Adriana touched the wavy brown hair that stopped just at the base of his neck, as if grateful for his affection.

"And you're so beautiful," she continued.

There were those who had already remarked on his large velvet eyes, his nose that sloped gracefully, and the fine muscles that swelled around his mouth and suggested the curving mustache he could never have. He was always aware that he lacked the common protrusion over the ruffled collar of the soutane, that he had no "Adam's apple" as other men, but the smooth throat of prepubescence. Yet, in spite of his speaking voice, his breadth of chest and shoulders gave him a certain masculinity. Innocence and sensuality warred in him, as if the boy struggled to become the man.

Adriana laid her hand on the side of his beardless cheek. He smiled, first at her then, more shyly, at the man by her side.

"Oh, forgive me, Domenico. This is Michelangelo Buonarroti, who is painting the chapel ceiling. Maybe you've seen him working."

The artist stroked his own beard, as if to reassure himself he had it. He was slightly shorter than Domenico, and when he extended his veined and sinewy arm to shake his hand, the contrast with his own smooth unblemished skin was extreme. Michelangelo seemed made of knotted rope, Domenico of tan silk.

"*Maestro*," he said. "I am honored."

Michelangelo withdrew his hand and stood awkwardly. "I've heard you singing in the mass. Extraordinary. Sublime."

Domenico let his gaze linger on the artist's face. "Thank you, Signore."

The older man seemed to search for words. "How did you come to the Papal Choir?"

Domenico clasped his hands behind his back, revealing the wide expanse of chest that came, mysteriously, with the surgery that had made him a castrato. "That is the signora's doing. She and Signor Borgia brought me here from Spain."

Adriana grasped his upper arm, claiming him. "He means my husband, Juan. We heard him singing in a little church in Jativa and convinced Alexander to admit him to the Chapel Choir."

Michelangelo had not taken his eyes from his face. "Then Signora Borgia has done us all a great service. Did she also give you the fine cross you wear?"

"No, that is a gift from His Holiness." Domenico fingered the jeweled gold at his throat. "But Signora Borgia gave me Rome."

Domenico took Adriana's hand again. "Madonna, it's so lovely to see you. And now that you're back, you must not leave. The choirmaster's waiting for me and I dare not offend him by being late. Will you come again tomorrow, after the mass?"

"Yes, of course. Let's meet at the fountain in the atrium." Adriana embraced him once more and the two visitors stepped through the doorway, leaving him in the midst of the dull roar of the dining room.

❖

Domenico Raggi watched the painter and the lady disappear along the dim corridor. The first person he had ever loved was the Lady Adriana Borgia. The shock of seeing her again sent his mind racing to his first overwhelming days in Rome where he had followed her, back to the last days in Jativa, where she obtained his release from the conservatory, and farther back still, to the life he led before singing took him from it.

It was childhood alternately blissful and wretched, for he had been born illegitimate to a village girl and an Arab sailor. By the time he was five his mother had found someone who would marry her, although new children soon came and the stepfather openly abused her "Bedouin bastard."

But nature had cursed him in one way and blessed him in another, for half-caste though he was, he sang like an angel. In the choir school to which his parents gave him, or sold him, as he later realized, he finally had enough to eat and soft clean clothes to wear. In his innocence, he thought he would be safe forever.

His knees weakened at the memory of his "rescue," and he sat down on the nearest bench recalling the sound of soothing voices, the taste of opium-laced wine, the wicked pleasure between his legs from the warm milk in which they bathed him. Then, nothing. He had no memory of the actual violation, for while they soothed him, an unseen hand pressed on the pulsing artery at his throat and rendered him senseless.

But he remembered the headache afterward, and the horror when he looked down under the blanket. The grotesque stories the boys had told were true. The blood that seeped along the edge of the bandages and the throbbing pain in his groin confirmed it. They had castrated him.

In shock and terror he wet himself, the urine scorching the wound until he cried out in agony. The surgeon returned with his assistant to attend him. And after he was cleaned, the choirmaster came in and comforted him.

"It is for God," he said. "You belong to His Church now and this is your sacrifice."

Domenico chuckled bitterly to himself. He had only now learned what it meant to "belong to the Church." It was not the way someone like Michelangelo belonged to it. He could tell by his firm handshake. A robust, self-sufficient man like that wouldn't submit to being owned. Definitely not.

A hand on his elbow caused him to turn to see a bearded face, ruddy and affable.

"Oh, Bernardo."

The chorister tugged on his arm. "Come on. We have the new mass to learn, and you know how the choirmaster hates it if you're late."

"You're right. That's all I need—another dressing-down."

He left the dining hall and hurried to the rehearsal, cheered by the coming reunion. Was the artist her lover? Perhaps she would tell him. She used to talk to him, in the last year before she left. He wondered how it would feel to be loved by her. Or by him.

IV

Lifting her skirt to avoid tripping, Adriana climbed the broad stone steps to the atrium of St. Peter's Church. She had been stunned, as all of Rome had been, to learn that the new Pope had ordered the church razed and another one built in its place. But now she understood why. The ancient basilica was crumbling in vault and foundation.

Inside the atrium she strolled around the arcade, noting the foundation that had been poured outside the current structure. The great court held planks and stacks of bricks in one corner and blocks of marble in the other. Between them the peddlers had set up their stalls, and the noises of commerce and construction competed with each other, filling the entire atrium. She wondered what inspiration the pilgrims could possibly have from praying to the saint's bones in the midst of it.

A crucifix was suddenly thrust in her face. The tiny figure of the savior sparkled in the sunlight. "Buy a fine rosary, Madama? Blessed by His Holiness himself on Good Friday." The peddler tried to lay the circle of beads in her hand.

"No. No thank you." She brushed past him toward a row of booksellers.

The first book merchant stepped in front of her, a smiling, red-faced man in a Jew's hat. "A Bible, Madonna? Or perhaps a prayer book?" He pointed toward his table. "We have lovely volumes from France. Illustrated. Not expensive. Come, have a look."

"No. Please." She raised a hand to block him.

The crush of people only seemed to get worse. A few steps away men were hawking copies of the Veronica cloth, a dozen identical squares of cloth with the ghostly brownish imprint of an eyeless face. Behind the cloth hawkers, cabinets held carved wooden crucifixes of all sizes and flagellant whips in knotted leather. She shuddered, recalling the flogging she had witnessed the last time she visited St. Peter's.

"Make way," someone shouted. Adriana glanced up to see two papal guardsmen emerge from the basilica. With their ceremonial pikes held out at a diagonal in front of them, they marched down into the square, opening an avenue for the funeral procession that followed. Not a grandiose one, but one for a lesser noble perhaps, a church functionary, possibly even a merchant. There were only two acolytes at the forefront, followed by half a dozen choristers in red soutanes and white surplices. All carried long poles with votive candles, their flames protected by cones of glass.

They shuffled by murmuring, *"Requiem aeternam dona eis, Domine,"* between sections of the prayer being spoken by the priest who followed them. Directly behind the priest, four pallbearers in white bore the bier on their shoulders, and Adriana suddenly sickened. The bier was nearly identical to the one that haunted her dreams. It was a sort of narrow bed, with a low wooden headboard, elaborately carved and surmounted by a cross. The cadaver was covered by a red shroud up to the chest. Where the shroud was folded back, withered gray-blue hands were tied together in the prayer position. The head, white-haired and beardless, rested on a tasseled white pillow, its jaw hanging slack, just like the cadaver of Piero Battista had done. Battista, a man whom she had scarcely known, but who would haunt her now forever. The man she had murdered.

Behind the bier the widow walked, this one with sons, though Battista had only daughters, one a babe in arms, and the whole hideous scene rose up again in her memory. Seeing the children, she had grasped what a terrible thing she had done. Not even the death of her own husband had touched her as much as this act, which she herself had committed.

It was supposed to be a small murder, of a small man, and by the laws of the Church, not even a sin. For the Pope had ordered it and she was merely his instrument, the poisoner. Obediently she invited the unsuspecting man to supper and did the deed. She watched him slowly expire. Her stomach tightened at the recollection. She did not expect the convulsions, the deep rasping sobs, the foam that oozed from his mouth, or his final defecation. She did not expect that death would be so filthy.

The Pope's reaction the next morning had sickened her as well. She knelt before him and said "Holiness." Only that, "Holiness." And she waited for absolution. But so little was his interest in the matter that he simply waved her off, as if she had smacked a fly for him and the insect still stained her hand.

Even now her mind was a jumble of questions. Could an act ordered by a Pope be a sin? She had taken a simple man's life, impoverished his wife and children. She felt the need to confess to someone, to answer for a murder, yet the Church where she would have to confess her sin had commanded her to commit it. Opposing forces struggled in her: the need to ease the choking guilt and the soothing voice of a higher authority, which told her she was not guilty. Was evil something in itself, or only that which the Church condemned?

"Lady Adriana, over here!"

Domenico waved at her from the back of the crowd and she hurried toward him. She embraced him again with affection, noting that without the somber clerical garb of the choir he looked even more striking. He wore black hose and a black velvet doublet in the Spanish style. Tiny gold buttons ran all the way from the waist up to his throat between the ends of an upright collar. A small Greek cross hung at his throat, gold with tiny rubies at the four ends, jeweled droplets of blood. The severity of the dress only drew attention to his astonishing beauty.

"The mass you sang, was it this man's requiem?"

"Yes, I thought I mentioned that. A merchant. His guild paid for the service."

"Ah," she said neutrally, and drew Domenico quietly to her side. Dust had settled on his dark doublet, and she stopped to brush it from his shoulder as if he were still an adolescent. "Look at you. You're covered with soot, and you smell of smoke."

"I'm sorry. It's incense and candle smoke. It catches in the ceiling of the choir loft and stays for hours. The whole choir smells of it, but I'm the tallest, so I get the worst of it." He laughed softly. "And now that you've hugged me, you'll smell of it too."

"It's good to see you again," she said as they walked into the cool darkness of the ancient church. "Can you forgive me for leaving Rome so suddenly and for so long?"

"There's nothing to forgive." He curled his fingers over her hand. "As long as you promise to stay this time."

"I promise." She nudged him playfully with her shoulder. "So, tell me what's new in the Sistine Choir."

He became animated. "Oh, a great deal. We have a new music master, and he's teaching us the masses from Flanders in a new style of singing. Not pure polyphony. We sing all together. The high and low voices blend in layers."

She frowned. "Everyone sings at the same time? Isn't that confusing?"

He laughed again, a soft sibilant chuckle. "No. Not at all."

They strolled wordlessly under the long row of silver chandeliers where the air smelled pleasantly of the hot wax.

"Have you had word from the other Lady Borgia?" he asked.

"No, but I understand Lucrezia thrives now as Duchess of Ferrara, and has two sons. I must visit her one day."

"I always thought it would be lovely to have children," he mused. "To be the head of a large family. I know that must sound ridiculous."

"No. Not at all. One wants family—of some sort. Mine are all gone now, but I understand the longing."

"Oh, I'm sorry. I was so self-absorbed I forgot you lost your father. Signor Buonarroti told me this morning before the mass."

"We were so estranged, I hardly knew him. Of course that doesn't lessen the outrage of his death. Let's not talk of that." Adriana took his arm again as they reached the shrine over the sepulcher that held the bones of Saint Peter. Four columns of precious metals hammered together rose up, studded with gems, to a marble baldachin.

"This is the center, the heart of the whole Church," Domenico said. "A sacred place."

Adriana was less awed. "My father thought so when he arranged for me to marry here. At the age of fifteen, surrounded by a host of courtiers, I knelt there with Juan Borgia. But in fact, there was nothing sacred about the marriage at all. It was a financial transaction that involved the transfer of a significant amount of the Falcon fortunes into the Borgia coffers."

"I had not realized it was so…business-like."

"It was *only* business, on both sides. Juan's father, Rodrigo Borgia, was still only a Cardinal at that time, but my own father was sure he'd be Pope one day and was willing to pay a lot to be connected to a papal family."

She drew him behind the shrine to the apse. "This is also where I became a widow, six years later. At least this is where they found Juan's bloody gloves." She pointed toward the steps that led down to the catacomb below. "His body was found the next day in the Tiber."

"Yes, I remember that. It must have been terrible for you."

She shrugged. "I was bereaved and frightened, but even then I knew that Juan's death was business too. The business of power."

The high altar at the center of the apse had drawn his attention. Its silver surface, encrusted with countless precious stones, glowed with the reflected light of the surrounding candles.

"Don't you feel it, Lady Adriana? That God is close? Look, I'm so happy today that I want to make a sacrifice here on His altar." He lifted his hand, revealing a thin silver ring on his last finger. He twisted it off with difficulty and held it up between them.

"Ah, the child's ring I gave you in Spain, just after we got you from the school. For your saint's day."

"It was my first gift ever from a lady, and I treasure it. When my hands grew large, I wore it on the last finger all the years you were gone. But now you're given back to me, and for joy and thanksgiving, I'll return it to God."

He slid the ring toward the back of the altar, where the opulence of the altar surface rendered it nearly invisible.

"What a strange man you are, Domenico. All right, if it pleases you, go ahead. We will see how long it takes before some altar boy finds it and you see him walking around with it on his finger."

They walked into the south transept. In the French chapel they halted before the white marble sculpture at its center. A young woman in voluminous robes held the angular form of a dead man draped awkwardly across her lap. His head cradled in her arm fell back, limp. A sash ran diagonally across the woman's heavily draped chest and held the deeply engraved inscription "Michelangelo Buonarroti Florentine made this."

Domenico stared dreamily at the incandescent marble. "It takes your breath away, doesn't it?"

"Beautiful, yes, but it also seems cold. The face of the virgin looks empty."

"Empty?" His voice registered surprise. "Oh, no. It's serenity, I'm sure. The Madonna has accepted God's will. Don't you see? If God's will is perfect, then there's no sorrow, only the peace of obedience."

She hated the word "obedience" but did not reply as they turned from the tableau and made their way around a wide column. Domenico looked back over his shoulder. "Does Michelangelo come often to the Sistine…oh—"

He halted suddenly to keep from colliding with a man who knelt at the balustrade of a chapel. "Pardon me, Signore."

Domenico stepped back and bowed gracefully. Adriana caught herself in mid-stride and stopped behind him. A portly well-dressed man drew himself up with difficulty to a standing position and bowed in return. Adriana searched her memory. She knew him.

"I am sorry, Signore, if I disturbed your prayers," Domenico said.

"Oh, no. We were not praying." The familiar stranger picked up the sheet of paper covered with lines and numbers that had lain in front of him. "We're only taking measurements." He held out his hand. "Donato Bramante. A pleasure, Signore."

As the men exchanged courtesies a young woman stepped out of a side chapel into view. Bramante summoned her with a brisk wave of the hand.

"And this is my daughter Raphaela."

❖

Adriana concealed her surprise. How lovely Raphaela Bramante had become, with a slender frame that was somehow robust. The years had taken away the girlishness and added a certain solemnity to her face. She wore her hair differently too, or perhaps working alongside her father had caused it to fall loose. But the warm honey color was the same.

Raphaela tilted her head back and her lips fell slightly open as if she were about to speak. But she did not. Her eyes merely swept over Adriana with focused interest as they had in the Sistine Chapel five years before.

Domenico finished the introductions. "And this is Lady Adriana Borgia."

Bramante inclined slightly from the waist, a faint raising of his brow the only evidence of surprise at her name. He had changed too, Adriana noted. The top of his head was bald now, while gray hair curled upward over his ears, like Mercury wings. Yet something magisterial about him kept him from looking comical. His height, demeanor, and intelligent gray eyes could not be mocked. She reminded herself that this was Michelangelo's rival, the man charged with rebuilding the basilica in which they stood.

"Ah, Signora Borgia," he said amiably. "I worked on several projects for His Holiness Pope Alexander before he died."

"Yes, he spoke of you once, and I recall seeing you at his requiem mass."

"Requiem mass? Ah, yes, a…disagreeable experience, if one may dare to speak so of a mass. Fortunately the new Pope is also in need of architects and so I am once again employed."

Adriana found the man charming, but wondered if even talking to him was a sort of betrayal of Michelangelo. She smiled back but did not continue the conversation.

Bramante cleared his throat. "The Holy Father pays me to work, not to chatter. Signora. Signore." He nodded in both their directions and offered his hand again while his daughter rolled up the page of calculations. She smiled briefly and fell in step with her father as they retreated down the nave of the church.

Watching the pair walk away, Adriana said, "Twice in five years this woman has stared at me that way, and I've never heard her speak."

❖

They stood at the eastern end of the basilica over on the wide stone steps, the afternoon sun warm on their backs. Below them the Piazza San Pietro was alive with activity, and beyond the square the panorama of Rome itself spread itself out in the afternoon haze. The gray Tiber formed a wide V-shape in the distance, curving abruptly northward on the one side past the Castel Sant' Angelo and stretching out more gently toward the southeast around the Trastevere. A slight breeze wafted up from the river.

"Is Rome any better now than it was under Alexander? I hope
so," Adriana said, touching Domenico's arm. "It cannot be any more
corrupt."

He shrugged lightly. "I've only known the life of the chapel,
nothing of politics."

"It wasn't just the politics." She pressed her lips together. "Do
you remember Cesare's supper party in the Apostolic Palace, when he
invited all those prostitutes? You sang during the supper."

Domenico nodded, frowning.

"Late in the evening when all were drunk they danced naked and
then coupled with the guests. An orgy, in the Sala Reale in front of
God's highest priest."

Domenico stared into the distance, conceding. "We're all sinners,
Adriana." He squeezed her hand. "One longs for purity, reform. But
some of the holiest relics in the world, St. Peter's bones, are beneath our
very feet, and pilgrims come here in the thousands to revere them."

She shrugged without replying.

"I myself sometimes have doubts and temptations. But always,
when I'm singing in the mass, my heart rises and I feel His presence."

She studied him for a moment. "How pious you are, Domenico,
to still see the good. I can't. The last Pope I served was corrupt and
he corrupted me, that's certain. You may repent of your doubts, but I
cannot repent of my certainties."

"Who can know of God's greater plan for us?" he persisted. "There
are things we don't understand, but must accept as an act of faith."

"Act of faith? You mean like the auto-da-fé? I saw one of those
in Spain."

"That is not what I meant," he said, but Adriana was not
listening.

Three clerics in long black capes were climbing the steps to the
church, their shadows jutting out like blades behind them. Against
the pale marble steps, they seemed specters, black things that walked
upright, but she recognized the face of the gaunt Dominican in the center.
He looked pointedly in her direction, then nodded before ascending the
last steps to the church portal.

"I'm sorry, I have to go now." She gave Domenico a brief kiss on
his cheek and stepped around him.

"Why so suddenly?"

"It's nothing. I just can't stay any longer." She started down the staircase.

"When will I see you again?" he called after her. "Will you come back to Rome?"

"I live in Tivoli now. You should come to visit *me*. There are too many dogs in Rome," she called back over her shoulder and hurried toward her coach in the Piazza San Pietro.

❖

Domenico remained standing before the portal of St. Peter's, staring after the coach that rolled toward the Ponte Sant' Angelo. Pious, she had said. How little she knew of him.

Oh, yes, he definitely remembered Cesare's supper party. He came perilously close to joining in the lasciviousness. For that night, Gaetano Alberti let him know he wanted to share his bed and passed a note suggesting where they might meet.

Domenico had slipped away discreetly, just as the coupling with the prostitutes began, intent upon finding Gaetano. But, stupidly, he blundered into the wrong dark room. How could he have misread the note? He found himself in a nursery where, by the light of a small candle, an infant slept. The child awakened at his entry and began to cry. And, stupidity upon stupidity, he did not flee, but picked it up.

Miraculously, the baby stopped crying. Content to be held, it sighed and began to suck its fist, its tiny head nestled in his neck. As he smelled the pleasant odor of its damp curls, first wonderment and then sorrow rose in him. This child was some man's heir. Some man could look into its tiny face and see himself reflected. He held the warm bundle closer, his hand covering the entire span of the infant shoulders, with a tightness in his throat. Never had he felt so incomplete, so cheated, as at that moment. He would have wept if the sound of the opening door had not interrupted him and he spun around to an old woman's angry face.

"Signora. Forgive me. I heard the child crying," he lied, and handed over the bundle before she could raise alarm. He had fled, not only the nursery, but the palace and the whole evening's misadventure.

He wondered how long Gaetano waited, or if he waited at all. Perhaps the whole thing had been a cruel hoax, and the Roman princelings had amused themselves at his expense. He knew what they thought of him. Away from the safety of the chapel, he was always merely a sport among whole men, a source of amusement.

And then there were other hands that caressed him. They troubled him far more, but he could never speak a word about them.

Lust or laughter, that's all he had ever gotten from the world.

Who would ever really love him, except God?

V

Michelangelo stumbled as something scrabbled over his boot in the darkness. He wished for a moment he had a lantern, but at midnight in the Trastevere that invited robbery, or worse. No, he would make do with the faint light that came from overhead windows, or from the lanterns marking the prostitutes.

He passed the women in their doorways, one by one, avoiding their glances. Some were haggard and worn. A few, the more expensive ones, were younger and more shapely, but all their expressions, when he could see them, were hard.

There it was, the upturned cart that signaled the crossing into the darkest part of the netherworld. He turned a corner and made his way carefully down a narrow, crooked alley that stank of urine. The first stirrings of lust, tiny coals ignited in his groin and sent out heat to the rest of his body. Then came the niggling shame. He told himself it was not his real person who waded into the swamp of sin.

This is only my skin, my outer form, my willful burning flesh, which pulls me. My soul sleeps under it, and one day will be free.

One day, but not tonight.

Halfway down the street a young man slouched in a doorway under a lantern. His shirt was open to the waist, and his threadbare breeches were stretched tight over the visible bulge of his manhood. He was beardless, though a patch of hair showed in the opening of his shirt. But what drew attention more than anything was the short red cloak he wore in spite of the warm night. Hooked on his left shoulder and tucked into his belt on his right side, it caught the night breeze and billowed for a moment, giving him a brief theatricality.

Agreement was quick. Michelangelo laid a hand on the narrow purse at his belt. "You have time for someone like me?"

"It will cost twenty grossi."

"That's a lot."

"You don't come here often, do you? That's what it always costs."

"All right."

The young man took down the lantern and strode along an inside corridor to a rough outbuilding. The place reeked of animal ordure and rotten hay, and the lantern light revealed it was a stable. A small one, with two stalls. A donkey in one of them shuffled a little as they entered but made no other sound.

Michelangelo held the leather purse under the lantern, ready to pour out its coins where they could be counted. Then he saw the open hand. Half the index finger was missing and only a stub up to the first knuckle remained. "What happened there?"

"An accident, sir. With a meat axe. I'm a butcher, you see. With my brothers."

"I don't want to know more." Michelangelo shook the coins into the man's palm, and they disappeared into a vessel hidden under loose straw.

The young man unhooked his cloak and draped it over the plank between the stalls. With a graceful motion, he drew his shirt over his head, revealing tight musculature. The patch of black hair at the center of his chest narrowed to a line that went down his midsection to his navel and continued into his breeches.

He took Michelangelo's hand and drew it across his own naked chest. "What would you like, sir? I'll do whatever pleases you."

Michelangelo's hand trembled as it rested over the warm curve of the chest, and he took a step closer. He rubbed the rough surface of his thumb over the small nipple and with the other hand began to unfasten the other man's trousers. They were held together by a single cord and so opened completely and slipped to the ground. The stranger's dark sex was half swollen and curved outward from a thick bed of black hair.

Still without speaking, Michelangelo pressed himself against it and lightly bit the stranger's neck, tasting the salty sweat.

The butcher's hand, adept in spite of its stubby finger, stroked

Michelangelo through the coarse fabric of his own breeches, then unfastened the buckle that held them, freeing the hard hot flesh to the night air.

Their mouths met in something more like bites than kisses, as if each resented the desire for the other. Lust welled up in Michelangelo, then anger at the flesh that now dominated him. It was as if the devil had incarnated himself in that single part of him that stood erect against the handsome prostitute. Enflamed, he could not stop himself. The furnace of the young man's body called to him; it needed only to be opened.

Michelangelo slid his hands around the muscular hips down the curve of buttocks to the legs. The swarthy skin was pungent with new sweat, like his own that trickled down the small of his back. His dry breathing became louder as he felt the stranger's turgid member press on his own, man to man. Michelangelo pulled the young body tight against himself, squeezing the hard young buttocks and spreading them.

He whispered hoarsely, "Turn around."

VI

Silvio Piccolomini stepped back, satisfied, from his mirror. His rose-colored satin doublet, gathered at the waist, had soft yellow sleeves slashed along the length and buttoned at intervals. The doublet skirt ended high, revealing a hose of the same pale yellow, which molded his well-muscled thighs and the provocative swell of his masculinity. He wore no codpiece, finding them vulgar, but the careful tailoring of his hose amply flattered his natural endowment. With his head of thick blond curls he was, he had to admit, as handsome as any man in Rome.

When his manservant opened the heavy door, Silvio met his two guests directly in the entryway.

"Michelangelo, you old stone smasher. It's been far too long." He offered his right hand, resting the other fraternally on the artist's shoulder. After several vigorous pats, he stepped up to Adriana and took both her hands.

"Adriana, you are even more beautiful than I remember. When Father said he thought he saw you at the Vatican mass the other day, I could scarcely believe my ears."

"You're looking very fine yourself, Silvio. The years have served you well."

He laid his hand over his heart and lowered his head, purposely displaying his crop of curls from another angle. "You shame me with praise. However, I understand this is not a visit to me, but to my art collection."

Michelangelo pressed Silvio's shoulder. "Take it as a compliment, old man. Everyone knows you have one of the best collections in Rome.

Besides, you're all got up in your best clothes for us. Yellow and rose together, who'd have thought?"

Silvio put his hand to his chest again. "I'm so pleased you noticed. Why don't you come into the library now, while the light is still good. Father will join us in the garden afterward for lunch."

He led them down a long gallery into a room where the inlaid wood paneling and the quantity of books subtly displayed wealth and taste. The midday light shone through two windows and lightened the wood to a rich honey. On the far wall the paneling on both sides of the door ended at shoulder level, and on the plaster above were two large frescos. In one of them, the god Apollo, with Silvio's long straight nose, well-formed lips, and pale curls, posed beside his chariot.

Silvio regarded the image for a moment, then explained. "I had in fact contracted for a simple portrait, but Signorina Bramante suggested Apollo. I think her likeness of me is quite good."

Michelangelo chuckled. "Yes, she's captured your superciliousness rather well."

"Bitter words from a man with a crooked nose, Michelangelo." Silvio clapped his friend on the back and looked toward Adriana for approval.

But she stood riveted before the second fresco.

A half-nude woman sat on the back of a garlanded bull, which leapt toward an ocean wave. Her dark blue gown was open to below the navel, exposing her shoulders, upper arms, and youthful breasts. Her pale flesh darkened provocatively below her belly, suggesting the eroticism that had drawn bull and woman together. She held on to the bull's horn, and the ocean wind seemed to blow through her long black hair as they plunged together into the sea.

"An odd painting, from a woman. So very sensual," Adriana remarked.

"Do you recognize it?" Silvio asked, at her side. "Zeus as a bull, abducting Europa. Signorina Bramante insisted on painting that story. She started just after Pope Alexander died, so I asked her if it was supposed to be the Borgia bull. The image had been all over the papal banners, you know, and it got to be a joke."

"And was that her intention?" Adriana asked. "I mean, to paint the Borgia bull?"

"I'm not sure. She just smiled and said I was too clever." He chuckled. "I don't see any resemblance to the Pope, though."

Michelangelo joined them. "Take a closer look at Europa. You'll see a Borgia face there."

Silvio scrutinized the fresco. "You're right. How very strange. It could almost be your portrait, Adriana. I never noticed, but the eyes are painted pale blue. Just like yours."

Adriana stared at the painting, speechless. It was not only the face that disturbed her. The dress that hung open around Europa's hips, somber blue with a single black stripe running from the crumpled bodice down to the hem, was identical to the dress she had worn at Alexander's requiem mass.

Michelangelo traced a line with his finger around the head of the princess. "The work is excellent in places, but inconsistent. Look, on the figure of the woman, every tiny element is painted with precision. But in the setting, the details fall away. It's the individual that interests her, not the scene. She remains the portraitist."

"A good portraitist, though, you must admit," Silvio countered. "I recommended her to a Venetian acquaintance who engaged her as well."

"Yes, she's clearly gifted. You did well to patronize her, Silvio."

Silvio nudged Michelangelo's shoulder. "You should take her on as an assistant."

Michelangelo shrugged, dismissing the subject as the two of them meandered from the library. Behind them, Adriana remained standing, bemused, before the fresco.

"Adriana, will you come?" The sound of her name roused her and she hurried to join her host.

Silvio led them to a shady portico on the west side of the palazzo where a table was set for lunch. The air smelled pleasantly of the honeysuckle that grew at the side of the house, and sparrows chirped from a nest on the roof. As Adriana approached the table, Annio Piccolomini made to rise, but age and infirmity made it a gesture only. From his seat at the head of the table the patriarch offered his hand to his guests, his eyes bright with interest.

"Good afternoon, Signora Borgia. Signor Buonarroti. I trust my son has not bored you too greatly." His voice was soft, as if he used it sparingly, his manner dignified and gallant.

"Not at all, Signor Piccolomini," Adriana replied. "It is a pleasure to be in your house and in such company."

"You are very kind." The old man took her hand in both of his. They were dry and trembled slightly, but they had a pleasant warmth. "I am very pleased that Signor Buonarroti could convince you to come, Lady Borgia." He swept a hand toward the lunch table. "You see, we wish to detain you as long as possible."

The guests were seated and a servant poured wine into silver goblets. They ate leisurely, remarking on the weather and the profusion of flowers in the garden. Then Silvio beckoned his housemaster, who came carrying a large volume bound in dark leather.

"Now, my dear friends, the trap is sprung. You cannot leave until you have admired our most recent prize. By Marsilio Ficino, a Florentine. I assume you know him, Michelo."

"I knew the man himself. In my time he was head of Lorenzo de' Medici's academy at the Villa Careggi. We even attended a dissection together. He had some rather radical ideas about the importance of the body in understanding divine principles."

"Ficino had radical ideas about a number of things." Moving aside his plate, Silvio slid the volume in front of him and opened its heavy cover to the first page. "This is his bilingual edition of the Platonic Dialogues. *Euthyphro, Crito, Apologia.*"

Silvio leafed reverently through the first several pages. On each recto was the Greek original in clear black letters, and on each verso its Latin translation. The first page of Greek was topped by a decorative frieze, and garlanded columns ran down the vertical margins. Though it was printed, the volume looked for all the world like a manuscript, lacking only the bright colors.

Michelangelo was not impressed. "I remember. Ficino said Plato taught that the divine exists within man himself. Though I never quite understood what he meant by 'the divine.'"

Silvio nodded enthusiastically. "Which is why you might have spent a bit less time cutting up cadavers and a bit more reading Plato. And now you *can*, without learning Greek. Look here, the *Euthyphro* talks about exactly that question."

Across the table Adriana set down the piece of sweetmeat she was about to taste. She was out of her depth here. "The nature of the divine? Isn't that why we've got a clergy, to tell us all that?"

Silvio looked disdainful. "Oh, please. When we're children, they chant phrases at us that *they* learned as children, and none of us examine the meanings. Plato asks us to consider whether moral behavior is moral because it's God's command, or whether God commands moral behavior because it's moral."

"What difference does it make?" She bit into the sweetmeat.

"Every difference in the world." Silvio became animated. "If moral behavior is moral *only* because God commands it, then morality is nothing but obedience. But if God commands moral behavior because it is *already* moral, then morality is independent of God, and men do not need God to make them moral, only understanding."

Michelangelo set down his wineglass. "Why do you dwell on these questions, Silvio?"

He continued to turn the vellum leaves tenderly, his brow furrowed. "Why not? Shouldn't we want to know those things? Why else do we have thought and language?"

Michelangelo shook his head. "A man feels contentment when he obeys God." He dropped his glance. "And suffers guilt when he doesn't. No words are necessary."

Silvio closed his heavy manuscript, inserting his last two fingers between the pages he had been reading, and tucked the entire volume under his left arm, as if protecting it. Pointing, he twisted back around to the artist on his right and recited, "'And do you mean to say, Euthyphro, that you understand piety and impiety so accurately?'"

The elder Piccolomini chuckled amiably. "Do not be offended, Signor Buonarroti. My son loves to quote Plato."

"But your ramblings border on heresy," Michelangelo chided his friend. "I should remind you that Ficino's academy fell silent under the rule of Florence's other great spirit, Savonarola. I heard him preach once, about the wrath of God, and there was a lot to take to heart."

"Savonarola? You consider for even a *moment* that he was anything more than a fanatic?" Silvio snorted. "You're beginning to sound like a Spaniard."

Adriana studied the twisted pose still held by the young Piccolomini, the curled finger, the look of slight disdain at his opponent's apparent ignorance. She could imagine that these two friends had fought in like manner for years. Yet while the nobleman played lightheartedly with words, Michelangelo was deeply earnest, as though he grappled inwardly with something.

She took another sip of the light luncheon wine and thought of Gian Pietro Carafa. Would he bring the Spanish fires to Rome after all? And if he did, could she herself withstand torture for even a moment before confessing? The thought was deeply troubling, but so too was the image of a blue-eyed woman with her own face and in her own dress, and borne on the haunches of a bull.

❖

"In the name of the Father, and of the Son, and of the Holy Spirit." The voice of the priest intoned through the grillwork of the confessional.

"Bless me father, for I have sinned," Domenico murmured into his clasped hands, pressing the glass beads of his rosary onto his chin.

"All men are sinners, but those who freely confess will be forgiven. How have you sinned, my son?"

"I have let myself be caressed. I have given myself in lust and do repent of it."

The voice of the priest was without inflection, as if he had heard the same admission a thousand times. "The flesh is the prison of the soul and you must mortify it when it rises up against you. Separate yourself from those who tempt you."

Domenico felt a quick pang of dread. He could mortify the flesh, but never separate himself from the tempter. The dilemma tortured him.

"Father, can the same act be a sin for one person and not for another?"

"Of course. Consider the commandment not to kill. It is a mortal sin in most instances. But for the holy crusaders, it was a blessing to kill the infidel and the heretic. It is God who determines what sin is, for only God is all-knowing."

Domenico worked the rosary beads between his fingers. "But if I am enjoined to do something that seems wrong, how shall I know if it is a sin?"

"God has given us the Holy Mother Church, my son, to reveal His laws. That is why the gravest sin is doubt, and the greatest blessing obedience."

Dismayed by the answer, Domenico finished the ritual mechanically. "Lord Jesus Christ, have mercy on me, a sinner. I will pray this night for understanding and hold myself from sin."

"What the priest speaks on earth is confirmed on high. I absolve you. Now go in peace and sin no more."

❖

The Via Giulia clattered with carts and men on mules going about their business. Taking Adriana by the arm as they crossed, Michelangelo asked, "Did you like what you saw?"

"The book? Quite impressive, and Silvio's argument was too. Although it leads to dangerous questions."

Michelangelo shook his head. "I meant the frescos, Adriana. Did you like them?"

"Oh, those." She laughed nervously. "The Apollo is pure flattery, which I suppose is the point. As for the other one, I don't know. The similarity may be just a coincidence, but you're right. Raphaela Bramante is very gifted. Why did you laugh when Silvio said you should employ her?"

"Because she said the same thing a few weeks ago. She came to me just as we were setting up the first scaffolding and asked if she could work with me."

"Really? You didn't say that earlier. Why don't you want her?"

"I *do* want her. But how can I have a woman working in the chapel with all those men? It would cause a scandal."

They had crossed the Via Giulia and wandered past a worksite where men on a scaffold painted the façade of a palazzo. One of the painters, in baggy trousers, glanced down at her.

"Dress her in boy's clothes," Adriana said abruptly. "She'd need them anyhow, climbing all over your platform. With a big hat to protect her head from paint. She's tall. She'll look just like all the others."

"You can't be serious. This is the Pope's own chapel. What if he found out? What if she were hurt? Besides, there's no money left to pay her."

She touched his arm. "I'll cover her salary. It won't even show up in the accounting."

He shook his head. "Look, I'd love to employ her. But Bramante would never consent to having his daughter work on high scaffolding with a dozen men and boys." The whine in his voice showed he was running out of arguments and waited to be convinced.

"He doesn't have to be told every detail. You know he would be glad for her to be instructed by you, the great Michelangelo. It would oblige him to you."

He scratched his beard, obviously considering the idea. "It's asking for trouble, you know. But if you do something for me, I'll take her on."

"What's that?"

He studied the ground for a moment, clearly preparing his case. "Convince the Pope that I should work on the basilica."

"What? You can't do both the chapel and the basilica at the same time."

"Yes I can. I can make designs. I already have ideas. Adriana, I *want* the dome of St. Peter's. It's the greatest project Rome has had since the coliseum." His hand closed in front of him, clutching air.

"Michelo, I'm all but an outcast here. What possible influence do you think I could have on this Pope?"

"You said yourself that Julius owed you a favor for getting Cesare to sway the Spanish Cardinals. That got him elected Pope. He can't have forgotten." He took a breath. "Look, just tell him the new basilica is a glorious project, worthy of him, but that it's too big for one man. And that I should be involved too."

"And if he refuses to see me?"

"I'm sure he won't. He can't. And the argument is so simple, he's got to agree. If he does, I'll take the girl on as an assistant."

Sighing, Adriana grasped his arm so that they walked together, like siblings or a couple, toward the Albergo dell' Orso.

"Fair enough, Michelo. I agree. One madness for the other."

VII

Strange to be in Sala Misteri again, Adriana thought as she paced. On the last occasion she was one of those in power, not the supplicant. In a different time, with a different pope, she sat here with Cesare while he gave the appearance of waiting on His Holiness's pleasure, but got what he himself desired.

She tried not to be impatient. Even with the small obligation Julius might have had toward her, he delayed for ten days before even replying to her request for an audience. Obviously, the hated name Borgia preceded her like a banner. And the favor she had to call in was as threadbare as the hem of her court gown.

She studied the Swiss Guardsman standing in bright yellow and orange stripes before the door to the Sala dei Santi. Alexander had kept a palace guard as well, but his well-armed veterans were far less visible. She wondered whether the pretty costumes made them better soldiers or worse.

"Signora Borgia."

She spun around as she heard her name. A priest stood at the door to the audience chamber and motioned to her. Adriana gathered her skirts and followed him into the Sala dei Santi. Pope Julius II sat without cushions, somber with ecclesiastical authority under the blues and golds of Pinturicchio's fresco. He wore no ceremonial vestments, only the pleated white alb tied at the waist by a cord, which covered him down to his silken slippers. The satin mozzetta rested on his shoulders, and the red camauro, bordered in ermine, covered his head. His only ornaments were the jeweled pectoral cross and, on his right index finger, a cameo ring.

Beside him a massive oaken table was covered with maps, books, and documents. She wondered, briefly, what he read. And yet he seemed breathless, as if he had just come into the room a moment before she did and the regal pose was quickly staged.

"Holiness." Adriana knelt before him and kissed first the papal slipper, then the ring of the Pontiff, noting the gnarled strength in his hands.

She recalled the soft hands of Alexander VI and marveled at the difference between the two popes, the voluptuary and the warrior. There was a curious odor about him, though, not unpleasant, that she could not place. Julius glowered down at her from his throne, a wooden chair with a tall narrow back. Its supporting posts were carved at the top with the acorns of his family crest. As if anyone needed to be reminded.

"Lady Borgia," a voice said behind her, and she glanced over her shoulder at the familiar red face of Cardinal Giovanni de' Medici, as massive in his crimson cassock as Julius was in his white alb. Together they seemed to fill the room, like giant chessmen. But the Cardinal was welcome, as far as she was concerned. In spite of his bullish appearance, the Cardinal was of a calm nature and, more importantly, a friend of Michelangelo.

"Eminence." She genuflected quickly and kissed the Cardinal's ring.

"Lady Borgia. A pleasure to see you at the Vatican after these several years."

She listened for sarcasm, but did not hear it. The man was a master of neutrality.

"Signora Borgia has a request?" the Pope said, moving to the substance of the audience.

"Holy Father, I speak on behalf of the artist Michelangelo Buonarroti."

"Ah, yes, our *Maestro della Sistina.*"

"Yes, Holiness, but Signor Buonarroti has asked me to speak about the new basilica."

"Has he?" Julius's voice was cold.

Adriana took a breath. "He has asked me to convey that he is aware of the apparent delays in the execution of your wishes, and that he proposes a collaboration with Maestro Bramante, in order to carry them out with greater speed."

"Maestro Buonarroti has our commission for the Sistine Chapel. For an enormous sum, I might add. He knows full well that Signor Bramante is in charge of the reconstruction."

Adriana glanced briefly over his head at the fresco of Saint Catherine converting the scholars of Alexandria. The saint seemed to look down at her, laughing.

"If I may be so bold, Holiness. The reconstruction of St. Peter's is a task beyond the capabilities of a single man, however gifted. Maestro Bramante's genius is beyond question. So is Michelangelo's. He wishes only to put the full force of it at your service in such a noble task."

"He does not find the painting of our chapel to be sufficiently noble. Is that it?"

His ring tapped as he beat softly on the wooden arm of his chair. She searched for something to say that he could not twist into accusation. "That is not what I meant, Holiness. Maestro Buonarroti merely offers his talents to the basilica as well. He holds Signor Bramante in the highest regard."

Was there any subtle way to remind him of the service she had rendered him? The scowl he already had suggested it would be useless.

"Signor Buonarroti is a man of great talent, but God has seen fit to enrich Rome with a plenitude of such men. I shall use each one according to my will, which is God's will."

His face began to redden, and he stood up exhaling exasperation. He was vastly more imposing standing than he had been sitting. It was easy to imagine him at the forefront of an army. He did not raise his voice, rather he lowered it ominously, but the intimidation was the same.

"Signor Buonarroti has been chosen to serve us by painting." He paused dramatically. "And paint is what he shall do."

The audience, which had lasted less than five minutes, was over. He raised his hand and she expected a benediction. But it was only a gesture for the other prelate to escort her to the door. Deeply chagrined, Adriana genuflected once again and kissed the papal ring. In the brief moment his hand was before her face, she recognized the scent. It was a mix of incense and candle smoke.

She backed toward the door and heard Cardinal de' Medici beg his leave as well. The gaudy new guardsman snapped to attention. Reeling from the abrupt dismissal, Adriana lowered her eyes as she moved past him into the anteroom. When she looked up once more, she halted. At the opposite end of the room, waiting for her to leave so he could enter, was Gian Pietro Carafa.

He seemed ageless, but his gaunt face held no vitality, only a forceful trimness. His tonsure was extreme, exposing most of the top of his skull and leaving only a thin ring of closely cropped hair around his head. He had draped his black cloak over a chair as if expecting to stay awhile in the Papal Palace, and he stood slightly hunched in his white Dominican robe. His expression of courteous respect directed toward the other Cardinal shifted to disdain as it fell on her.

At a faint cough from Cardinal de' Medici, she turned away from the doorway and fell into step beside him. "Eminence. If I may ask, what is Gian Pietro Carafa doing in Rome?"

"Carafa? Ah, the reformer. The conscience of the Church, perhaps, or its watchdog. He has come to urge His Holiness to a more rigorous defense of orthodoxy. I believe he also hears confessions at St. Maria del Popolo."

"More rigorous? Does this Pope plan to bring the Inquisition to Rome?" Adriana felt a rising dread.

"Why do you ask? Do you have something to confess?"

"No, not at all." She caught herself. "I ask only because I was recently in Spain, in Seville, while he served with Torquemada. My own family was tragically affected."

"I'm sorry to hear that, Signora Borgia. But I cannot speak to the way the Pope may choose to enforce the Inquisition. Regarding Signor Buonarroti, however, I think you need not be so discouraged. I have great respect for him. He was apprenticed in his youth with my family in Florence, and I know him well. But genius alone counts for little with this Pope. He sees himself as the Caesar of God, and he expects the same obedience that a general expects in battle." De' Medici clasped his hands behind his back. "You must explain this to Signor Buonarroti."

"And so, the matter is settled then? I can give Michelangelo no hope with regard to the basilica?"

The Cardinal shook his head. "You miss my point, Lady Borgia. Great temples are built over generations. Michelangelo should finish painting his chapel and bide his time. His day will come. Perhaps with the next Pope."

"But Eminence, who is expected to be the next Pope?"

Cardinal de' Medici smiled.

VIII

Silvio urged his horse closer to the coach where a boy waited holding a cushioned armchair. A footman helped the elderly Annio Piccolomini climb down from the interior of the coach.

Silvio bent down in the saddle, causing the peregrine falcon on his arm to flutter. "Are you certain you want to do this, Father? It's surely a strain on you."

The old man supported himself on the footman's shoulder. "Of course I'm certain. I don't know what awaits me in heaven, but I do know what's here on my own land. Do you think I want to lie on a stinking sickbed when I can spend a day with you and your falcon?"

The coachman got down and carried the armchair to a slight promontory overlooking a wide expanse of meadow. With assistance, Annio settled into his seat.

"Go ahead," he commanded Silvio. "Set her loose. I'll have a perfect view of her."

"I'm glad we can spend the morning together, you, me, and Freccia. She's been whistling all morning, longing to be in the air."

Silvio gazed lovingly at the hooded raptor perched on his gauntlet, a handsome female haggard caught in the wild. Up close, he could see the subtleties of her plumage, the slate blue back, white feather beard, and high, striated chest. Her long trousered legs were concealed against the white belly crossed by undulations of gray. He lifted the hood and the falcon blinked enormous dark brown eyes, then tilted her narrow head as if deciding which part of the sky to patrol first. "Hoh!" Silvio called, thrusting her upward for her first flight of the day.

She rose at once to great heights until she was a tiny fluttering thing against the clear blue sky. Not hunting yet, she circled once in a leisurely spiral, savoring the rush of open air itself.

"Is anything freer than that?" the elder Piccolomini remarked.

"She's happy, you can see it. With nothing but the short jesses on her claws." Silvio shaded his eyes and watched her fluid movements. "And yet, she comes back to me. Like penitents to the Church. A few bribes and this splendid creature gave up her will to me. The pious are no different."

"I wish you would not utter such blasphemies. There are those who listen for it and would burn you for your sentiments. Think of our family. You are the grand-nephew of Pius II, a man whom many consider the greatest of Popes. If his successors had been as wise as he, the Church would not need its Savonarola or its Inquisition, and there would not be the rumblings of heresy in the north of Europe."

His head thrown back, Silvio followed the spiraling course of the falcon. "Popes are princes like any other, like the Duke of Milan or the King of Naples. They fight one another for power and win or lose. If the Pope were truly the instrument of God, how could he ever lose a battle? Why would he need an army of paid soldiers to fight on God's behalf?"

"You frighten me, my son. Sometimes it seems that you believe in nothing at all."

"I believe in books. A profusion of books. Books for every man who reads."

"What would that accomplish? If every man could read the Bible, there would be a thousand misunderstandings of it."

"Who's to say there aren't already? But more than Bibles, I would see books of every sort in circulation. Why shouldn't every merchant and mendicant read Plato, for example? Assuming they could all read. Imagine—"

Excited barking seized his attention, for the dogs had just been released. Within moments they flushed out a rabbit. Freccia shot downward nearly perpendicular, pulling up to the horizontal at the last moment. The rabbit pivoted toward another direction but it was too late. On her first swoop, the falcon seized her prey and held it down.

Silvio dismounted and dashed down the slope to where predator and prey still thrashed. He dropped to his knees and seized the rabbit by one leg, slicing its throat in a single clean stroke. Freccia still held its hindquarters in her beak. She would not let loose until he rewarded her.

"Good work," he said, soothingly, and cut out a section of meat on the rabbit's thigh. He tossed it to the side and the falcon pounced on it, releasing the carcass.

The footman arrived with the game bag and Silvio dropped the rabbit into it. Freccia leapt onto Silvio's glove again, ready for the next hunt.

"Signore!" A shout came from the promontory. One of the houseboys was running down the slope toward him.

He dropped to the ground some distance away so as not to startle the falcon and called out, "Signore, the excavators have found something. In the villa of Hadrian. Something wonderful."

❖

Livio Farnese slouched in the doorway on the Via dei Coronari until he saw her. It had taken him three days, but finally he had determined that she left her house around seven every morning. He stepped out in front of her.

"Good morning, Raphaela. You're looking lovely today."

She started at seeing him, but recovered herself. "Livio. What are you doing here?"

He ignored her question. "Where are you headed in such a hurry?"

She continued walking, clutching a large soft bundle to her chest. "I'm working. Why else would I be out here?"

He walked alongside her. "Working? A woman as beautiful as you shouldn't have to work. You should stay at home and let yourself be pampered."

"That doesn't interest me."

"The more's the pity. I would love to be the one to pamper you." He leered, tilting his head slightly.

"Livio, please. I don't have time for this."

"I bet you'd have more time for me if I were rich."

"No, I wouldn't. You don't know what you're talking about." She hurried on ahead of him. He followed a step behind for a few moments and then, seeing that she would not engage him, he halted and called after her, "We'll see about that."

She did not turn around, and Livio struggled with the conflicting urges of anger and lust at the same time. He dreamt constantly about intimacy with her, although he alternated between fantasies of her crawling toward him, begging him to take her, and of his ravishing her in spite of her resistance until she melted with desire for him.

Money. He needed money to impress her. It was a cruel irony that he carried the name of one of the most powerful families in Rome and yet was poor. Being a bastard son of one of many Farneses meant little, except that his name allowed him stay in the palazzo. If he wanted to advance in the world and receive the respect he deserved, he had to get his hands on some money. Well, there were always men who would pay for discreet assistance, of one sort or another. It was just a matter of finding such a man and offering his services.

Yes, he'd come back soon, in fine new clothes, on a horse, and she'd change her tune. He was sure of it.

IX

Penthesilea, Queen of the Amazons, with my face. I love it!"
Arabella Raimondi gleamed, studying her portrait. A woman
with bow and arrow sat astride a white warhorse, wind fluttering her
hair and leather skirt. "Who would have thought that a lady of my...
profession, would look so at home leading an army of women?"

Raphaela lifted the portrait from its easel. "Leadership suits you
completely, just as well as the leather and feathers. You have a natural
imperial bearing, you know. I just gave you a setting."

"Imperial? You really think so? It's true I do like being in charge in
the bedroom," Arabella said *sotto voce*. "I was known for being one of
the best, shall we say, 'disciplinarians' in Venice, and you'd be surprised
how many men, including a few senators, like that sort of thing." She
sighed. "But one wants to stop doing that at the age of forty."

"Age has not harmed you in the least, Arabella." Raphaela held
the portrait next to her model's head, comparing the two. "I've studied
your face for weeks, and I can assure you that you're gorgeous. You can
still attract any man you want, I'm sure."

"But my dear, I don't *want* to attract a man. Whether they want
me over or under them, domineering or docile, I've had quite enough
of them. Fortunately a few dozen of them, mostly the very old and
very rancid, paid handsomely for their 'imaginative' sex. And even
better, they taught me a thing or two about investment. I'm financially
independent now and can retire while I still have my teeth and my
tits."

Raphaela laughed out loud. "Yes, you *do* have all those things. I
believe I've done at least your bosoms justice in the portrait." She set

down the painting on a table and laid out a length of cloth next to it. "So what will you do now, with no gentlemen in your life? Have you given up love?"

"Heavens no. But it's much nicer with women. Have I shocked you? Well, it's time you found out anyhow. Women do with their fingers and tongues what men do with their clumsy cocks, and they do it lots better. They take their time and know how to torture you deliciously with delay. A skill few men master."

Raphaela was not sure how to reply. Her own experiences, with both boys and girls, had been furtive, leading to nothing but the conclusion that boys were awkward and self-centered. She already knew to whom she was attracted; only the physical aspect of coupling was still vague. It was pleasing to learn that, at least in Venice, there were women who pleased women. "Uh. Well, I'll have to remember that information. But surely that's not all you'll do. There are a lot of hours in the day."

"Well, when I'm not on my back, I will entertain artists, poets, philosophers. Venice is crawling with them. I have a small but handsome palazzo on a tiny canal that's impossible to find unless you are invited. I wouldn't want any old clients showing up at the door. But I would love for *you* to show up one day, my dear. I'm serious. For a short visit or a long stay."

She stroked Raphaela's shoulder in a manner midway between flirtatious and maternal. "You know, with your talent, you would have no end of work in Venice. I know a dozen vain people who would pay in gold to be painted as a hero or a god."

Raphaela patted Arabella's hand. "Thank you, dear Arabella. The day may come when I will take you at your offer. But for now, I've just been invited to apprentice here in Rome. With Michelangelo," she added quietly.

"Michelangelo! You're going to study sculpture?"

Raphaela laid the portrait in the cloth and wrapped it carefully for transport. "No. Painting, of course. The Pope has engaged him to paint the ceiling of his chapel, and for that Michelangelo needs assistants. He's even agreed to let me work with him on the platform, but I'll have to be disguised as a boy."

Arabella tossed her head back with an excess of glee. "I *love* it," she repeated. "Especially the dress-up part. You'll look adorable. I had a client who liked me to do that. I won't tell you what else he liked me to do, but let's just say it involved certain devices and…never mind. So when do you start?"

"Immediately. But I'm trusting you with a dangerous secret, Arabella. The other painters can't know, and my father *especially* mustn't. He gives me a lot of freedom, but if he found out I was in disguise and working alongside a dozen men, he would bring it all to a halt."

"I understand, my dear." The courtesan took her package under her arm and started toward the door. "Of course you can trust me. I've a thousand secrets *much* more interesting than that one, believe me. But listen, when you're done, please come and do a few portraits in Venice. You'll never locate my house without help, but you can reach me through the priest of Santa Maria dei Miracoli. He was a client and is now a good friend and will always know how to find me."

"Venice sounds just as immoral as Rome, only prettier." Raphaela offered her cheek for the departure kisses. "I'll be sure to remember your invitation." Softly she closed the door, it seemed to her, behind one of the freest women in Italy.

X

Lethargic and brooding, Adriana let herself into her stable to see to her horses. The creamy mare nickered recognition as she stroked its neck, before passing to the next stall to pat the sable horse that her lover Cesare had given her. The mature gelding still served her well pulling the ducal coach that Cesare had also left behind. She could not fathom how such valuable objects had not been seized. Presumably, during the weeks of confusion, the servants had simply hidden them. For her taste, the painted coach was more ostentatious than comfortable, however. For all its six carved posts, its fine woolen curtains, and its canopy, it was in the end just a wagon, and certainly rode like one, even with iron-rimmed wheels. But ostentation was Cesare's style.

From the very beginning, his imperiousness was breathtaking. She had been among the crowd at the Porta del Popolo when he returned like a conqueror from the Forli campaign. On his warhorse, in a coat of black velvet reaching to his knees, the son of Pope Alexander VI looked like the Prince of Darkness. His heralds blew a fanfare as he passed through the gate. Bishops and ambassadors followed with a thousand infantrymen, Swiss and Gascons, marching in ranks carrying halberds and standards blazoned with the Borgia arms.

The Castel Sant' Angelo flew his banners on its ramparts, and between each merlon a trumpeter stood in ornamental armor. The castle cannons sounded repeatedly, their concussions shattering windows along the entire length of the battlements. Rome was besotted with him, and so was she.

As the widow of his brother Juan, she was privileged to be present in the Vatican Palace when the Pope received him and bestowed the new titles. When Cesare strode from the room after the ceremony, as Captain General and *Gonfaloniere* of the Holy Church, he caught her eye and his expression was unmistakable.

Two nights later he came to her at her house in the Via dei Leuteri.

He entered her room without preliminaries and had only enough patience to undress them both before he took possession of her. She gave herself willingly, though. It made no difference that rumors said he had killed her husband, his own brother. The confusion around Juan's assassination made for uncertainty, and Cesare had too much power to be questioned openly. Their coupling under the windows of the Vatican was not so much passion as wild abandon. She could not say she ever loved him, but he burned between her legs like a torch and could do anything with her he wished.

She recalled the night that was the nadir of her sexual servitude to him, the night of the banquet in the papal apartments. The courtesans invited to the party had debased themselves ever more as the evening wore on, finally crawling naked on the floor in sordid games, where some of the guests mounted them from behind. His Holiness had merely laughed at the spectacle, but Cesare was clearly aroused.

Yet even he knew there was a limit to the lasciviousness to which she would stoop for him, and public sex was beyond it. So, while the party went on in the papal stateroom, she found herself in one of the service rooms of the palace, disrobed and entangled with Cesare and a courtesan.

She was used to granting Cesare his every sexual wish. But their sordid copulation that night with the courtesan strangely troubled her.

The first touch of the other woman reminded her of the sex play she had once engaged in with Lucrezia, the girlish tickling they had begun in a fit of giggles and that had evolved, finally, into a sudden surprising climax.

But the courtesan was experienced in prolonging excitation. Yet at the same time, it was Cesare they were supposed to entertain and satisfy. Cesare had entered her from behind, using her like a boy, so she tried to focus on him, matching her rhythm with his. But all the while she found herself excited to breathtaking pitch by the skillful mouth of the courtesan.

The climax, so expertly delayed by the other woman, had been long and powerful, but because Cesare had been involved, Adrianna could never be sure what sensations had caused it. In any case, it was by then almost morning, and the courtesan had departed wordlessly, leaving her feeling depleted and used.

Still, she followed Cesare, even after Rome, fearful of defying him. For years she was swept along in his violent wake, and now that the momentum of his life was gone, she found she had none of her own and was sinking. Who in Rome could pull her up again?

"Signora." Her housemaster appeared at the stable door.

"A visitor, Signora. He says his name is Piccolomini."

"Piccolomini?" The name came like a reprieve. "See to his comfort," she ordered, and she hurried behind him toward the house.

Her guest met her halfway, on the path to the stable, and he was grinning.

"Silvio, what a pleasant surprise." She flushed with affection as he took her hand. He looked dashing, in an elaborately slashed and stitched jerkin of the same soft green leather as his boots. Was there never a day when he was not elegantly dressed?

"What brings you to the country? Will you hunt? Where is your falcon?"

"Freccia is at home. Today I am hunting marble. My antiquarians have been searching in the new excavations at Hadrian's ruins, and it appears they've located something."

"One of Hadrian's statues? Well, I wish you luck. Most of them are broken."

He sighed with the resignation of a collector who had been disappointed in the past. But his gray eyes still glowed with hope. "Yes, it could be all in pieces, or missing a head. We shall soon see."

"Will you stop for some wine before you go on?" She gestured toward the house.

"No, there is no time. I thought you might like to ride up with me for the final discovery. Who knows? It might be another Apollo or Laocoön."

It took her scarcely a moment to decide, and she called to her housemaster, who stood a respectful distance from their conversation.

"Jacopo, have the stable men saddle my mare. Signor Piccolomini and I are going hunting."

❖

They rode awhile side by side in silence, and Adriana wondered about the reason behind Silvio's visit. Was he courting her? The thought was agreeable, though it took her by surprise. His lighthearted, almost effeminate nature was an appealing contrast to the men who used to control her, and she felt at ease with him.

And yet, whenever she stole a glance at his tousled blond hair, she thought of another blonde, two others, in fact, who attracted her as much. Cesare's flirtatious sister, Lucrezia, had been her best companion during her Vatican years. Now the face of the mysterious young painter hovered at the back of her consciousness. Raphaela, who painted a half-naked woman wearing Adriana's clothing. She shook the thought from her mind.

"This place was really a small city, wasn't it?" she observed as they came through the entrance archway of the portico into the complex of ruins called Hadrian's villa.

"Yes, it had everything an imperial city needed. Residences, temples, theaters, fountains, pools, baths."

They rode along a fractured marble pavement bordered by a peristyle of broken columns, and she tried to recreate the city in her mind's eye. It was scarcely possible, since almost everything that stood upright had been taken as building material into Rome, and what was left was covered by rubble and growth.

"What made you decide to look for statues here? There can't be anything left after so many years of pillage."

"When Raphaela Bramante was painting my 'Apollo' portrait, she mentioned that she and her father had been at Hadrian's villa and seen men digging out statues. I half forgot about it until Michelangelo showed me a marble medallion he made with images of a woman's face. The two events happening one after the other—I took it as a sign and sent my antiquarians here to search."

"A sign?" She laughed. "You reject the Catechism but believe in signs?"

"The falseness of the Catechism does not mean there are no divine forces that deserve our scrutiny. Of course I believe in signs, wherever they come from. The trick is to distinguish them from our longings."

"So you think my medallion—he's promised it to me, by the way—was directing you to Hadrian's villa?"

"*Your* medallion? Now I'm sure it's a sign. In fact, your return to Rome without Cesare could also be taken as one. Don't press me to say what it is a sign *of*, but I think it's a good thing. In any case, I'm happy to see you again. We must get you out more."

They descended sharply in single file into a semicircular area. It appeared to be a theater or a stadium from which most of the marble had been stripped. Adriana's mare was careful as she picked her way over the uneven ground.

"Remember, I'm still a Borgia. I'd rather keep to my friends, people I can be sure will not poison my wine or hand me over to the Inquisition."

"Well, I can promise that I won't poison you," Silvio said amiably. "But if you're nervous about the Inquisition, I'm not the best company for you. The Dominicans have their collective eye on me, and even having two popes in the family is no defense. Michelangelo can protect you better than I can. It's true he's always arguing with the Pope, but he's valuable to Julius and both men know it."

"He's a difficult man."

"Which one? The painter or the Pope?"

"Both, actually. But I meant Michelangelo. We made a deal a few months ago, for him to engage Raphaela Bramante, but since I couldn't uphold my part, nothing came of it, I suppose."

"It's too bad, then. She's a woman with an exceptional gift. One of these days she'll marry some fat merchant and start popping out babies, instead of paintings. But until then, Michelangelo should try to make something of her."

Adriana winced at the image of Raphaela holding one babe in her arms and pregnant with another, a faceless man standing smugly beside her.

"I should think Bramante himself would have something to say about his daughter's future," she remarked.

"You'd think so, but he's had to raise her alone and doesn't seem to know how to control her. Not that she behaves immodestly or anything of the sort. When she was painting me, her father escorted her in the evenings, but during the day she was alone when she came and went, just like a man. She's a bit wild that way."

Adriana tried to imagine someone like Silvio attending the young artist as she rode through the Roman streets. The faceless "gentleman" was scarcely more appealing than the merchant.

"It's too bad Michelangelo didn't take her in hand. Would've done them both good. Have you seen the work he's done in the chapel?"

"No. My last visit to the Vatican was pretty disagreeable. I won't go into Rome now unless I have a reason."

"Or a sign?" Silvio teased.

She could think of no retort and so murmured limply, "Maybe so."

They rode awhile over hard-packed ground interspersed with patches of patterned mosaic tile. The quiet of the somber winter afternoon was punctuated by the cawing of crows and the clopping of their horses' hooves on the ancient Roman stone.

A man seemed to step up out of the ground suddenly before them. "Good day, Signor Piccolomini. The men are just below. We're almost finished."

"Ah, here we are." Silvio dismounted and assisted Adriana. His hands were comfortingly warm where they touched the chilled skin on her forearms.

The workman led them down a narrow staircase into a subterranean chamber where two others worked by lantern light. Between them lay the discovery, mottled with dirt and algae, but unmistakable. The huntress Diana with her stag leaping at her side. Unbroken.

"Well done!" Silvio took the lantern. "Come here, Adriana. Come and meet my lovely new lady."

One of the workmen made room for her while the other wiped away the dirt that still adhered to the pits and grooves of the face. He trickled water from a gourd over the surface as he wiped, each swipe gently removing another layer of clay. Finally only the nostrils and eye sockets remained caked.

"There are still flecks of paint, Signore, here and there. It looks like her dress was gold."

"Magnificent." Silvio knelt down. "And nothing broken but the bow. Isn't she magnificent, Adriana?" he repeated. "You see, my signs were correct after all. Maybe this is *your* sign, to visit Rome again."

Adriana leaned over his shoulder just as the plugs of soil were washed from the two eyes. One eye was plain marble, its pigment lost, but the other still had its light green color. The goddess looked up at her, one-eyed and conspiratorial.

"Signs," Adriana murmured. "Yes, maybe so."

XI

DECEMBER 1508

Adriana entered the Sistine Chapel from the great hall and stopped under the first platform, letting her eyes adapt. The overcast sky sent little light through the high windows. Only a few candles burned on the tall candelabras before the chapel screen, and the artists' lanterns that hung at the top of the scaffolding shed scant light below.

Hearing voices overhead, she stepped out from under the platform and craned to peer upward, searching along the row of lanterns on the balustrade for Michelangelo. The shadows cast by the workers danced eerily on the curve of the vault. She turned slowly in a circle, studying what he had accomplished in the months since their last meeting and her disastrous audience with the Pope.

He had sketched in a fictive architecture supporting the vault, an intersection of illusionary columns with illusionary ribs, outlines of swags and medallions between them, and a few brooding figures in the lunettes. Hanging cloths, which presumably obscured the work during the services, were pulled aside at the moment, revealing the maze of chalk lines, strings, and sketches.

"Adriana! Is that you?"

She finally spotted him, or at least the toes of his boots jutting from the platform he stood on directly over her head. Between the feet, foreshortened, she saw the underside of his face, lit from below by lantern light.

"What brings you into Rome again?" Michelangelo called down.

"You do, of course. I came to see what you've been doing."

He made a wide arc with his arm. "Well, what do you think?"

"I don't know," she called back. "From down here it's all just lines and strings."

"I can't leave off working right now. Do you want to come up?"

She was startled by the invitation. Climb up? Ascend the scaffold to the vault of the holy chapel? She considered her dress, one of her more practical ones, for the days she rode horseback. She felt the devil grinning inside of her, urging her to dare it.

Michelangelo pointed a dripping brush toward a ladder leaning against the base of the platform. "You can get up over there, in the corner." One of his boys was just climbing down it with a bucket.

Adriana gripped the hem of her skirt, wound it once around her legs, and tucked it into her belt. The boy held the ladder while she climbed. Committed to the ascent, she ignored the panic that rose with each step. At the top of the ladder Michelangelo grasped her hand and pulled her firmly up onto the platform. It creaked and swayed slightly as it caught her weight.

Breathless with nerves and exhilaration, she glanced down at the floor far below, at the tile circles of the Papal Walk ending at the marble screen that divided the chapel in half. On the right wall was the choir loft where Domenico sang. Beyond the screen was the *quadratura,* in which only the Pope and the College of Cardinals were permitted. Stone benches were arranged around the square on three sides, where the Cardinals sat during mass. On the left was the papal throne, and at the far end, against the west wall, the altar. Sacred ground, and yet, in its murkiness, it seemed irrelevant to the work taking place where she stood, in the light-filled arc of the ceiling.

She stood on the outermost of several footbridges that arched across the chapel in parallel to the ceiling and were just wide enough to hold two men side by side. On the two first platforms boys were spreading plaster on the exposed masonry of the ceiling. They applied it with trowels, smoothing it in wide rhythmic sweeps, occasionally glancing over their shoulders at her. In the heat and dusty air high under the vault, the sour mixture of wet plaster and the workers' rancid sweat was oppressive. Holding her skirts close to her legs, she made her way gingerly to the innermost platform, where Michelangelo stood painting over his head. "It looks like you've found inspiration after all."

"Enough to start, at least." He spoke to her without taking his eyes from his work. "Over there, the boys are applying the base plaster that will support the whole thing. It will take a day to dry and then I'll move. I'm applying the *intonaco* now, the final layer."

He dipped a brush into a bucket of thin, creamy plaster and laid a smooth coating over the base plaster in a wide strip. When he was finished, he set down the bucket and stepped back to the previous band, which had begun to dry. He tested it with his thumb and found it satisfactory.

"Now the transfer."

He unrolled a parchment the width of the painted strip. It held a cartoon of two figures and a tree stump, sketched in charcoal. The lamplight behind it revealed that the lines were perforated. He pressed the parchment against the intonaco, tacking it at intervals. When it was well anchored he took a cloth-covered ball of charcoal from his apron and pounced it lightly over the surface until every portion was covered with powdered carbon. Then he slowly peeled the sooty paper away, uncovering the entire drawing behind it, as if it had been sketched there.

"I must work quickly now, while the intonaco is still damp," he said, rolling up the parchment and handing it to one of the boys. "Otherwise the pigment won't be fixed."

He picked up a palette made up of a ring of shallow bowls, each containing a different pigment, and with several brushes he began to paint in the scene he had just outlined. She was amazed at the speed and confidence with which he painted and then remembered that he was a sculptor. Compared to the blows of the chisel on unforgiving marble, paint, which allowed room for correction, must have seemed a relief. No wonder he was fearless.

The scene showed people in flight from rising waters. On the right side, on a strip painted earlier, a cluster of the doomed huddled together under a blanket. In the center, a shallow boat capsized, while in the background, a closed vessel floated. The first fresco on his ceiling was the punishing Flood, the ark sealed and inaccessible, repelling all who tried to enter. There was no hint of rescue, only of damnation. Michelangelo had made good his threat to "wash it all away."

He painted directly over his head, moving from the lightest shades to the darkest with finality, never going back to the light shades again. With three brushes dipped into paint pots of brown, red, and white, he created endless variations in tint and shading, rounding off every muscle, giving substance and vitality to the painted flesh. Before her eyes, he cast upon the emptiness figures of clay and breathed life into them. It was as close to a miracle as the human hand could accomplish.

She stepped back to study the gathering of refugees he had painted the day before. Among them, two men embraced, one hovering protectively over the other, whose head was loosely bandaged. The injured man reached up and held the other around the buttocks.

Michelangelo saw where her eyes went and said, "Two of the doomed."

"Shall I continue painting the water, Maestro?" Behind her, an alto voice spoke, too soft for a man, too resonant for a boy.

Adriana felt a shiver of pleasure even before she turned around.

In trousers, smock, and plaster-spattered apron, the androgynous form of Raphaela Bramante stood solemnly in front of her.

XII

Michelangelo spoke without looking away from his work, obviously for the benefit of the other workers. "Adriana, my background painter, Carlo. Carlo…the Lady Adriana Borgia."

The two women stared at each other while Adriana recovered from her surprise. Michelangelo had obviously upheld his end of the bargain in spite of her failure with the Pope.

"Honored, My Lady." "Carlo" lowered her eyes.

Adriana smiled at the lovely low register of the voice she'd wondered about for so long.

Michelangelo set down his palette. "I am sorry, Adriana. Carlo must paint while the plaster is still damp, and the platform was not built for three. I am afraid you must leave now before we all go crashing down."

"Oh." She looked down at her feet. "Yes, of course." Suddenly obedient, she attempted to step past the young assistant but stumbled to one knee and was caught in Raphaela's slender arms. The other woman's breath was warm on her ear.

"Madonna, I'll help you to the ladder."

"I can manage, thank you."

Chagrined, Adriana regained her footing and stepped as quickly as she could toward the ladder where she descended, embarrassment giving way to a sort of intoxication. She had been under the vault of the chapel and seen the beginning of what the world would soon wonder at, Michelangelo's vision of the Deluge.

She was drowning in it.

Dazed, she untucked the hem of her dress from her belt and moved to the door of the chapel. For several seconds, she stared out into the Sala Regia, then became aware of someone behind her. "Carlo" had followed her down the ladder.

"Madonna…" That lovely voice again. "Maestro said to give you this."

The creature held out one arm, the paint-flecked hand closed in a fist around something small. Adriana accepted the object, studying the face of the "apprentice." Amazing, she thought. The charade was of her own invention, yet her eyes could not decide whether she looked at boy or woman. Silence stretched between them again. Adriana wanted to talk, but the other workers were within earshot. She lowered her gaze to the marble medallion in her hand. The carved face of a woman looked up at her, haloed by a snake.

"Thank you…Carlo."

With a silent nod, the lovely boy-woman returned to the chapel interior to paint the waters of God's great punishment. Adriana watched her walk away, wondering what Michelangelo had told her. She was tempted to rush after her, to ask, but instead swept through the Sala Regia to the great stairs leading down and out of the palace.

As she emerged from the doorway the first clap of thunder warned of a coming storm. Jacopo sat scowling on his horse, holding the reins of her mare. He pointed toward heavy clouds on the horizon.

"We'd best leave right away, My Lady."

She mounted quickly and rode toward the Ponte Sant'Angelo. The wind over the Tiber was already strong as they turned eastward along the Via Giulia. The horses were fresh, and they covered the distance at a comfortable canter. The sky darkened with evening and the coming storm, but the route was familiar and she was not worried. Her thoughts crowded in on one another. Michelangelo's flood waters, a boy that was a woman, the strange medallion in her pocket. She felt no chill.

Then, as they reached the Via Tiburtina the sky began to rumble and flare with sheet lightning. With each flash, the high cumulous-cloud masses lit up orange-red on one side and stayed black on the other. Jacopo slowed his horse and peered upward, holding his cap against the wind.

"You might almost think the heavens were angry. Look, My Lady. When the sky lights, you can see the saints."

"What are you talking about?" Adriana reluctantly drew up next to him. The evening sky again flickered orange, causing her mare to dance nervously.

"Over there." He pointed toward the west. "Wait until the next flash. It looks like they're standing at the foot of God's throne."

She looked toward where he pointed in the darkness, waiting for the sky to ignite. In a moment it flashed again a jolt of yellow light and she saw it. The tall thunderheads did indeed look like colossal beings, gathered around a central light, and the crack of thunder seemed to give them voice.

"I see tall clouds. No saints," she shouted between thunderclaps. The wind had increased in strength and whipped at her cloak, causing it to flutter wildly behind her. She clutched it closed with one hand.

"Best to hurry now, My Lady," Jacopo said, kicking his horse into a run. They galloped wildly, she and the warm creature between her legs fleeing the storm. Once more the ear-splitting thunder exploded and the whole sky lit at once, as though signaling an end to the world. Then silence fell and for a few moments she heard only the rushing in the trees, the panting of the straining horses, and the thudding of the hooves on the still-hard ground.

An hour away from the cypress trees of the Villa Borgia they met the deluge. As if the vessel holding it had broken, the rain fell like a wall of water, drenching them.

XIII

She stood on the shore of the Tiber looking toward St. Peter's. Inside the basilica, she knew, a requiem mass was being sung. They were in there, her father and all the Borgias, Alexander and his sons, and the doors were sealed. A storm began, the wind billowed her shawl and water pooled at her feet. Across the water the edifice that had been St. Peter's melted into the shape of the ark. No port was visible and no ladder for the sinners thrashing in the water. At its prow, silhouetted against the sky at each lightning flash, was the form of Gian Pietro Carafa.

The Tiber suddenly swelled and overflowed its banks, and the surging water swept something large against her leg. She looked down to see the corpse of Piero Battista, his dead eyes staring up at her.

Shivering, she turned and fled the rising flood, joining a line of refugees that struggled up a steep hill. She clambered past them to the crest where two men embraced amorously at the foot of a dead tree. Michelangelo stood over them, the wind whipping his hair. He pointed to the refugees by the tree.

"This is my secret which I offer to God. Now you must offer yours."

Adriana looked back at the floodwaters where now a multitude of bodies floated, and at that moment a wave rose from the side and washed ice-cold water over her.

Heavy rain still clattered against the wooden shutter when she woke. The sound of the servants working downstairs told her it was morning, but she could not get out of bed.

Christiano Ferri, the house physician, stood over her, removing the leeches from her forearm. "A serious catarrh, no doubt of that," he observed.

It was the second time she'd been bled, and she noticed little difference in the heat that poured from her body. The honeyed rice and wine with a drop of opium made her sleep, but when she woke, she was wracked with a painful cough that only grew worse. Her fever, she could tell, was mounting, and each day she felt weaker.

Maria dutifully tended her, and Jacopo the housemaster, who berated himself for failing to protect her from herself.

As Ferri placed the seal over the leech jar, Adriana asked, "What's next, if I am not recovered?"

"There are other interventions, but first let us wait and let the leeches do their work. We can, if necessary, double the amount of opium. Rest is the best thing, Lady. That and all our prayers." He pulled the sheet up to cover her already over-heated body and took his leave.

❖

A week passed and she was no longer lucid, but babbled hoarsely during the day and had fever dreams at night. Domenico came, when he got word, and then Michelangelo, but in her delirium she did not know them. On the twelfth night Domenico took the watch and sat praying at her bedside. Finally, in the early morning hours, a priest was summoned from Tivoli to give the last sacrament. When the priest left, the entire household stopped working and waited numb with dread, for the fate of every servant and field worker was tied to hers.

The servants sat in the kitchen, talking quietly among themselves, letting disorder accumulate. Then in the early afternoon three men arrived, two in a cart and one on horseback. Jacopo opened the door and recognized Silvio Piccolomini. He did not know the visitor's two companions, but one of them, he noted with misgivings, was a Jew.

The man's head was covered by a fringed blue cloth, which was twisted once across his chest and thrown over his shoulder. Older and taller than the other two, he had a trim white beard, massive shoulders, and the bulk of an ox. Although he held his gaze down and kept a certain distance from the others, his very mass dominated the group. The third man was nondescript, but stood adjusting his clothing and affected an air of authority, which did not quite convince.

Jacopo, as housemaster, blocked the doorway, reluctant to admit them. "My Lady is mortally ill, Signori, and the priest has already given the rites. Master Raggi keeps the vigil now."

Silvio nodded. "Yes, I know, Jacopo. Michelangelo has informed me. These two men are physicians. Dr. Ligori has assisted my father through dire illness, and Dr. Salomano brings Moorish knowledge from Spain. I believe they offer hope."

At the word "hope" Jacopo relented. Without remark, he led them up the stairs to the bedchamber where Domenico and the maid Maria kept watch over the unconscious woman. The room was rancid with the smell of soiled bedclothes, and the fire burning in the fireplace together with the candles gave off a stifling heat. As the four men entered, the singer stood up, his face ashen and his eyes red-rimmed. Next to him the maid Maria wept quietly.

"Signor Piccolomini has brought two physicians," Jacopo said. Domenico hesitated for a moment, then stepped aside.

Dr. Ligori placed his hand first on her forehead and then at the center of her chest, which rose and fell slowly. "Morbid fever. How long has she been thus?"

"Two days, my lord," Maria replied. Jacopo nodded. "And since yesterday we have not been able to give her any water."

Ligori stood up and the two physicians conferred in whispers, although it seemed the Jew spoke more and the other man listened. Finally Ligori addressed Jacopo.

"Have a wash tub brought up. Large enough for the lady to be set in. And fill it with cold water."

Maria looked astonished. "But Signor Dottore. Surely a bath…at this time—"

"To lower her fever. Don't waste time. Do as I say." The Jew whispered in his ear again, and Ligori added, "Have the kitchen make her a strong tea of red pepper and lemon peel. Do you have these things?"

"Yes, my Lord," she replied, wiping her hands on her apron, as if she were about to cook.

"Bring it up as soon as possible. Please," Salomano added quietly.

Domenico spoke from the foot of the bed where he had stood. His black doublet was wrinkled and unbuttoned halfway down his chest, for he had watched through the night. "Do you have hope, Signore?" His voice was hoarse.

Ligori, bending over the patient again, did not respond. Standing behind him, Salomano said, "While the heart still beats there is hope, my son." Then he extinguished the fire in the fireplace and all the candles save those by the bed. The dimming light seemed an ominous sign, and Domenico pressed his fingers against his lips. Tears flowed again from his swollen eyes.

Jacopo located the wooden laundry tub and with the gardener dragged it up the stairs into the bedchamber. Servants followed with buckets and pitchers, and in relays they filled the tub with the frigid water. At Ligori's instructions, the Jewish doctor wrapped the unconscious woman in the sheet she was lying on and with massive forearms lifted her from the bed.

Jolted by the plunge into the freezing cold the mistress resisted feebly and her eyes fluttered open. As she was lifted out again, she seemed to respond to their voices and their touch when they dried her. Maria placed a cup of some sour fluid at her mouth, and she swallowed a mouthful obediently, then tried weakly to push the cup away. Then she lost consciousness once more.

"You must immerse her again in two hours," Dr. Ligori instructed Jacopo. He seemed well pleased, having determined that the patient was capable of response and thus not moribund. The dramatic gesture of her awakening had impressed her servants, who now gazed at the unconscious woman with hope. Wiping his hands dry on a towel, the doctor accompanied his colleague Baldassare Salomano down the stairs to the reception hall to accept lunch.

In the sickroom, Domenico and Maria resumed their vigil.

XIV

As his cart came down the slope toward the Villa Borgia the next morning, Baldassare Salomano looked out through the mist at the line of cypress trees and the land they bordered. He hadn't noticed the serene beauty of the villa the day before, the well-kept garden near the house and the lush vineyards and olive groves farther out. For the thousandth time, he gave thanks for his good fortune in being expelled from Spain and forced to begin a new life in Italy.

Memories of his final months in Seville still haunted him, though sixteen years had passed since he fled the land of his birth.

Their Most Catholic Majesties had aligned themselves with the extreme ascetic faction in the Spanish church, and together they undertook to purge all of Spain of doctrines that were not identical in word and letter to their own.

His family was not immediately affected, but other lax Jews, who felt no particular piety or allegiance to any dogma, had converted. Ironically, these were condemned, though it seemed illogical for the Church to persecute those who were lukewarm rather than, in its eyes, heathen. Or maybe not. Maybe the doubters were the most dangerous of all.

In any case, it was the *conversos* who were accused of fraudulent oaths or hidden practices of the old religion. It might have been true; he did not know the personal stories of all those condemned. Those he knew who had converted had done so as a matter of convenience. If they were bad Catholics, it was not because they were secretly good Jews.

He had no idea what the Inquisition sought and had wondered even in those days how the church could see into the soul of a man and know which image of God he feared, the one of the Trinity or the one of Moses. Didn't Christians also revere the Old Testament? And certainly they were ignorant of the quarrels about God in the Jewish community itself.

Whatever criterion they used, the agents of the Inquisition rounded up people from all over the city and surrounding towns. A few weeks passed and he heard nothing. He assumed they were in prison, a horror in itself. But then the terrified whispers began; there was to be an auto-da-fé.

Morbid fascination drew him to the square and to the platforms that had been erected. Twenty of them, with central posts, and to each one four penitents were chained. Eighty men and women in long white gowns. While he watched, priests went to each group of four and read their sins to them. Those who repented and begged for mercy were garroted on the spot. Only a few, scarcely a dozen, refused. Ironically it was the truly pious who were prepared to suffer for their beliefs, whatever they were. And suffer they would, burned alive.

He should have left the square then; he would have kept his peace of mind. But the urge to bear witness to the depths of depravity to which the Church would sink obsessed him, and so he watched while they lit the fires, one by one, and the overawed crowd fell silent.

For a long while all he could hear was the crackling of the flames on the straw and kindling. Soon it became difficult to see through the thick greasy smoke that carried the smell of roasting flesh. Then, though he could not see, he knew the flames had reached the living, for the screams began.

Normal screams at first, such as he would expect, but then they became more frenzied, animal-like. He heard sounds he did not know the human throat could make, that made him retch with revulsion and fear. Then the smoke seemed to choke them too as the shrieks became ragged and then weakened. By then the crowd was excited too, and their screaming combined with that of the burning victims.

He would never forget drawing the airborne residual of the dead into his lungs and tasting the horror in his mouth. That day marked him for the rest of his life.

No man had ever seen God. No man knew whether the Creator of the universe was one or three, and yet one set of believers tortured and burned alive another over such trivialities. The thought made him more than a religious skeptic. He did not have a word for what it made him.

The auto-da-fé, the "act of faith" was, ironically, the final ruination of his own. All the way home, smelling human smoke on his clothes, he asked himself how the absolute law of the Jews—with its vast list of regulations in Leviticus—was any better than the absolute law of the Church. How was God supposed to "favor" a people by making them suffer? He tried to imagine a world without God and realized that it would look just like the world in which he lived.

Then in 1492 came the great migration, when their Most Catholic Majesties drove the unconverted Muslims and Jews out of Spain. The Christians called it the Expulsion, but for him it had been deliverance.

Jewish travelers coming from the East had raved about the prosperity that Jews enjoyed in Constantinople. The Ottoman emperor was trying to rebuild his capital. He needed money, skill, talent, and Jews were invited along with Muslims and Christians, if they had these qualifications. The young doctor was tempted to seek refuge there, but he had children and a wife fearful of long travel. Fortunately, Rome offered similar rescue and was closer.

Pope Alexander, though whispered to be personally corrupt, had nonetheless wisely decided that Rome, filled with foreign pilgrims and their diseases, needed physicians more than converts. And so Baldassar Saloman romanized his name and moved with his family to the Holy City. In a short while, at the age of forty-five, he began a discreetly prosperous life as the Jewish "assistant" of a Christian doctor fifteen years his junior.

To be sure, he was scarcely a Jew any longer. Although he still covered his head, identifying himself as a Jew rather than a converso, he no longer believed in anything. And that was the problem.

For while Rome had a certain tolerance for Jews, it had none whatsoever for nonbelievers. He learned to be silent about his lack of faith in a way he never had to be about his Judaism. He still thought of Constantinople and wondered if the Turks scrutinized their Jews the way the Spanish and Italians did.

Salomano was startled back to the present as his carriage pulled up before the entrance of the Villa Borgia.

Although the morning rain had stopped, a cold dampness filled the air and the sky remained dreary. He had come alone, while Ligori tended other patients, and he was unsure of his reception. If the patient had died during the night, he, the foreign Jew, would surely be blamed. He had no idea whether the ice bath and the red-tea cure would help. The treatment could bring down a fever, but little else. In this, as in all other sicknesses, the patient's inner resources would make all the difference.

As he stepped down from the cart, someone came out of the house and a groom was just bringing a horse from the stable. Salomano tasted the bile of rising dread. The lady must have died; Signor Raggi was pale and bent with exhaustion. Briefly they stood face-to-face in silence and each took the measure of the other. With old eyes he looked anxiously into tired young ones, waiting for accusation.

"You have saved her, Dottore." The young man held out his hand to be swallowed up in Salomano's muscular grasp. "Whatever you gave her, it was miraculous. The fever has broken and God's mercy has sent her back to us."

Salomano released the breath he held. "That and her own strength. A physician cannot call upon the divine, sir. Only upon experience."

Puzzlement flickered for an instant across the exhausted face. "In any case, we are most grateful for your skill and kindness."

It was only at that moment that Salomano realized he was speaking with a castrated man. The high soft voice. The wide chest and slender, elongated physique. Of course, the singer from the Vatican. He had heard of him. What monstrous things the Christians did, even to their own.

"You are most welcome. But experience also teaches that recovery is not instant, and I must attend the patient still."

"Certainly, and I will keep you no longer. I have overstayed my leave and must return to my duties, but Signor Buonarroti sits with her."

Domenico clasped his old hand again in departure. A stable boy held the singer's horse while he mounted with difficulty. Slouching in the saddle, he pulled his cloak around him and rode down the avenue of cypresses.

❖

In contrast to the day before, this time the maidservant admitted Salomano with deference and warmth. The housemaster came hurriedly, called him "Signor Dottore" and led him upstairs to the bedchamber. The lady still lay feebly against two pillows, but she was lucid and could hold the cup of medicinal tea without assistance. A wiry, bearded man stood up from his stool at her bedside. The housemaster addressed him.

"Maestro Buonarroti, this is Doctor Salomano. He is one of the physicians who saved Lady Borgia's life yesterday." They shook hands.

The housemaster slid a chair behind Salomano and he lowered his great bulk onto the seat. He found himself directly across from the painter, who watched him as he attended the patient. He laid a hand on her forehead and noted that the fever had indeed fallen and some color had returned to her face.

"Have you eaten anything yet, Lady Borgia?"

She turned her head weakly toward him. Her long dark hair was damp and clung to her face in limp strands. "No. I've only drunk this vile tea."

He laid his ear on her chest and listened to her cough. "Mucus. That's very good. But Madama is obviously still very weak." He took the empty cup from her hand. "Vile or no, you must keep drinking the tea for two more days at least. And you must also have your cook prepare you a special broth. I have a list of ingredients." He drew a roll of paper from the pouch and held it while he spoke. "Have your servants wake you every two hours for the tea and for the soup. It is time to return to life, Madama."

"It looks as if God has given her a second chance. Though I wonder if it was your God or hers." Michelangelo glanced meaningfully at the blue cloth that covered Salomano's head, but the tone of his voice was light, as if he attempted banter.

Salomano was not used to banter. "The God of the Jews is not much inclined to heal the sick," he replied cautiously. "Jews try more to understand God than to call on his medical skills."

The artist folded his arms across his chest and asked very softly, in the same tone as before, "How can you know God's will, having no priest or sacraments?"

Salomano frowned. "It seems impolite to argue theology at the bedside of a sick woman."

"Not at all." Adriana glanced over at them through half-closed eyes. She still couldn't raise herself from her pillows, but her mind seemed to have cleared and her spirits much improved. "I don't mind. Salvation seems to be Michelangelo's current obsession. Next year it may be love poetry."

Salomano thought for a while, stroking his white beard. He would not be drawn into an argument, but this Christian artist seemed more interested than hostile. "Rabbis and scholars have debated God's will for centuries, but they do not so much mediate between man and God as do your priests. They simply interpret scripture and advise. Maimonides, one of our greatest, did set out basic principles, but many Jews disagree with him."

"You mean you don't all believe the same?"

"The basic ideas, yes. But there's always a dispute—in your religion too—of how literally to take scripture. Maimonides said that God and the afterlife are intellectual events and the Bible is only symbolic."

"But you've got all those laws."

"Yes, more than six hundred. But Maimonides argues that most are just meant to fulfill the first two, belief in God and rejection of idolatry. Otherwise, God is unknowable."

Michelangelo's gaze became more intent. "An unknowable God. A dangerous idea."

Salomano rolled up the paper he had been holding and weighed his words. "It shouldn't be dangerous. Not being able to define God opens the way to focus on the world and discover His reverberations here. It's the 'God's backside' idea."

Adriana watched them, seeming interested though drowsy.

Salomano leaned toward Michelangelo with an open hand. "In Exodus 33, God tells Moses that He can't show His face. It would be too much to bear. But He *will* let Moses see his backside as he passes."

"God's backside." Adriana chuckled weakly. Sleep was overtaking her again, and the nearly empty tea glass tilted precariously in her hand. Salomano took it from her.

"Maimonides says it means we can see God's earthly *effects*, but not His *essence*. Myself, I like to think of God more like Ficino does, as the incomprehensible perfection behind beauty, behind the things we love."

Michelangelo sat up, with unconcealed surprise. "You read Marsilio Ficino?"

"Do you think only Christians can read Latin?"

"No, of course not. But Ficino was a priest."

"Well, there are priests and priests, aren't there? He was also an interpreter of Plato, who belongs to neither Christian nor Jew." He glanced over at the patient. "But I think we have exhausted Lady Borgia."

Taking her hand, he said, "You seem out of danger, dear Lady, so I'll leave you now and look in again tomorrow. Remember about the tea and soup." He laid the rolled-up list on the bedside table.

Once the doctor had left, Adriana's energies were depleted. When Michelangelo turned back to her, she was dozing off again, and sentence fragments in his voice drifted into her sleep-addled mind.

"Going to Florence," she thought she heard him say. A gift someone had for him. Back in a few days. Visit him in Rome when she was well. Ideas to share, memories, secrets.

Maria closed the door behind him and Adrianna drifted off. With her last glimmer of consciousness she thought, "God's backside. So that's what it's all about."

XV
SECRET THINGS

Michelangelo had timed it well, arriving at Santo Spirito just at sundown. Good old Niccolò Bichiellini, prior and friend, was waiting at the monastery gate. He could be relied on to be discreet. If he was disgusted, good manners kept him from ever revealing it.

"Fra Bichiellini, good evening. I take it everything is ready. He didn't cause you too much trouble, did he?" Michelangelo dismounted and one of the lay brothers took his horse silently.

"No, Signore. Nothing the usual bribes couldn't take care of. He's waiting for you now, as before. But I urge you to hurry. It will not escape notice that you are here, and people will ask questions."

"Yes, of course." He took up his satchel and followed the prior into the main building. The reception area was lit by only a few candles, and the prior took up one of them in passing.

"He's in the basement, where you'll have privacy. I've instructed the sacristan to admit no one." He led Michelangelo down a flight of creaking wooden stairs to a completely dark space. The light from the single candle held aloft was not sufficient to light the other end of the room where the coveted one waited.

Bichiellini strode forward, taking with him the sphere of light. When he reached the figure in the far corner, he held the lantern high and pulled off the linen cover with a single dramatic gesture.

"Here he is, Maestro," he said. "Freshly dead."

As the prior set about lighting additional candles around the table, Michelangelo bent over the hooded cadaver. "He's magnificent. I couldn't have asked for better. Look at that chest." He ran his fingertips along the musculature that was bulky and well defined in spite of the relaxation of death.

"They hanged him at dawn yesterday," Bichiellini added. "Unfortunately, the birds got to him and picked off most of his face, so I asked the bailiff to cover his head. Not a nice thing to look at all night long." The prior lit a final candle inside a lantern that hung over the table. "Will you be doing a full dissection?"

"Like the old days?" Michelangelo shook his head. "No. All I'm interested in this time is the musculature. I'll be out of here in a day and a half."

He rolled up the sleeves of his shirt and drew a leather apron from his satchel. Opening a small pouch of scalpels, he said, "I would be most grateful, Fra Bichiellini, if you could provide me with a pitcher of water for washing. And perhaps a flask of watered wine to see me through the night?"

After a nod of thanks, Michelangelo adjusted the candles for a maximum of light and set to work. Someone, either the bailiff or more likely Bichiellini himself, had done him the favor of washing off the urine and defecation of the dead man, for which he was grateful. But he noted the early signs of decomposition, the greenish-yellow coloration of the abdomen and the swelling from pooled blood in the lower extremities, an artifact of the hanging position. Only the feet showed evidence of advanced decay, with blistering around the ankles and a covering of foul-smelling brown paste that had leaked through the skin. The odor of the corpse was still tolerable, but by the second night, he would have to work with a mask over his nose and mouth.

Michelangelo made the first incisions, a horizontal along the surface of both clavicles and a long vertical down the sternum. Then, with the efficiency of a man long familiar with the knife, he cut two more verticals along the sides of the corpse and two diagonals along the lower edges of the rib cage. With the flesh marked out like the panels of a short jacket, he proceeded to flay the upper chest, starting at the throat.

The leanness of the cadaver allowed him to slice in a series of rapid, small motions under the fatty layer of the skin and gradually roll it back. He was careful not to penetrate the underlying layer of membrane that held the muscles in their living shapes, for that was what he needed.

The fatty tissue was slimy with a slightly reddish mucus that oozed out with each slice of the blade, but there was otherwise no blood to obscure his view. The unembalmed corpse might still have blood in the deep arteries, but it, too, had decomposed, and as long as the dissection was only cutaneous, the cadaver would seep but not bleed.

By the time the prior returned, the entire pectoral area was exposed, and the panels of skin lay folded neatly in a wooden pail on the floor. Michelangelo wiped his hands on his apron. "A pity he never modeled for me when he was alive," he said, and allowed himself a long drink of the sweet wine. "Now we'll give him a second chance."

❖

Michelangelo gently folded the last panel of skin and set it into the bucket at his feet. He let out a long exhalation and felt as if he had been holding his breath for the two hours he had been cutting. He had flayed the entire front of the cadaver, including the male member, which he regarded as skin. But he could cut no more now without the assistance of Bichiellini to turn the cadaver over. That would be tomorrow. Now he came to the reason for the entire procedure.

He laid out the flayed arms and legs in a pose to his satisfaction before rinsing his hands of mucus in the pitcher of water. He adjusted the candles, redistributing the light over the subject, then took up his sepia pencil and sketchbook.

After a few moments, though his hand moved rapidly in the sketching, the familiar tranquility settled over him. It was a pleasing trance that came to him at no other time. He had thought at first it was the endless tap-tap of the chisel when he sculpted that transported him. But he had felt it too when he fell into the rhythm of painting a fresco.

Then he realized that the same euphoria, the same sensation of rising up over the mundane world came over him even when he sketched. It was not the monotony of movement or the sound of the instrument; it was the very act of bringing forth an image, pulling something out of nothing. Creating a form lifted him to a place from which he could contemplate higher things. Not hunger or discomfort or the whims of his patrons, but the color, line, and light of his creation, and the perfect beauty within.

His transport was so real that he fell into the habit of talking to his subject as it came into being, even *before* it came into being. For the creature was already in the material, and Michelangelo talked to it as he urged it from the darkness into the light. Or in this case, from the dissecting table into a sketchbook and finally to a fresco.

"Sorry to burden you with my troubles, brother. Obviously your last few days have been worse than mine. But it hasn't been easy for me either. I work for a tyrant, send all my money to a thankless family, live in poverty, and endure constant pain from painting over my head." He held the drawing at arm's length. Yes, the pose was good. "And no one listens to me when I complain."

He adjusted the cadaver's limbs a second time and turned to a blank page in the sketchbook.

"The birds took away your face, my friend, but you know, that's not such a bad thing in the end. I finished their job by taking off the rest of your skin and the flesh of temptation between your legs. Whatever your sins were, you're innocent muscle now, and I'm going to make you into something new. What would you like to be: a soldier, hero, pagan god?" He glanced up at the corpse, as though awaiting a reply. "How about an angel? That should compensate you. A man could not ask for more."

Almost cheerful, Michelangelo finished the second sketch and posed the limp cadaver yet again. He lifted one of the meaty legs and one of the arms into a sort of twisted pose, the best he could do given the slippery flesh. "Whatever you were before, my friend, you're beautiful now."

He took a long drink of the wine and stepped back for a third sketch, though increasing fatigue made him dreamy and philosophical.

"Beauty is divine, my friend. Like sunlight searches for a tree or a meadow or a face to shine on, beauty searches for something to shine *from*. It's my gift, to sense beauty where it hides and to draw it out for the world to see."

He paused over the sketch. "Also a curse." He sighed. "I cannot find God in prayer or in the mass. Only in the material. This weakness plagues me, as much as my flesh, that I find the divine in cellars like this one talking to the likes of you."

He turned the page for a fourth drawing, though his eyes had begun to burn. Talking about his curse had cast a pall over his mood. He fell silent, but his mind still rambled. *Is this all I'll ever have to share my secrets with? A cadaver or the phantoms in the stone?*

He was suddenly terribly lonely.

❖

The crowing of the cock in the monastery hen yard woke Fra Bichiellini in his chamber. Rubbing consciousness back into his face, he dressed and descended the cellar stairs once again.

Michelangelo was just setting aside his sketchbook. "Dawn already? I lost track of time."

Bichiellini stepped toward the dissecting table. The corpse, now in its shiny gray-red flesh, lay in a new position. The two arms were folded back with both hands under the neck of the still-hooded head. The body was tilted slightly sideways, and one flayed leg was raised. Though the entire front of the cadaver was skinned down to the ankles, it looked for all the world like a sort of macabre vanity, a monster displaying himself, nude and provocative, for a lover.

Bichiellini mused that if anything could be more naked than nude, he now beheld it.

"I've got what I need tonight. If you would be so kind and help me turn him over, I'll dissect him from the back tomorrow." The two men grappled with the limp corpse. As they finally maneuvered it into place, facedown on the table, someone called from the top of the stairs.

"Fra Bichiellini, the bailiff is here. Just stopping by, he said."

"Morbid curiosity, I'm sure," the prior muttered. "He's already got his bribe." Then, louder, "Send him down, if you please."

In a moment the bailiff was at the door, holding a rag over his nose and mouth. "Everything all right, here?"

"Yes. The dissection is half finished," the prior said. "We'll be done tomorrow and we'll see to it that he has a Christian burial."

Michelangelo arranged the half-flayed limbs alongside the prostrate body but stopped abruptly and raised a candle over the man's back. The entire surface, from the edge of the cloth hood to the buttocks, was crisscrossed with countless scars.

"This man was flogged," Michelangelo said.

"Yes, and little good it did him." The bailiff snorted, approaching the table. "You'd think he'd have given up the habit after that. But he just couldn't stop himself, I guess. The last time they caught him, it was the noose."

"What was his crime?" Michelangelo asked cautiously.

The bailiff hooked his thumbs in his belt. "This one's a sodomite. Hanging's what they do to them here if they don't change their ways. He didn't."

XVI

Gian Pietro Carafa stood on a balcony on the Piazza Venezia and swept his solemn gaze over the streets being cleared of animal ordure for the parade. He pictured the coming frivolities of Carnevale, and his resolve was unwavering. It would have to be, for the task he had set himself was no less than the rescue of the Holy Mother Church.

If anyone should know of Rome's depravity, it was he, for he had seen the effects while Alexander VI still reigned. That despicable libertine had defiled the Throne of Peter, not only fathering children on his various whores, but parading them in the court. Worse were his unashamed display of pagan symbols and Egyptian idols in court frescoes, and the opening of Rome's door to heathens expelled from Spain. But Alexander's unforgivable crime was the excommunication and execution of that saint among men, Girolamo Savonarola.

A brother of his own order, blessed be his memory, the Dominican friar had ten years before taken up the flaming sword against the paganism and the vice, the foreign thoughts and licentiousness of the Florentines.

Eyes half-closed, Carafa recalled the great bonfire he had seen on the Piazza della Signoria. A fire dedicated to God, consuming the Carnevale masks and wigs, the volumes of filthy Latin and Italian poetry, the vain ornaments and scents and mirrors, the chessboards, lutes, and harps that lured men to frivolity. And, on the highest tier of the scaffold, the obscene paintings of women. The whole collection of worldly temptations rose in a spiral of glowing flakes and ashes, and as the bells of the campanile pealed in celebration, his young soul swelled with a sense of the presence of God.

But Savonarola's most courageous act was the one that doomed him, the vilification of the Borgia Pope. Alexander had excommunicated him, accusing him of heresy when, in fact, he spoke the purest truth. The saintly man was hanged in the very spot where his great bonfire had raged, and his still-twitching body was burned in turn.

Carafa's heart quickened in outrage at such injustice. He himself had resolved to reclaim the fire, and this time it would be on behalf of God as the Church of Spain used it, to purify the faith and the believer. Pain was good for the soul. He had known pain himself, the suffering of long fasting and mortification of the rebellious flesh, and he welcomed it as the sharing of the agony of Christ. So he rejoiced to witness the sufferings of the tortured penitents. Every scream was an affirmation of their growing piety, the parting shriek of demons.

He glanced down again, envisioning the revelers similarly consumed. Yes, with fire and the rack he would bring God back to Rome, he swore it on his soul.

❖

Adriana arrived in the Piazza Rusticucci in the late afternoon, unsure of her reception. She had after all sent no notice and hoped Michelangelo would remember he had invited her. She knocked and within moments the door was opened. The housemaster's face registered surprise.

"I'm sorry, Madonna. The Maestro is not due for another hour. Would My Lady wish to visit him at the Vatican chapel?"

"No, no. I don't want to disturb his work. I'll wait for him here."

The servant led her into an anteroom where two high-backed chairs were pushed against a long table. He pulled one of them out to offer her a seat and returned a moment later with a glass and a bronze ewer of wine. When he was gone, she poured herself a tall glass and surveyed the room where courtesy required she wait. It had a sterile and depressing air. She did not relish the thought of spending the next hour there.

Taking both glass and ewer, she crossed the corridor to Michelangelo's workshop. Here was life—the agreeable clutter of used objects, the smell of paint, the inviting sight of chairs with worn cushions. One table held drills and mallets and next to them a box of chisels. On another were rolls of vellum, notebooks, an earthen pot with a bouquet of paintbrushes. Beside an inkwell and a pair of spectacles, a smaller vessel contained half a dozen quills.

The walls held shelves bearing jars of colored minerals. In among them were mortars and pestles and a slab of porphyry for grinding. Everything had a covering of gritty marble powder and ordinary dust.

She draped her cape over the end of a long table, taking pains not to disturb anything, and poured herself another glass of the soothing wine. She felt at home in this room, or perhaps it was simply the wine that was causing her to relax. She wished now that Michelangelo had invited her sooner, for she could imagine herself in warm conversation with him here. About his work, his thoughts on his papal employer, his "secrets," whatever they were.

A sketchbook caught her attention. She sensed she was in some way trespassing, but the wine made her venturesome. Michelangelo surely would not mind if she admired his drawings. With the tips of her fingers she opened the volume and turned the pages delicately. She was horrified.

A man, or rather what had once been a man, lay on his back, his head covered by a sack. The striations across his muscles, the protrusion of the clavicles, the strip of white cartilage down the center of the chest made it clear he had been skinned. The red chalk used for the drawings emphasized all the more the exposed red meat of the body.

Page after page held the same figure in varying macabre poses, lying with legs drawn up, slouching, twisting.

But on the last page, there was something less sinister, even amusing. A male figure, heavily bearded and copiously robed, in two twisted poses. On the right, he curved in midair, as if blown along by some great wind, with arms outstretched, his long robes flowing behind him. In the left sketch, the same figure was in reverse and seemed to fly away, his elbow, back, and foot soles sketched in detail. In the center of the figure, his garment blew against him, outlining well-muscled buttocks.

Adriana laughed out loud, remembering the conversation that had taken place at her bedside. It was a sketch of God's backside.

She was startled when she heard someone outside the door.

Abashed, she hurriedly closed the notebook and glanced up. A woman spoke, and she knew the voice. Adriana caught her breath as the door swung open.

Raphaela Bramante stopped on the threshold, her expression registering alarm.

❖

Adriana raised her hand. "It's all right, Signorina Bramante. I know of your disguise."

The young painter paused for a moment, absorbing the revelation, then came into the workshop. She set a bundle of rolled-up cartoons on the worktable.

"Lady Borgia, good afternoon."

"You remember me from the chapel?" Adriana realized the question was foolish. The Borgia reputation was not yet eradicated, and few people forgot encountering her.

Raphaela pulled off the bulky cap that had contained her hair, and honey-colored curls suddenly ringed her face like a wreath. "Oh, I recall you from long before that."

Her voice was only slightly less husky than that of a real male and held a surprising authority. Although she had the appearance of a boy, her manner was adult, assured.

Adriana was uncertain how to speak to her. The late-afternoon sun that lit and warmed the studio seemed to offer a place for intimate conversation, but they were, on the face of things, strangers. Distant sounds from the street drifted through the window.

Raphaela took off the loose jerkin she wore over her work clothes and dropped it over the back of a chair. "I understand you were infirmed recently. You are recovered, I trust?" Her hand lingered on the jerkin, the fingers tapping on the soft leather. "You look recovered. I mean, you look as I remember you. That afternoon on the high scaffold…in skirts. Impressive." The fingers drummed again.

"Was I? I astonished myself climbing up there. And nearly killed myself climbing down."

"I remember. You wouldn't let me help you."

"I would have just pulled us both down to disaster." Adriana laughed lightly, nervously. Her fingers also took on a life of their own, brushing dust off the work table.

"Do you still have the medallion?"

"Yes, at home." She fingered the place on her bodice where it would have hung.

Raphaela glanced toward the door, as if awakening. "I'm sorry, but my father will be here shortly, and he must not know about the clothing. You understand." She opened a narrow wardrobe behind the studio door, took out a simple overdress, discarded the canvas apron, and pulled the long painter's smock over her head.

"Shall I leave?" Adriana asked.

"No. We can talk while I change." Standing in her undergown, she poured water from a pitcher into a wide bowl and splashed her face and neck. Her honey-colored hair was still pinned up tightly at the back of her head, the baggy trousers still concealed her hips, but her breasts, visible through the damp shift, revealed the woman. Adriana averted her eyes, but they were drawn back again, irresistibly.

Raphaela undid the cord holding up her trousers and let them drop to the floor. The light underdress that had been drawn up inside the trousers now fell to her feet. Smoothing the underskirt, she stepped into the sleeveless blue overdress and pulled it up to her shoulders. She reached back with one arm, struggling to fasten the buttons at the rear.

"I'm sorry. My arms are so very tired, I can hardly lift them. We have to paint over our heads for so many hours. Could you…?"

Adriana hesitated. The last time she rendered such a service was with Lucrezia, and that had ended in girlish intimacy.

"Of course." Nervously, she threaded the buttons into their eyelets, then retreated, clasping her hands as though to bring them back in line.

Raphaela undid the mass of hair at the back of her head, brushed out the plaster dust, and straightened the center part before twisting the long amber strands into a knot. She fastened it in place with a jeweled hairpin that briefly caught the light and sparkled, like a brilliant thought.

The upraised arms showed a subtle musculature, hinting at virility. Then with the efficiency of someone who did it frequently, she applied rouge and tint to her lips, and put on tiny pearl earrings. Raphaela

Bramante was complete, but Adriana had seen the boy Carlo and could see him still.

"Why did you want to do it?" Adriana asked, taking up the sleeves that hung over the back of a chair.

Raphaela's eyebrows went up slightly as she pulled on the sleeves and tied them at the shoulder. "Do what?"

"Paint for him. With all those men around."

"You must take risks. When some extraordinary thing comes along, you must seize it and not be afraid."

"Some would call that wild talk from a woman." Adriana suppressed a smile.

"Wild?" Raphaela seemed to consider the word. "Michelangelo is the one who's wild, not me, though he mostly paints it into his figures." She leaned back against the windowsill and her lips fell open slightly as she studied Adriana. "You convinced him to take me, didn't you? Why?"

Adriana hesitated. "I saw your work and thought it was good."

"My work?"

"Yes, the frescos you did in the Palazzo Piccolomini. Hippolyta and Europa. Perhaps it was my vanity, but I thought I saw something of myself in them."

"You think it was *you* I painted? Ravished by a bull?"

Adriana searched Raphaela's expression for playfulness that would have admitted to the game, that she had toyed with Adriana's image and had, in her painter's mind, shamelessly undressed her.

Raphaela's glance was penetrating, intensely interested, but opaque. Adriana would have to be the one to suggest that something intimate had gone on, and she lacked the courage.

"I don't know. Perhaps I imagined I saw—"

The clatter of horses' hooves interrupted them. Raphaela snatched up the bag of brushes and rags and hurried toward the door.

"It's best if he does not come in."

Adriana followed her out to the street. The sky was a blazing furnace of red, with horizontal streaks of scarlet and purple shot through it. In the foreground Trajan's Column jutted black and stark against the rare brilliance. The setting sun cast a deep orange glow across Raphaela's face, as if she smoldered. She mounted and looked down with a certain expectancy in her expression as though waiting for Adriana to finish her remark.

But the moment passed, and Donato Bramante nodded a polite but short greeting that suggested they were in a hurry. "I wish you both good evening" was all Adriana could think of saying. The Bramantes were halfway down the street as Michelangelo arrived.

❖

"I'm sorry if I stink of plaster." Michelangelo dropped a bulky sack onto the floor as they entered his studio. The dull wooden clatter suggested it was paintbrushes. He stared at the pigment on his fingers, distracted. "Have you come all the way into Rome just to see me?"

"You said I should visit you. That we had things to talk about."

"Did I? I don't remember."

He fished several brushes from the cloth bag and placed them in a ceramic basin. Clearly exhausted and muscle-sore, he fetched a pitcher of water and poured it over the brushes. Tendrils of red, green, and ochre curled out from them and blended into clouds of grayish brown.

Adriana had a sinking feeling of having misjudged his invitation and tried to laugh. "You said we both had our secrets. There must have been something on your mind for you to say that."

"No, nothing that I recall. Well…" His tone became matter-of-fact. "I did want to ask you about Domenico. Do you see him often, I mean outside the chapel?" Not meeting her glance, he arranged the brushes on a clean rag, wiping the shafts and pressing out the last of the color from the bristles with another.

"Not since he was in my sickroom, the same time you were there."

"Of course. But we both were so concerned about you that we hardly exchanged any words. I thought it would be nice if…" He hesitated.

"Nice if what?"

He continued to wipe his brushes, though they seemed to be dry. "The Carnevale parade is in two days, and the Piccolomini will sponsor a *carro allegorico*. Silvio finds you interesting, and Domenico seems like a close friend. I thought I'd propose that the four of us go to see the parade. You know, you, me, and Domenico. None of us get out much. It would do us all good to be a little wild for an evening."

Adriana shook her head. "Unless things have changed, Domenico will not be allowed out of the chapel school without permission from the Master of Ceremonies, and Paris de Grassis will certainly refuse it. He's not going to let his most important soprano run through the streets at Carnevale."

Michelangelo seemed disappointed. "All right. But what about you?"

"You mean stand in the street with all the drunks? I don't think so."

"Silvio and I will protect you. Besides, knowing Silvio, I'm sure his float will be something classical and arcane that no one will understand except us. We'll be the only ones applauding. Please say you'll come."

"I don't know, Michelo. It could be dangerous."

"Silvio did save your life, after all, by bringing those doctors," he cajoled. "You owe him this."

"Blackmailer." She folded her arms. "You know, a lot of things happen at Carnevale. It's not safe for a lady to be in the streets then."

Michelangelo pressed his right hand, which still held a paintbrush, to his heart. "On my honor, Adriana. No man shall lay a hand on you at Carnevale."

XVII
February 1509

Adriana stood with Michelangelo and Silvio Piccolomini in the jostling crowd of revelers in the Piazza Venezia. Distrustful of the hordes of anonymous and disguised people, she tucked her marble medallion inside her dress. "I've never been in the streets at Carnevale before," she shouted over the noise. "And now I remember why. It's madness."

"A little bit of madness will do us all good." Michelangelo set a Jupiter mask over his face and adjusted it on his imperfect nose. "As for me, I can use the inspiration."

"And you think staring at drunken men and women in costumes will stir your artistic visions?" Silvio's laugh was muffled by the silver mask that covered his face. When he turned his head the myriad tiny bells surrounding the mask tinkled softly.

Before Michelangelo could reply, the bells in the Campidoglio Tower chimed and the long-awaited salvo of artillery thundered, signaling the start of the *Trionfo* parade. The crowd surged toward the street in the roiling colors of their costumes and banners.

The parade itself began with the continuous rattatat-rattatat of marching drummers. At the front, ranks of *gonfalonieri* carried the heraldic standards of each guild and confraternity. Mummers followed with pennants, scattering confetti as they marched. Then the *carri* commenced, the great parade of chariots and horse-drawn floats.

Religious scenes led the procession. Archangel Michael, resplendent in golden breastplate and greaves, stood with buskined foot on the devil's chest. The crowd cheered. "The militant angel. Of course," Silvio muttered. "To remind us of the Church's triumph over Darkness." He sounded amused.

Other pious floats came after: the Annunciation with a kneeling Angel Gabriel in multicolored wooden wings, and Noah's ark, complete with tethered animals.

The Virgin followed, extravagantly haloed in a sparkling headdress and holding a real and slightly bewildered child to her breast. Four cherubs knelt before them singing "Laudate Virginum," though it could scarcely be heard above the street noise. Silvio chuckled again.

"Enough of Rome's Christian conscience. Now we'll see what Carnevale is really about!"

In fact, the noise of the crowd rose a degree in volume as an enormous golden she-wolf, the ancient animal symbol of Rome, drew past with her Romulus and Remus beneath her. Two dwarfs wrapped ludicrously in golden swaddling pretended to suckle, to lewd shouting from the crowd.

The next float bore Mt. Parnassus and the god Apollo, his curls bubbling up from his head, his clamys draped over his arm, and his nine muses in a circle at his feet.

Silvio grasped Michelangelo by the shoulder. "Look, there's the Piccolomini float." A new tableau edged toward them. Five burly women sat in a circle. Each one wore bright exotic dress, and each one struck a pose with a great manuscript made of wood. The pages, more than a meter square, were woven straw painted to look like vellum. "How do you like it?"

Adriana leaned between them and watched as the float rolled past. "What is it?"

"Don't you recognize them? Those are the sibyls. From Virgil's *Eclogue*. It's my best joke. The Church says the sibyls prophesied the coming of Christ, but they did no such thing. They merely repeated the same old stuff the ancients were always prophesying. No mention of Christ. None. The Church simply laid claim to the sibyls, spreading Christianity backward, as it were."

"What's the joke, then?" Adriana asked. "Your sibyls are not even women. They're men in dresses. Ugly, too. What's the point?"

The tiny bells of Silvio's mask tinkled as he shook his head. He spoke slowly, against the background noise of the crowd. "The joke is that the Church took pagans and dressed them as Christians. I've hired men and dressed them as women. Don't you take my jest?"

Laughter came from under the white Jupiter mask. "Silvio, there are not twenty people in all of Rome who read Virgil and will recognize who these women are. And only three of us who 'take your jest.' It is just as well, too, for if anyone heard you talking like that, you'd be hauled off as a heretic."

His words were drowned as a great roar broke out from all around them and Michelangelo pointed with his thumb.

"Now there is someone that everyone recognizes!"

In gold armor, his shining helmet topped by an opulent mass of red plumes, a Roman general swung his sword over his head. A phalanx of centurions clanked behind him, dragging a string of captives.

"Caesar, of course. The Romans do love their emperor," Silvio commented dryly.

"Yes, but they love *him* even more." Michelangelo looked toward the final float, the feathered chariot of Bacchus, drawn by six men in panther skins. A wreath of grape vine sat tilted on the god's head, and he held a goblet of wine. He took a long pull from the goblet, then tossed the dregs in a wide arc into the air.

The crowd screamed approval, massing together behind the chariot and closing up the avenue.

"Ah, that reminds me." Michelangelo uncorked the wineskin he had been carrying on his shoulder. He held it up high and tipped it, letting a long stream pour into his mouth. Then he wiped the back of his hand along his lips and offered the skin to Adriana.

"Here, this will wash the parade dust from your mouth."

"Don't be shy, Adriana," Silvio said reassuringly. "Everyone's drinking, and it will be a long, dry wait until the banquet." He took the wineskin from Michelangelo and pressed it into her hand.

"All right. Just a little. To wash out the dust." She swallowed the strong Corsican wine and immediately felt warmth and a lightness of head. She ought to have eaten beforehand. But no matter, there would be a feast later, at the Palazzo Venezia. She handed the wineskin back to Silvio, who held it up in salute.

"To Adriana, then." He undid his mask, which tinkled in protest, and hooked it onto his belt. After sweeping his fingers quickly through his thick hair, he struck a pose and raised the skin to take a long drink.

"I see that the crowd cheered the old gods more than the saints." Silvio dabbed at his lips with a silk handkerchief and set his mask back on.

"The crowd cheers everything." Adriana scoffed. "If the devil himself had appeared on horseback they would have applauded him."

Silvio laughed. "Now that you mention it, I'm sure I saw the devil in the crowd, with his hand in a woman's dress."

Adriana laughed with him. "There will be thousands of *that* kind of devils on the streets tonight."

"No doubt." Silvio took hold of her hand and pulled her along toward the Piazza del Popolo. "All the demons are loose now. Who knows what the night will bring?"

❖

Donato Bramante coughed into his handkerchief and fell back against a pile of pillows.

"This is the third time since summer that you've taken sick, Father." Raphaela turned away from the window and came to his bedside. "It's the dust you breathe knocking around all the city's ruins. You've got to stop doing that." She handed him the cup of lemon and wine that stood on his bed table, and he took a long drink. "I don't want to lose you."

"You're right, I know." He sighed. "But there's so much to do."

"Well, you can't work during Carnevale anyhow. They have the ruins on the Palantine roped off. They wouldn't let you cross the line."

"They're just the petty rules drawn by men for their own convenience. I'd find a way to cross them."

Raphaela smiled, thinking about her daily ruse working with Michelangelo. "I'll remember that you said that."

He settled back on his pillows again. "A man must take a few risks, or he will spend his whole life in shallow waters."

"A woman too," Raphaela added.

Her father glanced sideways at her and frowned. "I did not mean that to be paternal advice, my dear. Risk does not suit a woman. You already take too much risk living as a painter. I would much rather see you married to one."

"Oh, Father. We've had this discussion a hundred times. Stop worrying. The only man I need to look after me is you. And besides, my commissions have contributed to this household."

"Yes, they have. You have clearly made a name for yourself. But you would have been better going back to Padua when you were supposed to five years ago. You'd have children by now." He thought for a moment. "Wasn't that Farnese boy hanging about? It wouldn't hurt for you to be married to a Farnese."

"Livio? Oh, no. It would be awful to be shackled to a simpleton like him. I can take care of myself just fine. I have plenty of commissions."

"That reminds me, how goes your work in Michelangelo's studio? Does he treat you well?"

"Well enough. He's gruff sometimes, but he has a great vision for the chapel and I want to share it."

"Ah, yes. It must be fascinating for you to watch a painter like that. He doesn't like being called a painter, but it suits him better than architecture. That's why I recommended him to His Holiness." He took another sip of the honey drink and settled back again, drowsy.

Raphaela pulled his blanket higher over his chest and kissed him on his cheek. "Yes, Father. I'm sure you're right."

When he began to doze, she crept from his chamber to her own.

Her window looked out onto the Via dei Coronaria, and as the evening came on, she could hear the muffled sounds of the Carnevale celebrants in the streets below.

Raphaela stared out at the gathering crowd, thoughts turning in her head. Her father was frequently ill. She dreaded the thought of losing him, but she had refused all opportunities to marry and start a household of her own.

She knew her refusal set her apart from every other woman in Rome and was grateful that her father did not try to force her, as so many other fathers did, to choose between two prisons: the convent or the marriage bed.

Raphaela loved portraiture. She was happiest playing with colors and light to render a dull face beautiful and create a little fantasy around it. When she painted a heroic setting, she did not so much tell a lie as reveal a tiny bit of truth inside the sitter's soul, a picture of their highest aspiration.

How dreary it would be to produce a horde of children rather than paintings. She detested the idea of being at the beck and call of a man, and sexually at his disposal.

But the convent, she knew, was an even worse form of servitude. Mumbling prayers into the air all day long between waiting on the tyranny of some mother superior who herself had been imprisoned a generation before.

Strange, the way the Church managed to perpetuate the servile state of women even as it pretended to elevate it. The flash of realization had recently come to her like a bolt of lightning: the Church's veneration of the Virgin was not a glorification of women at all, but rather a gloss over its disdain for them. That the holiest woman in heaven had kept her virginity while producing a child was an insult to every female, chaste or unchaste.

She could not understand why an untouched woman was so revered. If virginity was deemed so precious, why were so many women forcibly handed over to men to be deflowered as soon as they reached puberty? The contradiction infuriated her. Women were thwarted from all sides.

Of course a few lucky women turned the tables of power. Women like Arabella Raimondi and Adriana Borgia, who used their sexuality rather than let themselves fall victim to it. Like Europa, Adriana rode the Borgia bull, and when Cesare was killed, she somehow got herself back to Rome unscathed.

Raphaela was not sure if that sort of risk made Adriana a model to women or a traitor. She only knew that the thought of her was exciting.

A man must take a few risks, or he will spend his whole life in shallow waters. A woman too. She turned the words over in her mind and made a decision.

XVIII

Rough hands seized the sleeping Domenico Raggi by the hair and pressed the point of a knife between his shoulder blades. In a jumble of arms and legs, he was jerked sideways from the prostitute's bed and thrown to the floor.

Now he could see them, four of the night watch. One held a lantern and the others wielded knives.

"Filthy bung-boy," one of them snarled over the cowering prostitute, then slashed through his exposed throat. The helpless man thrashed for a moment, his blood spurting through his fingers over the bed linen and the wall, then gurgled helplessly and fell limp.

"Luca!" Domenico tried to rise from his crouch but was seized on both sides by the guard. The lantern man said, "They didn't tell us he'd be bare-assed. Are we supposed to take him back like that? It'd teach him a lesson, though, wouldn't it?"

A mustached man, who seemed to be in charge, replied, "He'll get plenty of 'lesson' in jail. And we don't want to draw attention." He snatched up the bundle of clothing that had been dropped over the only chair in the simple room and flung it at Domenico. "Put this on, and hurry up or we'll drag your skinny naked ass through the streets."

Trembling at the sight of the dying man, Domenico forced his legs into the loose trousers that had been handed him. They were not even his own. He barely had time to throw the shirt over himself when the men shoved him through the doorway.

At the other end of the street, a few men lurched drunkenly toward them, obviously celebrating Carnevale. They showed no interest in the guard detachment loading its prisoner into a covered horse-drawn cart.

Nor did the celebrants swarming along the Ponte Sant' Angelo with their candles seem to care about the cart that rumbled past them into the Castel yard.

A guard opened the main portal to the prison at the Castel Sant' Angelo and stepped aside to admit the night watch. "Carnevale night and that's all you got?"

The arriving officer ignored the remark. "Who's in charge tonight?"

"That'll be me. Sergeant Bueti." A burly red-haired man a head taller than the porter emerged from the guard room. "What's going on here?"

"Order of Cardinal Carafa," the night officer said. Mustache man pushed his prisoner forward. Domenico stumbled, then caught himself with tied hands, on the stone wall. "Sodomy, we caught him in the act. I guess the Cardinal will stop by sooner or later to make it formal. We just checked the bawd houses and this is what we got."

"They killed him," Domenico said. "The man I was with. That's a crime, isn't it?"

The night officer sucked air through his teeth. "Yeah, there was another one but he, uh, resisted arrest."

Sergeant Bueti held his lantern close to Domenico's face. "He's a pretty one."

"Yep, and now he's yours. My job's done, and me and my men are going off duty. In case you hadn't noticed, it's Carnevale." He set his lantern on the floor and stepped back toward the portal.

Bueti blocked the door leading to the courtyard. "Far as I'm concerned, tonight's no different from any other night. Carnevale or no, you got to enter him and the charge in the book. Else your Cardinal's going to arrive looking for him and he won't find him, will he? My son will take care of the prisoner." He signaled a young man standing farther down the stone corridor. "Claudio, take this man to a cell and give him some water."

Claudio lifted a large ring of keys from its hook on the wall. Tall and wide-shouldered like his father, the boy was perhaps eighteen, still young enough, or sheltered enough, to be unscarred. He wore his long light brown hair tied back with a cord that hung down his back. When he got close to Domenico he stopped and looked directly at him before taking hold of the chain that hung from his wrist shackles. Awkwardly, as if he had seldom had this responsibility, he picked up a lantern and led Domenico down a wooden staircase, glancing back at him every few minutes.

They descended to a second level, and then a third. Each time they passed one of the doors, with its crosshatched bars, the odor of dank straw, rotten and infected flesh, and human waste assaulted them.

Finally they stopped before an empty cell and Claudio entered first, pulling Domenico in behind him. "I have to lock you to the wall," he mumbled, as though the task embarrassed him.

Domenico glanced around, dread rising in him. The stone walls were streaked with black mold, and the straw on the floor was rancid. He noted that the width of the cell allowed him to lie down and recalled rumors that the lowest cells were too narrow even to allow that. Would he want to lie down anyhow, with the rats? In the corner, a wooden bucket stood empty, though the stench that came from it revealed its purpose.

The young guard finally managed to turn his key in the rusted padlock, fastening the chain to a ring near the floor. Domenico was now anchored. At that moment he realized with a sudden nausea that he would be there, sitting or lying, in pitch blackness. His heart pounded with terror. "Please. Can you leave a candle? I have friends who will pay you."

"I don't know if I can. But I'll leave the lantern here on the floor while I get you water. You're allowed to have that."

"Yes, thank you." Domenico still stood, fearing to lower himself onto the stone floor, as if that would signal an acceptance of the terrible confinement. When the boy returned with a clay bowl of water, Domenico begged, "Please, stay a little longer."

Claudio hesitated and held the lantern up before his prisoner's face. "Your voice. I *know* you. I heard you sing once. At Whitsuntide, in St. Peter's. My God. How did this happen to you?"

"A sin, a foolishness. Please don't make me recount it. A man has already paid for it with his life."

"Do your friends know you are here? Can anyone help you? The choirmaster?"

Domenico shook his head. "Definitely not him. He follows orders of the Master of Ceremonies, the one who locks us up at night. Some of us find ways to get out, but it's dangerous—obviously." Domenico stared at the lantern for a moment. "But maybe…Michelangelo Buonarroti."

"The sculptor? You know him?"

"Yes. He's painting in the Sistine Chapel for the Pope. He's not really a friend. But he might have pity. I don't know."

"Do you want me to carry a message to him? I get off duty at ten. If you know where he lives."

"His workshop is in the Piazza Rusticucci, near Santa Caterina. Here." Domenico lifted his shackled hands to the cross at his throat. "Take this to him. He should remember it. Tell him where I am and that I beg him to help."

"And if he's not home?" The boy tugged at the short column of hair behind his neck, as if trying to pull an answer from it.

Domenico closed his eyes for a moment, then asked weakly, "What is the punishment for sodomy?"

"Ah, that differs according to the mercy of the judge. I've heard of men executed for it, and others flogged. But a flogging in a place like this…" He stopped. "Look, I have to lock the cell, but I'll leave the lantern here. It should last the night."

He unclasped the cross from Domenico's neck and slid it inside his leather jerkin. When he withdrew his hand, he offered something. "Keep this in exchange for the cross. At least for tonight, for comfort."

It was a small rosary, with simple wooden beads. Domenico took it silently.

"My name is Claudio," the young guard said.

"Yes. I'm Domenico." The guard's kindness, the exchange of names, it was a straw of hope. "God bless you for this," he said with quiet fervor.

"May God bless us both," Claudio said, stooping through the doorway.

Then Domenico was alone and the lock fell into place with a heavy, heartbreaking clank. He stared into the unwavering flame of the lantern and began the rosary, his own thoughts intruding. "*Pater noster, qui es in caelis…* Teach me obedience. *Sanctificetur nomen tuum. Adveniat regnum tuum.* Why do you wait so long to come? *Panem nostrum quotidianum da nobis hodie.* Not just bread. Teach me also what sin is, Lord. Is it the act or the thought or the pleasure from it? Do

I offend Thee in the surrender of my flesh, which is in Thine image, or already in the desires of my heart, which I cannot hide from Thee? And if I obey Thee and Thy servants, will that free me from sin? But what if the *obedience* is the sin?"

No answers came, no understanding, and so he drew the next bead forward and began the Ave Maria, mumbling the words he had said so many times he could pray while his mind wandered elsewhere. Where was the soul of Luca now? Had a prostitute any hope of salvation? And what about the thousands of Romans celebrating Carnevale in the same way? Was every act of the flesh a sin, if it was not under God's sacrament? Was there no form of love or need, however intense, that was exempt from the rule? Did not Christ also surround himself with men who adored him, who left their wives for him?

Domenico sobbed into his clenched fists. Surely there was a place for him in God's kingdom. If he came out of this purgatory alive he would ask the one man who seemed to wrestle with the same hard questions: Michelangelo.

If.

XIX

BACCHANALIA

The horse race had just finished and Michelangelo's wineskin made its way around the group once again. Darkness had fallen and Silvio fumbled for a moment in the leather purse at his belt, then withdrew candles with little collars and handed them around. The three stood together, waiting. Finally someone in the street shouted *"Moccoletti! Moccoletti!"* and it came, spreading up the street from the Piazza Venezia like a grass fire. One by one the candles were ignited until each person held a flickering light. *Moccoli* flickered in windows, atop walls and on balconies, until the entire Via del Corso seemed a lava flow of flames.

The melee began. Strangers threw themselves at each other, each trying to extinguish the other's *moccolo* while keeping his own alight. Masked figures in fantastical costumes chased each other and fell into an embrace. Rome scintillated and gave itself over to licentiousness. In the wild back-and-forth a bearded man staggered against Adriana. He was gold-clad, crowned and bejeweled like a Babylonian king, and exceedingly drunk.

"Scusi," he mumbled with foul breath and lurched sideways into an alley. He slouched against a wall for a moment and then slid gracefully down to lie in drunken stupor. His polished metal crown tilted precariously over his brow, reflecting the light of passing candles.

"I think someone wants our attention." Silvio nodded toward a pair of boys coming toward them. As the two neared, they opened their doublets, exposing the swell of breasts. Women, Adriana realized with a shock. Prostitutes dressed for the lawless appetites of Carnevale. One of them pressed herself against Michelangelo, who flinched in apparent distaste. Silvio, however, allowed the fraudulent boy to caress him from chest to groin.

Adriana suddenly felt the other prostitute's hand slide across her and squeeze her breast. A woman's voice whispered in her ear, "For you, I cost nothing, Lady." Shocked, she twisted away from the prurient hand and staggered against Silvio, who caught her.

"By the saints, Adriana. You've had too much wine. We've got to take you back to the Piazza Venezia to get some food in your stomach."

"Yes. Food would be good," she breathed, and they retraced their steps, passing the alley where the kingly reveler had fallen unconscious. The old man half lay, half slouched against the wall, but his finery had been stripped from him. He snored loudly, oblivious to everything. Three young men stood over him; two of them argued over his cloak and crown.

"Son of a whore!" the taller one shouted. "I saw him first."

"Take your hands off it, you pig's ass, or I'll send you to hell," the other one snarled. The first man began to pummel the other, who shielded his face with his forearms. The third man stood swaying on uncertain legs and pointed at the unconscious victim, mumbling something incoherent.

Silvio held his candle out in front of him, illuminating the scene. "I know those boys. From the Farnese."

At the word "Farnese," the attacker paused and glanced over toward the light. At that instant his victim sprang forward and pounded his fist onto the distracted opponent's chest. When he raised it again, he held a bloody knife. The wounded man staggered back while his attacker lurched into the crowded street. The third man careened after him.

Michelangelo caught the wounded man from behind as he collapsed, and both went to their knees. Blood poured over the man's bulky chest and trickled over his knuckles as he covered the wound with his own hand. He looked down at himself in astonishment and then lost consciousness. Silvio knelt in front of the two and pressed a wad of the crumpled shirt against the wound. The naked king, on whose account the whole quarrel had arisen, still slept.

Onlookers gathered, forming a ring of candlelight, while someone ran for guards in the Piazza del Popolo. At the periphery of the crowd,

Adriana stood dumbfounded. Everyone she could see—the belligerents, the spectators, and herself—wore masks, as if in a Carnevale tableau. She seemed suspended in a world of myth where Cardinals and satyrs, pagan gods and serpents celebrated bloody pandemonium.

At that moment a gloved hand encircled her wrist and yanked her into the crowd.

His sheer momentum pulled her with him, in among the revelers. She thought at first the assailant had returned, but then she recognized the doublet of a masked boy she had seen at the end of the parade. Excited, she let herself be dragged through the river of candle flames, wondering how far he would take her.

Half a street away, he abruptly swung her into a church. Without stopping, he pulled her along the outside aisle of the sanctuary into an open confessional. He seized her hands and, pinning them against the wall on both sides of her head, he covered her mouth with his. For a brief moment she tasted wine on his lips, and then she wrenched her head to the side. She tried to push him away but could not, for the angle at which he held her gave him an advantage. And yet, he did not molest her further. Instead he rested his head almost sorrowfully against her neck, both of their chests heaving from the sprint. His breath warmed her throat.

Curiously, he did not smell from the exertion, as had every other man she passed close to on the street. He was beardless, and even the way he leaned against her was gentle. The only discomfort she felt was the hardness of her own medallion pressed between her breasts.

Something was strange about him, about his too-soft skin. Did she know him? A new sort of dread assaulted her. Under the layers of clothing between them, the thick doublet and the folds of her own dress, she felt a slender body press against her. The hands that gripped her by the wrists loosened and slid down until he held her gently by the forearms still pressed against the wall, and his fingertips pulsed where they touched her inner arm. In the quiet of the confessional she could hear his breathing and her own.

Then the warm mouth covered hers again, not forcefully but with ardor. With all fear gone and with wine in her blood she kissed him back. She felt the slight touch of his teeth and inhaled his breath, tasted wine on his tongue. Heat spread upward through her and ignited a delicious awareness of her sex that she had not felt since Spain.

At a loud crash behind them, her captor sprang away from her, lurching from the confessional and running toward the altar. Three men had burst through the doors of the sanctuary.

Adriana stepped in front of her friends. "Let him go. I'm unharmed." She took hold of Silvio's arm. "It was only a Carnevale prank. Really, it's nothing. He'll simply have a brave story to tell his friends."

In a moment, the abductor was gone.

They stood in a little group in the nave between two lanterns, and she pulled off the narrow silk mask she had worn the entire evening. The others were already unmasked, sobered by the stabbing. Still breathless, she focused finally on the third man who had come in. Urbino, Michelangelo's manservant. All three were somber.

"What's going on?"

Urbino spoke. "There is something you must see, Madama."

He held out a callused hand. At the center of his palm lay a small Greek cross, with tiny rubies, like drops of jeweled blood at the four ends.

"Domenico's cross?" Confused, Adriana looked in the direction where her abductor had just fled, then back at Urbino. "Where did you get this?"

"A young man from the Castel Sant' Angelo brought it to the house on behalf of Signor Raggi. It was good that Signor Buonarroti told me he would eat at the Piazza Venezia. I was able to find him."

"What does that mean? Is Domenico all right?"

Michelangelo laid his hand gently on her arm. "Adriana, Domenico has been arrested."

"Arrested? When?" Adriana stammered. "For what crime?"

"It was Carafa. God's hound. He sent out men to patrol the streets for prostitutes. Domenico was found with one in the Trastevere."

"That's impossible. He could not...could he?"

"I assure you, many can," Silvio interjected. "If the surgeon cuts skillfully. Women who know from experience have told me this."

"Where is he?" she asked weakly, dropping down on a bench.

"In the prison at Castel Sant' Angelo, Signora. They brought him just a few hours ago, Urbino said."

Michelangelo sat down next to her. "Do you have money? If we can get to him before Carafa does, he has a chance."

"Money?" She patted the silk purse that hung at her waist. "Do you think that will help? Here, take it all." Fumbling, she untied the coin purse and pressed it into his hand.

"Consorting with prostitutes is not a crime, especially not at Carnevale." Silvio tried to sound reassuring. "It is only an offense because he belongs to the Church and has taken vows. I'll talk to my father. He still has friends at the Vatican who can help. But you must go to Sant' Angelo immediately, before he's formally charged."

Michelangelo hefted the coin purse, measuring its weight. "If justice can't save him, let's see what avarice will do."

XX

Adriana was well acquainted with the Castel Sant'Angelo, a vast stone silo surrounded by an exterior wall and four bastions. It had been a mausoleum, a fortress, and a wartime papal residence. The elegant apartments the Borgia Pope had made in the middle of it all surmounted a dungeon, the stuff of nightmares. Tonight, against the star-filled sky, the Castel was black and terrifying, the crenellations on its battlements like a row of teeth. She was nauseous with fear.

"Will they even open the door to us?"

"I know a sergeant with the prison guard. He was a stonecutter once in the quarries at Carrara until the blasting powder took away half of his foot. He should remember me."

Michelangelo hammered on the heavy oaken door. A porter opened it, pale under a layer of grime. He peered at them through bloodshot eyes, uncertain of their rank.

"I look for Sergeant Bueti. Bruno Bueti. Tell him Michelangelo, who owes him money, is here to pay him."

Muttering, the porter closed the door again and they waited in silence. Bats fluttered overhead and something small scurried along the bottom of the wall.

Finally the oak slab swung open. A giant of a man stood in the doorway and squinted out at them, his mottled face frowning in consternation. "Who claims to be…oh! Signore. It *is* you. What are you doing here?"

Michelangelo interrupted him. "Signor Bueti. I've looked for you everywhere. Here, I am a man of honor and I owe you this for the special block of marble that you cut for me." He pressed several coins into the man's right hand. The other guard, still behind him, tried to peer past his shoulder at the transaction.

"Uhh...all right." The sergeant's hand closed around the coins. "Is that it, then?"

"No, my friend. I have another offer to make. Can we talk inside?"

"Offer? Yes...all right." The two of them stepped into the prison corridor. The other soldier disappeared into a side room. Rough male laughter wafted through the briefly open doorway.

Michelangelo came quickly to the point. "You have a prisoner, Domenico Raggi, arrested just hours ago. We'd like to see him and will pay for the privilege."

"No need for that, Signore. You've already paid." Bueti took up a lantern, glancing sideways at Michelangelo. "Because I never cut a special block of marble for you. Come on. I'll take you down to the cells myself."

The giant led them down a wooden staircase into a narrow corridor, rocking noticeably each time his weight shifted onto the mutilated foot. His lantern brought a train of light into the dismal passageway. Gargoyle shadows danced diagonally alongside them as they walked. Adriana was assaulted by the stench and held her handkerchief to her mouth. She could not see into the tiny cells, which she knew were too low for a man to stand up and too narrow for him to lie down, but the moans that came from some of them were worse than the sight of the prisoner himself.

With her other hand she held her skirts away from the stone walls, grimy with soot from the smoke of the lanterns at both ends of the corridors.

The taciturn sergeant led them ever deeper through the labyrinth, each level more suffocating. "You can't stay long. Five minutes, or you'll get me in trouble." He unhooked an iron key from his belt and opened a narrow wooden door.

The cell, mercifully, was larger than most, with room for them to enter. A lantern already there shone on a man huddled on the straw of the stone floor, one hand clutching a rosary. Adriana knelt down next to him and touched his shoulder. "Domenico, dear. Are you all right? Have they hurt you?"

Domenico blinked for a moment, then took hold of her arm. "Lady Adriana. Oh, my prayers have been answered. No, I'm not hurt."

Michelangelo sat down across from him on the straw and placed the lantern between them. "We must find out if you've been charged by the magistrate. If not, we'll try to get you out."

He took hold of Michelangelo's hand. "But I'm guilty, Signore. They know it."

"That's between you and God, Domenico. If you—" Michelangelo stopped, sudden dread apparent in Domenico's face, and looked behind him.

The gaunt form of Gian Pietro Carafa stood in the doorway. Lit from the lantern on the floor, his bony face was a death's head. Wordlessly, he slid his glance from side to side across all three of them.

Domenico pressed his hands together. The rosary still dangled from the right hand. "Father, these are my friends who counsel me to repent before God."

The Dominican ran his hand down his white robe to his crucifix. "I know who they are. You, Madama, are one of the Borgia fornicators. And you, Signore, are His Holiness's painter who has overstepped his authority here."

Michelangelo struggled to stand up in the crowded cell. "Eminence is correct. But this boy is also the Pope's servant. If I can bring him back chastened, surely His Holiness will be pleased. Besides, to lie with a woman at Carnevale is not a mortal sin."

Carafa exhaled slowly and tilted his gaunt head. "He polluted himself with a *man*."

Michelangelo dropped his eyes for perhaps too long a moment. "It does not matter, as long as he is contrite, Eminence. God has mercy on those who struggle with themselves."

"Your knowledge of Scripture is faulty." The Dominican raised a bony index finger. "'Whosoever shall commit this abomination shall be cut off from among the people and cast into the fire.'" He let the word "fire" hang in the air for a long moment. Then he added, "However," and paused again to make sure he had everyone's full attention. "His Holiness takes a personal interest in his chapel singer, and of course we reported the arrest to him immediately." Carafa spoke directly to the prisoner. "Out of his inexhaustible mercy, he has decided to pardon you. Therefore, the Holy Office will look with clemency on the sinner this one time. But you are confined to the chapel for a month. Any hint of a violation will result in the direst consequences." The Cardinal paused again, to let his words have their effect before he unlocked the shackles around Domenico's hands.

"As for you, Signora," he turned his tight face toward Adriana. "The Borgia have been purged from the Vatican, and Providence has punished the crimes of Alexander's children. But be warned. The Church turns its righteous eyes upon the sinner and the sodomite, and the fire shall consume them." He pulled his black cloak around him with a gesture of finality and marched back along the hellish corridor. The cell door behind him remained open.

"I think you are free now." Michelangelo pulled Domenico up to his feet. "Let's get out of here before there is any doubt about that."

Domenico rubbed his chafed wrists. "Signore, there was a guard, Claudio, who showed me a great kindness. It was he who brought the message to your house. Please, can you grant him some reward? I'll find a way to repay you."

As they came out of the cell, the sergeant stood in the corridor. Michelangelo addressed him. "Signor Bueti, you have a soldier named Claudio who sent the message to me, and we would like to thank him. Is he on duty?"

The big man looked puzzled. "Claudio is my son. He's been off duty since ten, but he usually returns to accompany me home. It's possible he's in the common room with the others. They'll be washing off the smell of the prison."

The sergeant led them up the several wooden staircases to the guardroom next to the portal. Without comment, he ushered Michelangelo inside, leaving the door behind him slightly ajar. Through the opening Adriana could see some half-dozen men sitting on benches in various states of undress. They washed from basins of water on the floor and laughed raucously at some remark. Close to the door, a young man bent his right arm awkwardly backward to scrub his lower back.

"Claudio," the sergeant said. The man near the door twisted around awkwardly, threw his drying cloth over his shoulder, and leaned back on his arm. Extraordinarily, the face atop the muscular body was almost feminine and completely at odds with the brutal surroundings. The sergeant stopped in front of him.

"That's him," Domenico said from the corridor. "The man who helped me."

Michelangelo touched the naked shoulder lightly. "For your kindness," he said simply, and handed the man a silver coin.

The young soldier looked at the coin in his hand and then up at his benefactor. "You're Michelangelo, who is painting in the Pope's chapel?"

Michelangelo nodded and the guardsman continued. "We're not all beasts and torturers down here, sir. Some of us dream of being in the palace guard in a pretty uniform."

The gruff sergeant's voice interrupted his son. "Signor Buonarroti is not interested in our dreams, Claudio." He drew Michelangelo toward the doorway, terminating the meeting. "Signore, it's better you should take your friend away before the morning guard arrives. You'll just have to explain everything to them."

"I'm grateful to you both, Signor Bueti. If there is ever something I can do…" Michelangelo pulled the door behind him, but a hand drew it back again and a voice said behind him, "Signore, if you please, I'm a good Christian. Paint me in heaven." A second, rougher voice added, "Paint us all in heaven!" The laughter came again.

Michelangelo said nothing as he threw his weight against the prison portal and guided the shaken Domenico to freedom.

XXI

They walked awhile in the pre-dawn light without speaking, for the air held a dozen questions and all of them were dangerous.

Finally Adriana broke the silence. "I just don't understand. Why did you do it?"

Domenico was slow to reply. Then he said with obvious frustration, "The night watch—they butchered the man I was with, like a dog."

"That does not answer the lady's question," Michelangelo said.

"I'm sorry, Lady Adriana." Domenico took a breath. "I suppose it was just loneliness."

Michelangelo became conciliatory. "We're all lonely. God has given you this fate as He has given a fate to me and to Lady Adriana. You have His precious gift in your throat, but it comes with a price."

"A price? Forgive me, Signore, but you have little appreciation of the price I've paid. I am a servant of the Church, not by choice but because of a brutal transaction that was forced on me as a child. They say I owe them my life in return, but it's a debt I never did contract and cannot answer."

"These are not the words of a man who is contrite," Michelangelo said coolly.

"I don't know what I am. My head is full of locusts." Domenico rubbed his forehead.

Adriana put her arm around him. "You'll have time to sort things out during your confinement, and it can't be so terrible being in the chapel."

"Do you think locking me in the Vatican will change anything?" His voice was suddenly plaintive. "You don't know."

They came to the alley that led to the basement of the Sistine Chapel. Outside the open doorway, Paris de Grassis stood with his hands on his hips. The Master of Ceremonies was obviously furious, and Adriana did not envy Domenico the berating he would have to endure. She kissed him again and the softness of his face reminded her suddenly of another soft cheek that night. Was it the same night, only a few hours before? She felt a small guilt-ridden pleasure at the memory.

Domenico shook hands with Michelangelo. "Pray that the Virgin keeps us all safe. Good-bye," he said, and walked like a condemned man toward the Master of Ceremonies.

As they made their way back to Adriana's lodging, Michelangelo was hunched over with weariness. "Sin is always close by, isn't it, always breathing in your ear. A man was murdered tonight in front of us for a little bit of greed, and another was killed for…" He seemed to search for the right word. "For unpermitted pleasure."

"Why is that particular pleasure unpermitted, I wonder?" she remarked.

"A strange question, but speaking of that, just what did you do with that masked boy last night, anyhow?"

"Nothing. A simple embrace. I don't want to talk about it. Carnevale is over and we've seen how temptations lead to disaster. I wish to live within the law."

"I do too," Michelangelo grumbled. "And I can tell you that if you want to keep temptation away, you must exhaust yourself with occupation. Build something or tear something down. Myself, I cut stones and spread plaster. After a day of that, there's no time for anything but sleep. And if you should fall nonetheless, seek forgiveness."

"In the confessional?" She thought again of a mouth that tasted of wine. "No, I don't think so."

❖

Later in the morning Adriana's coach pulled up to the Villa Borgia. Ever alert, Jacopo stood waiting even before the horses had stopped. "Is My Lady well?" He offered his hand.

"I'm fine. How goes the household?" She gathered the folds of her skirt and let herself be helped to the ground.

Jacopo did not reply at once, but as they walked along the path to the entrance he said gently, "I don't wish to alarm you, My Lady, but the lower aqueduct collapsed yesterday afternoon. We brought water by bucket for the house and the garden this morning."

"That too," she said softly. She walked with the housemaster through the garden and noticed at once how quiet it was. With the fountain stilled, she could hear only the buzzing of bees and the crunching of gravel under their feet. They followed the course of the clay pipeline to the beginning of the stone aqueduct. Holding the bottom of her skirt over her arm, she bent over the sodden ground. The damage was grave. Not only had the concrete juncture with the villa pipeline disintegrated, but the remaining masonry had also crumbled. A large stone was rolled up against the cavity and straw packed around it, but water still trickled through.

"'Exhaust yourself,'" she muttered. "'Build something, or tear it down.' All right, Michelo, we'll try it your way," she said to no one in particular and clambered down the hill.

❖

The sun was set by the time she had fully inspected the problem, unpacked, and eaten her supper. She stared out the window onto the villa grounds and could hear the gardeners talking as they stopped work for the day. The sky was cobalt, and against the murky backdrop of the garden, Carnevale images still haunted her. A raucous parade and a river of flames, forbidden fondling, the dungeons of the Church, and the memory—which seemed never to fade—of the blood on her own hands. Now she had found the perfect penance.

She lit another taper and set out pen and paper. She listed the craftsmen she would hire—masons, hydraulic engineer, garden sculptor—then sketched out the whole fountain complex together with its water source. At the foot of the garden, she drew a curving colonnade and before it a rectangular pool. In the center of the pool, there would be a statue of the Madonna.

XXII

JANUARY 1510

Much had been accomplished in the many months since Carnevale, and Adriana was satisfied. Tilting her straw hat to shade her face, she walked along the ditch that held the new pipeline. Clever, she thought, the way the ceramic pipes were designed. Each pipe length was identical to the others, yet by their sameness they could be coupled. Was there some mathematical "principle of sameness"? She smiled inwardly. Silvio would know. He probably had an entire Greek manuscript about it.

She rubbed sore muscles in her neck. It was a good kind of soreness, the kind that could be assuaged by a bath and a good sleep. Michelangelo was almost right. Hard physical labor did take her mind from forbidden reveries. And though the nightmares persisted, of Battista and of her father, they were fewer.

"Madonna!" Jacopo hurried toward her. "A letter, Signora." He drew a fold of cream-colored paper from inside the bib of his apron. "From Ferrara," he added breathlessly.

Anxious, Adriana noted the Este coat of arms on the wax seal. She unfolded the large single page and recognized at once the florid and highly slanted script of her sister-in-law. Spoiled, sweet-fingered Lucrezia. As she perused the letter, dread gave way to relief. "The Duke and Duchess of Ferrara will visit us, Jacopo, but unfortunately they've given us little notice. They arrive in three days. Can we prepare for them in time, do you think?"

The alarm in his face showed his rapid assessment of the burdens of hosting nobility. "Do they travel with any of their court?"

"It's not so bad as that. It appears the Duke has business with His

Holiness. He will deposit his wife here for a few nights while he attends the Pope in Rome. I haven't seen my sister-in-law in years. Do you suppose we can have the pipeline to the house and the bath working by then?"

"Only a bath and not a banquet, Madama?" He broke into a rare smile. "It will be done tomorrow."

❖

Lucrezia Borgia, Duchess of Ferrara, shifted her position for the hundredth time, trying to bring some sensation back to her buttocks. Two days in a rumbling coach, even in a princely one, could benumb anyone's derriere. The trip had been organized so precipitously that she had not even been allowed to bring a lady-in-waiting. She sighed in resignation and began to play with her hair, curling it around her finger. There was no point in complaining to her husband, who rode ahead of the coach, since he had covered the same distance sitting rigid on a horse's saddle.

They were nearing the Via Tiburtina, though, and she recognized the countryside. Only a couple more hours and they could rest. It would be lovely to see Adriana again. They'd always had so much fun together, the two of them, in their Vatican days. She would not have called it an age of innocence. Not with all the killings and betrayals. She had not even always felt safe, though as daughter to the Pope and sister to Cesare Borgia, she should have.

But Alexander had been an attentive and responsive father, had groomed and pampered her, if only to increase her value in marriage. That was the way of things. Even given her fear of Cesare's wrath, and the sorrow of being assigned to husbands and then forced to divorce them or see them murdered, she'd had the unmistakable pleasure of being at the top of things.

Adriana had understood the game too. Her own father, Don Pedro Falcon, had certainly calculated the value of her marriage to Juan Borgia. The only thing that shocked Lucrezia was the ruthlessness with which any miscalculations were "corrected." In Adriana's case, her husband Juan was murdered, and both she and Lucrezia knew, though they never spoke of it, that Cesare was probably the cause.

Lucrezia had also seen her husband, the Duke of Bisceglie,

murdered in his bed. Again, the assailants were unknown but suspected to be acting for Cesare. That too was the way of things, and for the Borgias, such acts were not even a crime. She had learned from earliest childhood that the laws of God and state applied only to common men. The papal family enjoyed a mantle of divine protection, a state of grace that exempted them from sin.

Lucrezia felt she had held up well as the Borgia fortunes declined. She wondered if Adriana had over the last six years. Was she still as beautiful and exotic as at the Vatican? Lucrezia had sometimes been a bit jealous, but only a little. Adriana was always affectionate to her and obedient to Alexander, and there was never a hint of competition from her. In fact, she often helped Lucrezia with her "secret," the regular soaking of her hair in a special lemon wash to keep it blond. She stroked it again, grasping a thick swath and drawing her hand luxuriously along the length of it.

It was a happy day when Lucrezia realized that Cesare had chosen Adriana as his mistress, for that meant that even after the death of Juan, she would stay in the family. But she could not help but wonder what went on between the two lovers. It titillated her to imagine her brother conquering Adriana, riding her to the height of ecstasy. Did she moan and cry out? She would surely look appetizing, lying with her legs spread, inviting him in. Lucrezia felt a slight tingle, recalling their girlish wrestling in her chamber that once or twice ended in sudden sexual play.

Lucrezia shrugged inwardly. Well, she herself was a Duchess now, and well loved in Ferrara. She could have any man she wanted, as long as she concealed her infidelity from the Duke. She drew back the curtain and smiled up at the captain of the guard who rode alongside the coach. He was new and more amusing than the last.

She looked forward to exchanging news with her sister-in-law. There were new things in the air, aside from the tedious battles between France and Venice and Rome, a shift in the political and artistic winds. She welcomed the new poetry and art in her court, but she had complete contempt for the Church "reform." It was all political machination, and the "reformers" just invented a new set of rules to favor themselves.

The sky had been overcast for most of the morning, but as they turned onto the Via Tiburtina, the clouds opened up and sunlight poured down over the winter landscape, welcoming her.

❖

Fresh from his victory in the Battle of Polesella and preceded by six advanced guards, Alfonso d'Este, Duke of Ferrara, rode on a black warhorse in front of the coach bearing his wife. Behind the coach a detachment of ten more liveried guards and a standard bearer followed in formation.

Adriana hurried to meet her guests. At the front of the villa, the Duke dismounted and stood beside the coach. He was a coarse-looking man, with a mane of black hair that curved around his face and joined with his beard. His doublet of fluted green brocade was gathered in a wide belt embossed at intervals with gold eagles. Ah, yes, she thought, the Este eagles. The bulky sack tied to the back of his saddle suggested armor, and if it was, he had obviously chosen comfort over safety during the two-day journey on horseback.

"Your Grace." Adriana hinted at a curtsey. "It is an honor and a pleasure to welcome you. Lunch is prepared. Will you rest awhile and take a meal before continuing to Rome?"

The Duke's intelligent brown eyes swept over her with only a hint of disapproval. "I thank you for your kindness, Lady Borgia. But I have urgent business in Rome and cannot delay. My wife, however, is most anxious to accept your hospitality."

Lucrezia emerged, her full satin skirts bursting out like pale blue viscera from the coach interior. The guard captain assisted her down. Narrow-hipped and with a well-trimmed beard, he had the courtier's shallow virility. Lucrezia let go of his hand, but her lingering glance toward him told all.

"Sister!" Lucrezia ran past her husband into Adriana's arms. "How beautiful you are, after all these years."

"I see that my wife is content and in good hands," the Duke said. "With your permission, Lady Borgia." He gave a barely perceptible bow and remounted his horse.

At his signal, the driver turned the Duchess's ornate coach around to the villa stables, while Alfonso d'Este and his sixteen guards rode off toward Rome.

Nonplussed, Adriana said, "Not very chatty, is he?"

Lucrezia linked arms with her. "You have to get used to him."

Adriana led her to a table in the garden where a meal was laid out. "Look, I have all the things you like. Venison, goose, olives, even almond cakes." She poured wine into tall silver cups.

Lucrezia took a long gulp, then wiped her lips with a delicate fingertip. "How wonderful to finally be on the ground, after days in that bone-rattling box. But I won't complain. It took all my charm to convince him to bring me along at all."

Adriana filled her goblet again. "What business does the Duke have with His Holiness? What's so urgent?"

"It's the Venetians again. His Holiness was extremely impressed with Alfonso's command of the papal forces against them last year, but now they are in disagreement about something. Salt, I think. I am not privy to all Alfonso's plans, but I suspect he is looking for concessions from Julius in exchange for continued support."

"Alfonso dares to negotiate that now, with the Vatican so powerful?"

"Power comes and goes," Lucrezia mused, stroking her hair. "The Borgias were once the most powerful family in Italy, but when Alexander died, that disappeared. Poof." She popped an olive into her mouth as a sort of consolation and continued.

"Julius *appears* strong now. He has his Swiss army and his Spaniards. But Alfonso also has an army, and the best cannons in Christendom. He's a hard man to refuse these days, even for a Pope." She spat out the olive seed.

"Rather like Cesare?" Adriana offered more olives, amused.

"Yes, Alfonso does remind me of my brother, sometimes. But he's less reckless, so I expect he'll live longer."

"Do you love him?"

"Love? Oh, no. Love is the cruelest error. But I'm satisfied. A woman must belong to someone, and besides," the Duchess curled a strand of blond hair around her finger, "I have my diversions."

"Yes, I noticed." Adriana refilled her guest's wineglass from the ewer.

"How is your little choir boy? Domenico, wasn't it?"

"Domenico is not so little. But he's well. He attended me when I was sick last winter. For now he keeps to his duties."

"And your ill-tempered Florentine?"

"Michelangelo? You do him an injustice. He's undertaken to paint the Pope's chapel, though Julius, as I understand it, abuses him greatly. He has an amiable side too, in spite of his reputation. He invited me to watch the Carnevale parade with him and Silvio Piccolomini."

"Carnevale?" Lucrezia looked astonished. "You were in the streets, with the mob?"

"Yes. It started cheerfully enough but then things got out of hand. A man was stabbed to death right in front of us. And then I was... accosted."

"Accosted?" Lucrezia's eyes twinkled. "That sounds intriguing."

"It was nothing, really. Just a stolen kiss."

Lucrezia cupped her cheek with her hand. "If a stolen kiss makes your face all red like that, I think you haven't been getting 'accosted' nearly enough since Cesare died."

Adriana shook her head. "It is not that simple. These days I have no opportunities." She paused, puzzled by her own disinclination. "Or even desire."

Lucrezia wobbled her glass in reproach. "You're still young, Adriana. You need another man in your life, to keep you satisfied. Why don't you marry that Piccolomini fellow?"

"Silvio? Curious that you should mention him. I had considered it. Vaguely."

"Consider it precisely. He's handsome, has a well-formed leg, and other parts too, if I recall correctly. Besides, you shouldn't be alone. A woman must marry."

"I'm not sure if I want another husband."

Lucrezia set her empty goblet on the table with an unsteady hand. "Well, I know what I want right now, and that's a bath."

"You're lucky you arrived today and not a few months ago," Adriana said, rising to take her arm and guide her. At least one of them could walk in a straight line. "I still have no fountain, but my men worked day and night to finish the bath for you. I'll tell Jacopo to light the fire."

❖

Finally the heat from the caldera had spread under the stone floor and up through the vents behind the walls, so that both the water in the marble pool and the air in the room itself were pleasantly warm. Adriana dropped two large bath cloths on a bench near the pool. Behind her, Lucrezia began to disrobe with the same aplomb she'd had in childhood. She undid the laces of her bodice, dropped her wide skirts, and tugged off her underdress and shift. Turning slightly away, Adriana undressed as well.

Without comment, they both stepped nude into the bath and sat down so that the water rose chest high. Adriana opened the bronze tap behind her and steaming water flowed into the pool.

"Ah." Lucrezia laid her head back and squeezed water through handfuls of dark blond hair. The luxuriant backward curve brought her breasts up and outward, breasts that were no longer firm and maidenly, but still provocative. Catching sight of Adriana's glance she sat up and pushed a playful wave toward her. "I know what you're thinking, that I've lost my figure, while you're still trim as a girl." She affected a slight pout.

"Not at all," Adriana lied. "You are as beautiful as when you ran through the Papal Palace and every man in Rome was in love with you. Only now you have your own court. Motherhood becomes you, and so does a duchy," she added, veering off the subject of the body.

Lucrezia's fears were well founded. She was not yet thirty, but she looked older. Her soft face hinted at weariness and, without the corset of her dress, she had a paunch from the several children she had borne. "You mean it?" she asked girlishly. "It's so difficult, you know, after motherhood and a certain age. But a woman must remain attractive. It's our form of power, after all."

Adriana settled back against the pool wall, sinking as deeply as possible into the delicious warmth. "All things turn on power, don't they? And that's what women must do when they want it. Be seductive."

"Seductiveness has served us both well. You have the Villa Borgia and I have my duchy." Lucrezia ran her fingers through her wet hair. "We have nothing to apologize for either, because when we have power over men, we improve them."

Adriana was skeptical. "Seductress and saint. That's what Michelangelo said about women. They all want us to be like the Madonna, but we always turn out to be like Eve. But you know? I have a lot of sympathy with Eve." She smiled. "Can't you just imagine her scolding him? 'Adam, get some sense. This is the tree of knowledge. Eat, for God's sake.'"

Lucrezia giggled, then pressed her fingertips on her lips. "Be careful, Sister. There are priests who don't care for talk like that."

"Yes, I suppose there are. But I can tell you I'm fed up with priests. I'm fed up with it all."

Lucrezia flicked droplets of water at her. "Listen to you! Have you fallen under the spell of the new sciences? Very dangerous, you know."

"New sciences? What are you talking about?"

"I mean artists, scholars, talking of earthly beauty as a sign of God. If such ideas have spread to Ferrara, they're surely in Rome. People are studying the Greeks and reading Saracen scholars instead of scripture. Those who glorify the body and nature and paganism are charming entertainment at court, but they lead the weak to wildness of the mind and in the end to heresy."

Adriana splashed water at her. "Wildness of the mind? You've drunk too much of my wine." She thought for a moment. "Do you remember Raphaela Bramante? The woman who helped us get out of the Pope's chapel after Alexander's funeral?"

Lucrezia shrugged. "The painter."

"Yes, the portraitist. In fact she also spoke once of 'wildness' of the mind. Do you know she painted me from memory, after you and I fled Rome? I saw the painting in the Piccolomini library."

"How do you know it was you?"

"Aside from the resemblance, which even Silvio remarked on, she painted the dress I wore at the funeral. It was blue with a black ribbon down the front, remember? She copied it exactly, but painted it torn open, showing me half-naked underneath. I was supposed to be Europa, abducted by Zeus as a bull. I think that might qualify her as part of that worldliness in the air that the priests don't like. Imagine, a woman who paints lewd pagan scenes. If that isn't wild, I don't know what is."

"She had better be careful. The Holy Office will only stand for so much." Lucrezia's words slurred. Abruptly she lost interest in the intellectual subject and slid closer to Adriana. "We used to have so much fun together. Remember being young in the Papal Palace?"

Adriana felt the cool damp hair, the heavy head resting on her shoulder. Warm breath, smelling of wine, wafted against her throat. The soft flesh that pressed against her arm, she realized, was Lucrezia's breast. She recalled girlish fondling and Carnevale prostitutes, and a sweet tightness formed between her legs.

She pushed the other woman gently from her. "Lucrezia, dear. You better get out of this bath before you become a prune. Why don't you rest a little in your room? I'll send Maria up later to fetch you for dinner."

"You're right. Shouldn't have drunk so much. Sleep. I need a little sleep. Do you mind terribly?" Lucrezia stood up, water streaming down her pale body. Dreamily indifferent, as though in her own chamber, she climbed slowly out of the bath and stood unashamed by the pool. She dried herself and then wrapped her long hair in the bath cloth. Below her slightly swollen belly, the triangle of curly light brown hair still held beads of water.

For the briefest moment, Adriana wondered what it would be like to kiss the intimate parts of another woman. She splashed water over her face and stood up. "No, go and rest. I don't mind at all."

XXIII

"Holiness." Gian Pietro Carafa knelt in front of the Pontiff to kiss the papal ring.

Julius withdrew his hand. Something about this gaunt, intense man put him off. It might have been his rigid asceticism, or the way he stared so penetratingly, as if detecting hidden guilt.

"Thank you for notifying me of the errant behavior of our chapel singer," he said. "He understands the error of his ways now."

"It is a tribute to your forbearance, Holiness, that he was saved, but he was only one of many arrested that night. Clearly, Rome teems with fornicators and sodomites."

Julius tapped his palm on the armrest of his chair. Where was this going? "To what do we owe this visit, Eminence? I have an important guest shortly and we must be brief."

Cardinal Carafa ran his hand along the chain of his crucifix to the body of Christ. He held it against his chest as he bowed toward the Pontiff. "As you know, Holiness, several of my men have been successful in seizing certain felons during the past weeks. However, our effort has been wholly insufficient, for the city is overwhelmed with iniquity. It is not just the brothels and the violence in the streets. Depravity and heresy happen in the drinking places, the markets, the stables, and even in private homes."

"Yes?" Julius said slowly. "What would you have us do?"

"With your indulgence, if Holiness would permit me to form a force with powers of surveillance to uncover these offenses." Veins stood out on the hand that clutched the crucifix. "I have under my authority a dozen good men who could undertake this vigilance. In brief, I humbly beseech you to allow me to create a force of 'guardians of morality.' With official papal authority."

"Surveillance? Of depravity and heresy?" Julius frowned. "Do you mean the Jews and false converts?"

"The converts must be examined, of course, but the Jews are a separate problem, through their very presence. How can we preach that God rewards the Christian when the Jew so obviously succeeds, putting Christians in his shadow?"

Julius was surprised at the tangent. "What would you do with the Jews? They are our best doctors, printers, and merchants. Rome cannot do without them."

"Let them stay, but isolate them. On the Tiber islands, for example. They prefer to live among themselves anyhow."

"We will have to think about that."

The Cardinal tried another tack. "But heresy also comes from without, from new books and pamphlets. Orthodoxy is attacked from all directions."

"Rome is a city of foreigners. They bring their iniquities with them," Julius replied.

"Yes, their foreign ideas, their naked statues that have become fashionable, their licentiousness. But they do not need to be physically present to be a threat. They send their ideas before them like a disease, the anti-papal rumblings from the north, the misinterpretations of scripture, their godless science."

"Godless science? What do you mean, Eminence?" Julius sensed another tangent.

"I refer specifically to a young physician, one who was nurtured— to our shame—at two Italian universities. A doctor of theology from Padua who has returned to his home city in Prussia. Though I have not seen his 'Little Commentary,' as he calls it, I understand it proposes that God's earth is not the center of the universe, but that it merely revolves about the sun."

"Who is this heretic?"

"The son of a copper maker, he calls himself Copernicus. No matter his name. You can imagine the ramifications of such a notion. It challenges scripture in the profoundest way, and we cannot let such ideas infect Rome. The Church must remain the absolute authority on scientific thought and doctrine."

"The Church *is* the absolute authority."

"Only insofar as the layman is kept from corrupted knowledge. We can do that only if the Church prohibits the reading of false science and even of the Vulgate. It is also urgent that we create an index of forbidden books." He clutched the crucifix again, absentmindedly stroking the crucified man with his thumb. "For those who violate these prohibitions, there must be trials by a body of experts. There is even a model for this, called *Conduct of Inquiry of Heretical Depravity.* Brother Torquemada used it in Spain."

Julius tapped his hand again. "I see that Eminence has given thought to this issue. Perhaps too much thought." He stood up. "Let me show you something." He led the Cardinal across the room to a table where a large map was laid out. "Do you know the *Universalis Cosmographia?*"

"No, Holiness. Cartography has never held much interest for me."

"A pity. It should. This is the new map from the Germans, drawn up by someone named Waldseemüller. As you can see, it reveals not only the land mass that Signor Columbus discovered, but it indicates a western coast there and proposes that the new land is not a part of Asia."

"Yes, Holiness. I believe some have come to hold that view. It does not challenge orthodoxy, though."

"If you can stop harping on orthodoxy for a moment, you might consider the effect this new land has on the authority of the Church of Rome." Julius tapped vigorously with a forefinger. "There are two continents here. Look, the cartographer has even named them after our own Vespucci. America, north and south. Now, consider the size, consider what Spain and Portugal are achieving with their explorations and their conquests. Do you see how urgent it is that we secure the Romagna from the threat of the Venetians, or the French, and take our place among these world powers before it is too late? It is this issue that concerns me, not the Jews."

"I see your point, Holiness. But surely, expansion cannot be bought at the cost of the souls of our own people."

Julius waved his hand dismissively. "Yes, yes, your zeal for the purification of the Roman faithful is commendable, and I will grant you your guardians," he conceded. "Organize your men, if you wish.

Dominicans, I presume. They have an appetite for enforcement. In the meantime I must concern myself with statecraft. Will that be all then, Eminence?"

Cardinal Carafa took a step back, still clutching his crucifix. "One more thing, Holiness. The Borgias. They've always been your enemies. Indeed, the enemies of all good Christians. Adriana Borgia meddled in the case of your singer's arrest, and she is implicated in crimes committed by Cesare Borgia. It is not a coincidence that her father was declared a heretic in Spain. With your permission, I would like to arrest her."

Julius recalled a very old favor. It was years before, to be sure, but he was not without a sense of honor. "No, you may not. Monitor her, if you wish, but you may not arrest her for past deeds or for her family. Only for a new offense. If she is as corrupt as you suggest, she will soon provide you with one."

"As you wish, Holiness." Carafa's voice was silken. "But what about the painters' guild? There are said to be many sodomites."

He cleared his throat loudly. "Eminence dwells overmuch on men's private urges and too little on their political ambitions. I have armies to fight, Cardinal Carafa. When I have subdued them, I will address venial sin."

Julius sat down again on his throne-like chair, brushing off invisible dust from the lap of his alb. In case the gesture was not enough to signal that he had no more to say, he added, "My Master of Ceremonies tells me that I have an audience with the Duke of Ferrara now. God be with you." He presented the papal ring again, terminating the interview.

The Cardinal made the obeisance and backed toward the door silently, clutching his crucifix and holding on to his small victory. "Thank you, Holiness."

❖

Julius still sat, tapping his armrest as Alfonso D'Este, Duke of Ferrara, strode into the Sala dei Santi. It was a stride no one could mistake for subservience. Clanking in his fluted and elaborately etched cuirass that fit him like a silver doublet, with fluid pieces of steel covering him from shoulder to wrist, he looked for all the world like a conqueror. The cuirass itself was a piece of priceless art, and Julius suspected the Duke had donned it just for the meeting.

Alfonso observed all the formalities, kneeling and kissing the papal ring, but when he rose again, perhaps a fraction of a second before he was signaled to do so, his expression was proud. Julius, already piqued at the earlier audience, felt his temper rising. But the Duke was not a supplicant, and there was an alliance to maintain.

"Welcome to Rome, my lord of Ferrara. I trust your journey was not too arduous."

"Thank you, Holiness. I am pleased to be here. Let me also thank you, again, for the Golden Rose you sent to me after the battle of Bologna. A very great honor."

"It was only fitting, since you were instrumental in helping us expel the Bentivoglio. And of course, more recently, we could not have subdued the Venetian galleys without your cannons. It was only last week that the Venetian ambassador was here, kneeling in the Piazza San Pietro, to offer his surrender."

The Duke removed his metal gauntlets and hooked them to the side of his cuirass, where they rattled whenever he moved. "Yes. My cannons. It is that subject that I wish to address with your Holiness."

"Indeed." Julius waited for the Duke's proposal to be more clear.

"The threats to the Holy See are never-ending, I know. Today you have Bologna and Venice in hand, tomorrow may find the French armies or even the German emperor at your gates. Clearly, it would be prudent for the Vatican to maintain cannonry for its defense, and the Ferraran foundries would be pleased to provide them. However…"

"However?" The negotiation was about to begin. But Julius was in no mood.

"Alas." Alfonso hinted at a shrug. "They are much in demand, and in order to continue their production at Ferrara, we must be able to draw on the income from certain industries."

"To what industries, specifically, do you refer?"

"The salt marshes at Comacchio, of course, which the Ferrarans had been working until your troops interfered."

"Surely the Duke is aware that the Vatican holds the rights to the mining of salt in the Romagna. The proximity of the marshes to Ferrara gives you an unfortunate advantage in exploiting them, and thereby you undercut the price of pontifical salt in the marketplace. The Curial banker, Signor Chigi, informs me that this has affected our revenues significantly. It cannot continue."

Alfonso D'Este bowed slightly, causing his gauntlets to clank again. "Holy Father, I deeply regret this unexpected market effect, but as I indicated a moment ago, Ferrara needs its salt income, particularly if it is to continue production of the very cannon which your Holiness is so keen to possess."

Julius sensed he had hit a wall, or was about to, and he was enraged.

"Am I to assume Ferraran mining of salt from the marshes is the primary condition of the continuation our alliance?"

"'Primary condition' is perhaps overstated, Holiness. Let us say that the resumption of mining operations would simply underscore our fraternity, while the continued blockade would sow disappointment. Particularly in light of the renewed pressure from King Louis XII."

"My Lord Duke." Julius gripped his armrest. "If you think to threaten me with the French, you miscalculate. I do not need you. While I would love to have a row of your cannon again, I can do just as well with the six thousand pikemen the Swiss Federation has granted me."

"Swiss pikemen?" Alfonso's voice went soft, hinting at derision. "I hear they are very tall and handsomely uniformed. You must be careful not to let them soil their pretty outfits, Holiness."

Alfonso D'Este turned on his heel and clanked out of the Sala dei Santi without waiting for dismissal.

❖

"Lucrezia." Adriana sat on the edge of the bed and gently shook the other woman's shoulder. "Wake up, dear. Alfonso has sent one of his guard to announce that he is leaving Rome. Apparently the Pope did not give him the answer he was looking for and now he's furious."

Lucrezia rolled over onto her back and stretched. "I'll *bet* he's furious." She pulled herself up, fully awake. "That means he'll go over to the French."

"Julius will soon realize that and send men to stop him. That's probably why Alfonso is in such a hurry. He wants to get back to his castle and his cannons."

Lucrezia rose and pulled a brush through her long hair. "A plague on both of them, Pope and Duke alike. It seems I am always running away from Rome. Just like the last time you and I were together there, when Alexander died. I couldn't even mourn him, my own father, before they chased us out."

"Yes, I remember. It was so rancid in the chapel that day. It seemed a comment on what we all had done while Alexander lived."

Lucrezia began gathering brushes, undergarments, creams, and dropping them into a trunk. "You are being overly dramatic. Those were difficult times and the Borgias had a lot of enemies."

"Everyone has enemies. We were simply better at removing them swiftly. I'm not laying blame. I take the guilt on myself, and I am doing penance for it. My fountain and statue—"

"Penance? You? Whatever for?" Lucrezia laughed lightly. "What could you have possibly done that would require penance now, after so many years?" She closed the lid of the trunk and did up the buckles on both sides.

Adriana helped her slide it toward the door. "For Piero Battista. Don't you remember him? He was at the Vatican when we were both there."

"Yes. One of the men Alexander suspected of planning to assassinate him."

"Yes, suspected only. But Alexander ordered him killed. By me. I poisoned him."

Lucrezia smiled with superior knowledge. "No, dear, you didn't. Cesare did. On Alexander's orders."

"That's impossible. Battista came to my house on the Corso at my invitation. He was ailing, but came all the same. That's how certain he was that he could have me that night. I put belladonna in his wine and watched him die from it. It was terrible."

Lucrezia shook her head. "He was a dying man when he came to you. Cesare had already poisoned him. All you gave him was a little sugar in his drink."

"What? Then why did Alexander force me to invite the poor man? Why didn't Cesare kill him directly to be done with it?"

"I suppose because your house was a distance away from the Papal Palace. Alexander did not want his visitors dying under his feet at the Vatican."

"So I haven't committed murder," Adriana said, half to herself.
"Not that night anyhow. Have you poisoned anyone since then?"
Adriana did not laugh. "No, of course not."
"Well, my dear. Your conscience is clear."

❖

The Ferraran detachment drew up to the Villa Borgia, their formation less ceremonial than before. The draft horses that had scarcely rested had again been hitched to the ducal coach and brought up to the road moments before the arrival of the Duke.

Alfonso d'Este did not dismount this time, but remained astride his warhorse. He was in armor and the sack behind his saddle was empty. His guard seemed nervous as well. Of the sixteen, half waited as a rear guard at the junction with the Via Tiburtina.

Lucrezia gave her husband no reason for impatience. Jacopo had already loaded her trunk onto the coach, and the coachman sat in place. She was dressed, coiffed, and ready to travel, and she took only a moment to say farewell.

"I wanted us to spend a few days together, no children or husbands or affairs of state. But all I did was drink your wine and give you a headache."

"No. You've given me a great gift. You've lightened my soul better than any priest could in the confessional." Adriana kissed her on both cheeks. "Rome is in your blood. You'll come again, I know it. And then we'll have our long visit."

"Good-bye, Sister." Lucrezia waved one last time as the captain of the guard opened the coach door and her attention turned to him. The officer remounted and, at the Duke's raised hand, the coach and its company rolled off toward the Via Tiburtina.

Adriana stood for a moment watching the detachment re-form at the highway and turn northward. She savored the fleeting sorrow of departure for a moment, then returned to her garden to cheer herself. In the far end she could see the piles of dirt from the pit that had been dug for the pool and the neat crates of tile and marble for the structure itself. Only the fountain statue had not yet been ordered.

The fountain.

Something formed in her mind, something daring and wonderful. She was exculpated, free from the guilt that had gnawed at the back of her mind for five years. Her fountain no longer was a penance.

When she returned to her chamber she sat down again at her table by the tapestry. The original design still lay there, marked by annotations and costs. She turned it over and began to sketch. The image was rough, but she could approximate the head ringed by curls, the softly curving body, the tipped goblet from which the water would continuously flow, the second figure nestled against it, supporting it from the rear. A channel would have to be drilled through the wider part for the pipe, but it would work.

She laid down her pen finally, deeply satisfied. The new fountain deserved celebrating. She would invite her friends on the day the water flowed, when her fountain and her entire garden would be nourished by the languid, androgynous figure of Michelangelo's "Bacchus." A charming concrete copy of what he had created in marble.

With the afternoon sun pouring through her window, she lay down, content, and planned the dinner party in her head. The guest list would be small but worthy. Michelangelo, of course, and Domenico, if his confinement was over. Giovanni de' Medici perhaps, who seemed an ally. And Silvio Piccolomini, who would certainly get the joke, if he came.

Would he? Lucrezia was right; he was a suitable match. He would satisfy her yearnings and keep them from wandering where they should not go.

A woman must belong to someone.

XXIV

By summer, the Villa Borgia welcomed its first festive guests. Michelangelo and Domenico arrived in the late afternoon, and Adriana met them as they handed over their horses to the stable men. She offered a light embrace to Michelangelo, a more familial one to Domenico, then guided them both toward the slope overlooking the villa.

"Was it awful, being confined in the chapel complex?"

"No, not at all. I spent all of my time watching Maestro Buonarroti paint the ceiling. We talked about music, painting, everything. They were my happiest days."

"We all seem to have been spared a hard penance," she said cheerfully. "But come along, you two. I want to show you my villa from above. I've improved it a bit since you were here last year."

She walked ahead of her guests along the rising footpath, lifting her skirts from the grass, and sat down finally on a stone bench at the top. Michelangelo sat on the ground next to her. "Splendid vista. If I were a landscape painter, this is where I'd work."

Slightly below them and to their left, Domenico Raggi stretched out his long limbs on the grassy slope and rested on his elbow. In the heat of the afternoon, he opened his doublet and shirt and gazed down at the Villa Borgia below. "It's perfect, Lady Adriana. You've created a small paradise."

"That's what Lucrezia said when she was here," Adriana replied. "She flew in like a Ferraran sparrow, perched here for one day, then flew out again. Her husband the Duke found it wiser to be back with his army. Another war is brewing, I'm sure."

She fell silent, letting the others hear the sounds that had become familiar to her. Birds twittered in the bushes higher up the hill, and closer by insects buzzed. Michelangelo pulled up a blade of grass with a soft snap and drew it slowly through his lips.

She tried to see the entire estate with a stranger's eyes. The house itself at the southern end was modest: a two-story quadrangle with a central courtyard open to the sky and an attached wing on the west for kitchen and house-servants' quarters. Behind the house was her small private garden, cut off from the far larger formal garden laid out in symmetrical segments and divided by gravel paths.

On the western side the stables, carriage house, and field-servants' quarters formed a row, and behind these, woodland spread westward up another slope. To the east, gardeners were working in the vineyard and orchard. At the northern border of the estate was the new fountain and the cloth-covered statue that awaited its unveiling.

"A divine place," Michelangelo remarked, gazing up at the cumulus clouds that formed a ragged cylinder. Sunlight poured through it in distinct rays, like radii from a vast wheel of light. Adriana saw what caught his eye. "Now there is something you should paint."

Already half lying down, Domenico tilted his head sideways to see what held their glances. "Oh, yes." He raised his left arm and pointed languidly, his index finger curving softly, at the spectacle overhead. "It's like God's light is pouring down on the world." He sighed. "Don't you wish sometimes you could be up there, closer to the light? It must be glorious!"

Michelangelo murmured agreement. "No painter can produce colors like that, not even with gold leaf."

Adriana watched Michelangelo study both the splendid sky and the boy. There was a curious expression on his face, a sort of serenity, as if he looked outward and inward at the same time. Then his glance dropped to the road that curved below them into the lane of cypress trees. "Here come more of your guests."

Adriana stood up nervously. "It must be Silvio."

"Oh, pox!" Michelangelo suddenly slapped his chest. "I'm so sorry, Adriana. I forgot to give you this." He pulled a letter out from the inside of his leather jerkin. "Silvio said to tell you he regrets that he cannot attend your supper. He was called upon to go to Sienna to see to the terms of his betrothal." Then he added, "His father ought to have been the one to do it, but as you know, the old fellow hasn't been well."

"Betrothal?" Adriana was dumbfounded.

"Yes. To the Lady Gabriella Chigi. I thought you knew about the Chigis. They've been after him for ages and it looks like they've landed him."

"I...didn't know that." Adriana managed a smile, put the half-read letter into her skirt pocket, and looked out toward the road again. "Well, then, it must be Cardinal de' Medici," she said with forced lightness. "We should go down to meet him."

❖

Adriana approached the Cardinal's coach as the footman opened the polished wooden door. The priest emerged, a shock of bright red against the pastoral landscape. "Eminence." She genuflected briefly and made a brief gesture of kissing his Cardinal's ring. Michelangelo kissed the ring kneeling on one knee, Domenico kneeling on both.

The Cardinal accepted the obeisance with minimal interest and looked over their heads. "A lovely refuge, Signora Borgia. Handsomely appointed. I trust we will be given a tour."

"Most certainly, Eminence. Tomorrow, by morning light."

"I look forward to it. By the way, Lady Borgia, I've taken the liberty of inviting Donato Bramante to your little gathering. I hope you don't mind."

Adriana swallowed the second surprise within ten minutes. "No, of course not. If it please Your Eminence." Regaining her composure, she led her guests into the reception hall of the villa.

The four walls of the hall were covered with a decorative pattern with the Borgia coat of arms, while a pastoral tapestry covered the wall opposite the entry. A low fire crackled unnecessarily—given the heat of the day—in the marble fireplace flanking the entryway. Before the fireplace a table was spread with fruit and ewers of wine.

De' Medici sat down with a sigh on one of the wooden chairs and exchanged his wide-brimmed Cardinal's hat for the smaller biretta. His bulldog face was already pink from exertion, and his whole form, from the hem of his cassock to his hat, was of a similar hue.

He continued on his theme. "My thought was that it could be of some benefit to my old friend Michelangelo…" He nodded toward the artist who had taken a seat across from him. "…to sit down at table with Maestro Bramante, face-to-face, rather than for both men to hear rumors about each other."

A serving boy poured goblets of wine for the guests. The Cardinal emptied his in two drafts and handed it back. "What do you think, Michelangelo?"

Michelangelo feigned indifference badly. "Well, if Bramante is coming, I'll be polite, but I don't know what can come of it." Clearly agitated, he drummed his fingers on his thigh for a moment, then seemed to think of something that needed doing. "Adriana, will you excuse me? If you don't mind, I'd like to use your garden table for a moment." He stood up with his saddlebag on his arm.

"Of course. I don't mind at all. Maria will show you the way."

Jacopo was suddenly in the doorway. "Signora, forgive me. It's getting dark. If all your guests have arrived, I'll have the boys move the torches to the courtyard."

Adriana addressed Giovanni de' Medici. "You are certain that Signor Bramante is coming, Eminence?"

The Cardinal shrugged slightly. "He said as much. He seemed quite pleased at the thought of attending. I can't imagine what has delayed him."

"Jacopo, send two of the boys along the road to the Via Tiburtina." Adriana turned back to her guests. "The turn onto the villa road is easy to overlook in the dark."

The Cardinal was reassuring. "I would not be alarmed just yet. Signor Bramante travels often and is a cautious man."

"Signora." Jacopo stood again in the doorway, holding a lantern. "Two more guests are arriving. Andrea is leading them along the road."

"*Two* guests?" Adriana excused herself and followed her servant to the portal of the house. She peered out toward the lane of cypress trees, trying to see the new arrivals. The trees and vegetation before her were greenish black against the cobalt sky. Stars were already visible. Cold colors everywhere underscored the breeze that rustled through the trees. But straight ahead of her on the road, a sphere of warm orange light drew nearer as the groom brought the unexpected guests ever closer.

In a few moments the riders passed through the garden gateway. The stablemen came out to them with lanterns and took the reins. Donato Bramante dismounted and pulled his long red cape around him. The second rider sat for a moment, face concealed under a rust-colored hood. The cape was thrown open on the left side, exposing one leg in tan leather hose and the skirt of a green wool doublet. A gloved hand drew back the hood, and Raphaela's ochre hair sprang out into the light of the flickering torches. The boy-woman of the Sistine Chapel was suddenly there.

"Maestro Bramante, Signorina, welcome to Villa Borgia," Adriana said graciously, wondering if the expression on her face betrayed how she felt. Then she realized she had no idea how she felt. A door to something dangerous that she had closed had just opened up again.

Donato Bramante bowed with great formality. "Apologies, Lady Borgia. My daughter's horse lamed right after departure, and we had to return for another. We are sorry for any inconvenience."

"It is no inconvenience at all." Adriana glanced back at the father. "My servants will carry your things upstairs."

"I travel very lightly myself, Lady Borgia, but my daughter carries a change of clothing."

"I brought a gown. Of course." Raphaela hooked her thumb in the belt of her hunter's green doublet, which in fact became her superbly.

Adriana clasped her hands together awkwardly. "Yes, of course. Well, now, since all are here, I will show you to your rooms." She went ahead of her guests and beckoned them to the stairway, which led to a row of bedchambers along the second-story galleries on two sides of the quadrangle. Each chamber was simply furnished with a large bed, a trestle table with a basin of water, and a supply of candles. "We are honored to offer you the first chamber, Eminence."

"Thank you," Giovanni de' Medici said. "I shall be most comfortable. I see it has a shrine carved in the Spanish style. Very fine."

"The second chamber is yours, Maestro Bramante, and the one beyond it is for the signorina. Please make yourselves at home and call upon my servants if you need anything."

As Adriana was leading Domenico to the north gallery, Michelangelo appeared. He slipped a roll of paper into his jerkin, the same place he had carried the delinquent message from Silvio. Adriana recalled that she had not yet read the entire letter and patted her pocket to assure herself she still had it. Well, it was scarcely of interest any longer. Whatever foolish plans she had had for Silvio Piccolomini, they were useless now.

"Your rooms are there. The first one is yours, Michelo, and the one beyond is for Domenico. You can see the garden from your window." She stepped back toward the stairs. "If you are content, I'll leave you to your preparations. Supper is in one hour."

Michelangelo glanced meaningfully toward the opposite gallery where Donato Bramante stood watching the preparations in the courtyard below. "This evening should be interesting."

Adriana looked in the same direction. "Yes, it might just."

❖

The inner courtyard was lit cheerfully by flickering torches on every pillar of the arcade. In the center a long table had been set up as in a refectory. Each place had its plate, goblet, and cloth, and a mysterious pointed instrument. The guests came down from their rooms and seated themselves along the cushioned benches. Michelangelo held up the tool that lay across his napkin and studied its bifurcation into sharp prongs. He gingerly touched its points and turned to Jacopo, who was setting down a pitcher of fruit wine.

"And this instrument of torture would be...?"

"A fork, Signore," Jacopo replied instructively. "To keep your hands off your supper and your supper off your hands." He bowed respectfully as he stepped away from the table.

"Clever device," he said, stabbing an olive and transporting it to his mouth. "Less risk of cutting your tongue off."

Cardinal de' Medici laid his down again. "I have heard of them. A charming fashion that will have its day and then disappear. I believe I trust my fingers better than this tiny harpoon."

All heads turned as Adriana stepped into the courtyard and came to the head of the table. Bramante stood up from his seat and Michelangelo, who had lifted his cup to his mouth, set it down again.

"Oh, Lady Adriana. You look magnificent," Domenico said.

She knew she did and it pleased her, after so long an isolation, to be gazed at again with admiration. It was in fact a dress that Cesare had bought for her in Spain, saying that the crimson velvet called attention to her "midnight" hair. Wide gold embroidery in a pattern of birds outlined the deep square décolleté, descending from both shoulders and stretching across the middle of her chest. Her breasts swelled behind it, covered slightly by gathered white silk. The crimson sleeves, tied at the shoulders, were deeply slashed and buttoned, revealing the silky white undergarment when she bent her arm. Her long hair was plaited with strands of pearls and turned in a large knot at her neck. For jewelry she wore only Michelangelo's marble medallion. He murmured as she sat down, "You are a vision, Adriana. I see now why Cesare Borgia was besotted with you."

Adriana nodded graciously and addressed the entire company. "Forgive me, friends. I've kept you waiting for your supper. Jacopo?" She signaled the housemaster, who threw open the kitchen door with a flourish. Four boys paraded in carrying trenchers on their shoulders. In brightly colored doublets and hose, they glided like peacocks past the tables with their culinary set pieces.

The first one staggered under a roasted boar, still tusked and lying in a bed of rosemary and mushrooms. The second carried three hares in a circle around their sauce, the third venison in wine, and the fourth several pheasants ornamented with their own tail feathers. Behind them, girls carried baskets of bread baked in the shape of animals.

Out of the corner of her eye Adriana observed Raphaela. The dark green dress was similar in color to the doublet she had arrived in, and it suited her amber hair as perfectly.

Raphaela seemed focused on the parade of food for a moment, and when her eyes met Adriana's, her expression remained unreadable. The guests ate, full of compliments, while she made the ritual hostess apologies. The woods, she lamented, had yielded little game that year.

The Cardinal finally paused between courses for a breath of air and turned to the Vatican architect. "Maestro Bramante. How goes it with the designs for St. Peter's Church?"

Donato Bramante laid down his supper knife. "Eminence is most kind to ask. The design I have presented to His Holiness is in the shape of the Greek cross and challenges the traditional basilica structure. However, the Holy Father desires to enclose an unprecedented volume of space, which presents a problem. The weight of the dome would be so great that the pillars needed to support it would scarcely leave room to walk between them."

Cardinal de' Medici glanced sideways toward Michelangelo, as if waiting for him to offer expert comment, but he remained silent.

The Cardinal continued. "But the ancient Romans built the Pantheon, didn't they? The principles for such a dome were known."

Bramante smiled wearily. "Known and then lost. I am trying to rediscover them by measuring the remains of imperial buildings."

Finally Michelangelo intruded. "If you will permit me, Signor Bramante. I share your interest in classical architecture. In an idle moment I made a tiny sketch—based on Euclid."

He drew from inside his jerkin a roll of parchment, no larger than his fist, and handed it to the architect. "If you find anything in it of use, please apply it at your discretion. If not, it's of no consequence." The last of his words were muffled as he drank from his wine goblet.

Bramante accepted the scroll with a slight frown. Inclining toward the right, where the torch was brighter, he unrolled the document, allowed his daughter to adjust his red cloak around his shoulders, and began to read.

The scroll held several diagrams, shaded in crosshatch and accompanied by measurements and calculations. Clearly they had been drawn especially for the occasion, and their presentation, in public and by a rival, bordered on the insulting. And yet, his intent expression showed that the diagrams did in fact reveal possibilities he hadn't considered.

"You may discard it if you wish. No harm will be done," Michelangelo added with a dismissive gesture. "It's merely speculation."

Relieved of having to comment, Bramante visibly relaxed, rolled the scroll up again, and tucked it into a pocket of his cloak. "Thank you, Signor Buonarroti. I'll give it my full attention later."

"I would be honored, Signor Bramante," Michelangelo said, avoiding Adriana's glance.

The Cardinal changed themes. "Signor Buonarroti, how goes the collaboration between painter and Pope?"

"Not as I'd like, Eminence. I'm sure it is a secret to no one that we have our differences. His Holiness has made many suggestions, but we have conflicting visions. He wanted apostles but I am pleading for Old Testament scenes."

The prelate leaned forward on both elbows. "Surely you are bound to obey the Holy Father's wishes."

"The Hebrews *are* his wishes, now." Michelangelo toyed with the fork, turning it between his thumb and fingertips, scrutinizing its carved handle. "A painter is not a carpenter, banging together a cabinet on order, Eminence. There are areas to which obedience does not apply."

"But there is such peace in obedience, Maestro Buonarroti," Domenico said innocently. "Differences in vision seem insignificant before the mystery of God. Don't you think?"

Michelangelo veered away from the disagreement. "If His Holiness paid his toiling servant, he would find me more obedient. But I have not been remunerated in months for the wages of my assistants, or even for my materials. These days I'm safe from robbers because I haven't got a penny."

Donato Bramante offered unexpected support. "I too am pressed for funds, yet the Holy Father always cites financial deficits of his own."

"The Holy See is aware of the problem," Giovanni de' Medici replied. "I have suggested to His Holiness that he expand the Church's income through utilizing the very commodity to which he has sole access. God's Grace."

"You refer to indulgences, Eminence?" Raphaela studied the grape she had just bitten into, as if the fruit were more important than her remark.

"Yes, of course, Signorina. That is exactly what I mean. The plenitude of grace granted by God through the throne of Peter."

Raphaela persisted, her head tilted back and her lips parted slightly, as they did when she asked difficult, challenging questions. "The forgiveness of God and the guarantee of heaven. These are normally granted for Christian sacrifice or suffering and for charitable acts—not as a source of revenue. Isn't that so, Eminence?" She pressed the other half of the grape in her mouth.

Donato Bramante cleared his throat.

Cardinal de' Medici was unfazed. "Yes, of course, Signora. As well as for any other act the Holy Father deems pleasing to God. Financial support for the good works of the Church is by its very nature pleasing to God." He discovered he had room for yet another portion of boar and filled his mouth, preventing a more detailed answer.

"But Eminence, doesn't God see into the hearts of men and know if an indulgence has been bought without contrition? Surely true remorse would have the same effect as the indulgence."

After a long moment of chewing, Cardinal de' Medici picked his teeth with the fork, apparently forcing patience on himself. Then he raised an authoritative hand, the one that displayed the Cardinal's ring, in front of Raphaela's face. Raphaela held her ground and did not cede him space, though the ecclesiastical finger was close enough to touch her nose.

"Signorina. Indulgences are not handed out in the marketplace. The Holy Church bestows them only upon confession and evidence of contrition. Though you may not understand them, these issues have been thought out for centuries by wise and divinely inspired men."

Raphaela inhaled and appeared about to reply, but Bramante cleared his throat again and she closed her lips. In the tense silence, Michelangelo raised his glass. "Well, then, I propose we celebrate something that's pleasing to both God and man, the divine voice of Signor Raggi. You'll sing for us this evening, won't you?"

Domenico brushed back a swath of dark hair and glanced around at the table. "If you wish."

"We very much wish," Bramante replied, with obvious relief.

Domenico stood up from the table, brushed invisible crumbs from his lap, and took a position between two columns of the loggia. The torches burning on both sides of him illuminated him with pleasing symmetry. His voice began as pure velvet, on a sustained note, then changed timbre, weaving a complex melody, each phrase a variation on the one before, all in the voice of a powerful contralto. Then, as from a fountain, the stream of sound rose and dropped and rose again, ever higher, into the soprano range, achieving sounds of such delicate sweetness it did not seem possible they came from the throat of a man.

Adriana studied his audience. The Cardinal had the look of a man being soothed, and Bramante also seemed to be transported.

Adriana allowed herself to glance over at his daughter and Raphaela stared back. The gray-green eyes took hold of her for a moment. She saw interest, disarming in its directness, as if Raphaela were awaiting something.

She shifted her gaze to Michelangelo, who never took his eyes from the singer. Only the slight motion of his beard revealed that he bit his lower lip. Domenico finished on a gradual decrescendo, the sound fading slowly, like gold stretched ever more thinly and finally disappearing. After a momentary pause he bowed, his dark brown hair falling loosely over his face.

"Bravo, bravo!" Giovanni de' Medici said warmly. "Come here and sit by me, young man. Tell me how they treat you in the Sistine Choir." He poured them both more wine.

With graceful steps, Domenico went to the Cardinal's side, brushing against Michelangelo as he passed.

❖

Bramante was the first to stand up from the table, pulling his red cloak around his shoulders. "Lady Borgia. Your banquet was sumptuous, and your villa is as gracious as its mistress. But I must to bed after so long a day."

"Of course, Signor Bramante. I'll escort you to your rooms." Taking a lantern, she led father and daughter along the southern loggia. The servants had already lit the candles and carried in basins of water for washing. Adriana bade him good rest.

Raphaela stood in the doorway of the adjoining room. "May I see you alone, Lady Borgia?" she asked quietly. "We haven't really spoken this evening."

Adriana detected the pleasant fragrance of crushed grapes. "You're right, of course. You arrived so late, and…" She trailed off nervously. "I must see to my other guests first, until they retire. But perhaps in the garden, later."

She gathered her crimson skirts and hurried down the stairs to the courtyard. Giovanni de' Medici had risen unsteadily from the table. Jacopo supported him on one side, Gianino on the other, and together they assisted the Cardinal up the stairs to his bedchamber.

Michelangelo and Domenico were shoulder to shoulder in quiet conversation.

"What are my Sistine genii conspiring in now?" she teased, sitting down with them. "A concert perhaps, for the unveiling of the chapel ceiling?"

Michelangelo brightened. "I hadn't thought of that, but it's a good idea. I'll speak to Paris de Grassis about it. It is something the Master of Ceremonies would have to arrange."

"Oh, I'd love to be part of the unveiling," Domenico said. "You must promise it."

Michelangelo stood up from the table. "I give you my word that you'll be there. But now I will say good night. Don't worry about me, Adriana. I'll see myself to my room." He bent and kissed her quickly on the cheek and turned away.

Domenico watched Michelangelo climb the stairs. "I suppose I should retire too," he said transparently.

Adriana considered reminding him of the punishment he had recently endured, but on a tender impulse, she caressed his cheek instead. Its smoothness brought a stirring recollection.

XXV

Adriana paced before the tree at the center of her private garden. Though it was nearly midnight, and she had drunk a great deal of wine, she couldn't sleep. She faced the old Roman fountain, watching the water trickle over the edge of the upper dish into the basin below. The cicadas chirped all around her, and a breeze rustled high in the trees of the nearby woods.

She heard nothing of it and listened only for footfall on the gravel of the garden path. When she heard it, her heart leapt. "Raphaela?" she whispered.

"I'm sorry to disappoint you," a man's voice said, and the wiry form of Michelangelo emerged from the darkness. He sat down on the bench beneath the tree and took her hand, drawing her down to him as he had done on her first day back in Rome. He was slightly drunk, she could tell, but then, so was she. She sat comfortably with him, as with an eccentric cousin, feeling the knots and calluses on his hand.

"What brings you to my garden in the middle of the night, Michelo? The privy is over there, you know, on the other side of the house."

He did not laugh, but instead took a deep breath. "Adriana, you've known me for years. Since you first arrived from Spain." He looked up to the stars, as if hoping for assistance. "You know I don't think about women. I'm at a loss with them. But I want to try to settle down. I have been thinking about this since you came back to Rome."

He was silent again for a moment, then took another tack. "Life can't be easy for you either. You're a widow."

"Twice widowed, in effect, if not in law." Her mouth formed an ironic smile, which in the darkness he would not see.

"Precisely. Aren't you tired of being alone?"

"Where is this going, Michelo?"

"There is something about you that has always attracted me, something forceful and audacious. And then tonight, you looked so lovely. If there could be any woman for me, it would be you."

"Are you proposing marriage, Michelangelo, or something less respectable?"

"Oh, no. My intentions are honorable. I only want respectability… for both of us. And though I have no money now, I will when the ceiling is done. And there will be other works, of course. I would offer you a man's protection." He began to ramble nervously. "A woman needs protection. We can help each other that way. Domenico is right, you know, there is peace in obedience."

He stood up in front of her and held her by the shoulders. It was an awkward position. Perhaps he expected her to stand up so he could kiss her, but she did not want to kiss him. She turned slightly so that she could lay one of her hands on his, and the heavy paper of Silvio's letter crinkled in her pocket. Silvio's letter, mocking her.

She sighed. "An honorable proposal, old friend. Yes, it would quiet both our lives and keep us from sin, wouldn't it?" She paused, choosing her words. "I care for you as much as I care for any man. But all things have their season. What is alive one moment is dust the next."

"Now it's you who are being mysterious. I don't understand what you're saying."

It annoyed her that she had to explain to him what she could scarcely explain to herself. She was full of uncertainty, and she had not even finished reading Silvio's letter yet. It annoyed her even more that Michelangelo would not sit down again, for while he stood so close before her, she spoke to his groin rather than to his face.

"You see, something has happened. A hope that was already frail has died in me. I'm no longer fit for domesticity. We can't help each other that way."

He still did not move.

"But…there's another one who needs your protection more than I do, and who waits for you now." She dropped her voice until it was barely audible. "I think you should go to him."

He stood motionless, his silence revealing his confusion.

A voice whispered from behind her. "Lady Borgia?" Adriana turned toward the sound.

The figure stepped from the darkness into the moonlight. Raphaela.

Michelangelo abruptly grasped a limb of the tree over her head, the suddenness of the gesture startling her. Exasperation, she assumed, at being interrupted in so sensitive a conversation.

Raphaela stopped. "Oh, I'm sorry." Adriana rose to her feet, acknowledging her. Michelangelo glanced back and forth at the two women, and the moment was unbearable. Finally, he bowed and marched with heavy footfall back toward the house.

"Forgive me. I've disturbed your conversation, haven't I?" Raphaela looked toward the departing man.

"It's good that you did. It was becoming very awkward." Adriana emerged from under the bough of the tree and motioned toward the wide stone rim of the fountain. They sat down, keeping a measured distance between them. Yet the long folds of their two skirts, the scarlet and the green, overlapped slightly on the mossy stone.

Raphaela trailed her fingers in the fountain pool, breaking up patterns in the shimmering silver water. The moon lit one side of her face in blues and whites and cast her gown in pale gray. They sat for a long moment, the gurgling of the fountain and the persistent chirping of the cicadas filling the night air.

Raphaela inhaled deeply and Adriana heard the soft sound of her long exhalation—an intimate sound, as if she shared her breathing. She toyed with a pebble on the fountain rim between them. "Your friend Domenico is amazing, isn't he? So beautiful in face and voice. And so pious."

"Pious? Yes. His devotion is absolutely genuine. He thinks of God as an actual Father who looks after him, weighing everything he does. He makes gifts to Him on his altar."

"Is that so?" Raphaela tilted her head slightly. Adriana could not be sure she was really interested or merely polite.

"Yes. On our first afternoon together after I came back from Spain, he was so happy that he sacrificed a ring on the high altar of St. Peter's. It was a tiny silver thing I'd given him when he was a child. For all I know, it's still there."

Adriana fell silent, uncertain of what to add. A minute passed, and the cicadas chirped again. She looked over at the confident hands of the young artist, then at her own, pale helpless creatures folded on her velvet lap.

"What is it that you want, Raphaela?"

"That is the first time I've heard you speak my name."

"No, I spoke it at Michelangelo's house. While you changed from boy to woman."

"Ah, yes, I had forgotten. You helped me dress." The pebble dropped into the fountain with a faint plop.

"That evening, you never answered my question about the painting. And you haven't answered what I just asked either."

"Of what I want?" Raphaela tilted her head back. Her lips fell open slightly. She brushed grit from the fountain wall between them. "Do you remember Pope Alexander's requiem mass, that afternoon, in the chapel?"

"Yes, of course I do."

"Then you will remember the air, the smell of corruption. It seemed the perfect symbol for Alexander's court. But the Vatican gave my father work, wonderful projects, so we stayed. Father could shut his eyes to the excesses, but I couldn't.

"You see, my father wanted me to go back to Padua. There was a young man there he hoped to marry me to. I was wavering, on the brink of agreeing to leave Rome. And then I heard you say my name."

"Yes, you looked at me for a long time." Adriana warmed, recalling the moment. "Did you know who I was?" She brushed at the space on the fountain rim between them, repeating the other woman's gesture.

"Yes, certainly. With Alexander dead, I wondered what you would do. And then, of course, you fled."

"Yes, the chapel and Rome as well, that same day. And for five more years I stayed with him."

"I knew you were with him, but it seemed you had called me for a reason, so I stayed in Rome and painted. Portraits mostly, but I also painted you. As I remembered you and as I wanted you to be. When I saw you again at St. Peter's it was a shock because, in a way, I had already recreated you."

"I know. As Europa, with Cesare as a bull. Very clever, using the Borgia symbol. But what you painted was your fantasy. It wasn't me."

"It was a part of you." Raphaela rubbed her fingers on the stone, as if polishing it. "There is a kind of truth to art that transcends our lives. Well, outlasts them at least."

"Why do you need me, then? Why do you...pursue me?" Her voice remained neutral, betraying no emotion but caution.

Raphaela considered for a moment. "Because I'm flesh and blood and feel desire. Because you do as well."

"Do not speak of my desires. It is presumptuous. You don't know me." Adriana drew her fingers through the pool of water, cooling them.

Raphael's reply was like a touch. "I knew you once, for a moment."

Adriana glanced up, perplexed, but the harsh chiaroscuro obscured the expression on the other woman's face. "I don't know what you mean."

"I think you do. At Carnevale."

Adriana felt a pounding in her chest. "Carnevale? I don't remember Carnevale. I drank too much. A boy accosted me. That was all. A masked...boy." She pulled her skirts closer to her.

"You knew it was a woman. You pressed against me."

"No. I had no idea. It was a night of excess. Of violence and lust. The kind you want to forget about the next day."

"It was a night when people revealed themselves. And what moved me that night was not lust, but devotion, the same devotion that guides me when I paint."

"You have portrayed too many pagans, Raphaela. I speak of excess and evil, and you reply with painting. You're twisting things."

"Don't disparage pagans. They knew something that we've forgotten, that desire is not evil."

"It *can* be. You yourself saw the debauchery of Alexander's court, where lust could end in death. There are lines, I think, too dangerous to cross."

Raphaela shook her head. "I crossed them long ago. And something wonderful happened. A candle seemed to light inside me." She touched the marble medallion over Adriana's heart, holding it for a moment on the tips of her fingers. "And I saw you, Adriana. In the midst of a vile funeral for a corrupt man, I saw you and wanted to tell you." She let go of the medallion and pressed her fingertips on the crimson dress beneath it.

"Tell me what?"

"That what we are taught, of good and evil, is false, that the God they threaten us with is cruel. And that the forbidden thing is the most precious thing of all, knowledge."

Adriana touched the encroaching hand, though whether to hold it back or caress it she was not sure, and so she held it lightly.

Raphaela's fingers crept on, over the white silk to the naked skin above. "What we were that night was neither good nor evil. For just a few heartbeats we didn't need God. We were like gods ourselves."

Adriana shook her head weakly but did not move away.

"You do remember, don't you," Raphaela murmured. "You let me do it. You knew, and you kissed me back." The insistent hand slid up to Adriana's throat, curled gently around it, palm resting softly against the pulse. Raphaela leaned close; her lips brushed the warm cheek.

Like gods, knowing good and evil. The biblical temptation flashed through Adriana's mind as Raphaela's mouth covered her own. Then she surrendered to the embrace. Nothing else mattered any longer. Nothing existed but Raphaela's mouth and the delicate light entry of the stranger into herself. She tasted wine again, as in the confessional, but now it was sweetened by fresh grapes.

A window shutter suddenly slammed and they broke apart. Overhead the window to Michelangelo's room had shut, as if in revulsion. Adriana sprang up. "You must go. Please."

"As you wish." The young woman stood up reluctantly, reaching out to touch the crimson velvet one last time. "But I'll wait. I swear to you. I will wait."

Adriana watched Raphaela Bramante walk back along the dark path to the house, her pale hair seeming to give off a light of its own, and she whispered after her.

"Do not."

❖

Domenico stood before the small shrine in his room and lit a second candle. He was used to praying to the Madonna when he longed for something but now, of course, it was out of the question. He couldn't pray for a sin, and the long silence since dinner made it clear that there would be no temptation.

He slid off the calfskin boots that came above his knees and set them aside. Brooding, he undid the ties that held his soft leather leggings to his doublet and drew them off, draping them over a chair. It was just as well. He would surely have had to pay for such an infidelity. He would inevitably have been found out, and every such transgression was more severely punished. It had already cost one poor man his life. The urge for love was sometimes ferocious, but in seeking it, he walked a knife's edge that jeopardized his life and soul. Perhaps this night, he would simply pray.

Lethargically, he unbuttoned the long row of tiny gold buttons that ran down the center of his doublet and shrugged it off. It was pleasantly cool to stand bare-legged and in the wide linen shirt that was his undergarment.

Then the knock came. He caught his breath. "Come in."

Michelangelo stood in the doorway, backlit by the upstairs torch. "Do I disturb you?" he asked, and then came in, closing the door behind him.

"No, of course not." Domenico's voice was almost a whisper.

Michelangelo carefully latched the door and leaned against it, stroking his beard.

"I am puzzled."

"Puzzled, Signore?"

Michelangelo closed the distance between them cautiously. "Seeing you from afar, in the chapel service, makes me feel the presence of God. But closeness to you does just the opposite. It pushes God away and tempts to impure thoughts."

"I cannot help other men's thoughts, Signore. I struggle enough with my own."

"Struggle. Yes, that's the right word. And when the temptation is so beautiful, one is bound to fall." Michelangelo touched the front of Domenico's shirt. "Are you as attractive in form as you are in face?" His hands trembling, he undid the ties that held the shirt closed.

"Some men see me that way, but others find me strange." Domenico took Michelangelo's hand and slid it inside the shirt. "How do you find me?"

His chest was wider than that of a normal man, the musculature undefined, yet Michelangelo seemed to like the adolescent smoothness. His coarse hand moved all over the soft skin under the cloth, claiming him, pinching his nipples, hurting him just a little, just enough to arouse him. Then it withdrew.

"I can't say, until I see you."

Wordlessly, Domenico pulled the long shirt over his head and stood, almost defiantly, naked but for a hand's width of white linen tied with a cord just below his navel. Michelangelo's eyes went immediately to the bulge beneath and his eyes half closed.

Domenico liked being looked at that way. "You're curious, aren't you? To find out what's still there. I can tell you, there's everything necessary to please you."

"You already please me." Michelangelo kissed one of the dark nipples. His lips were kinder than his fingers were, but the flick of his tongue caused Domenico to shudder.

"I want to know what gives *you* pleasure," he breathed, sliding his hand down to gently squeeze the warm flesh that swelled under the linen.

"*That* gives me pleasure," Domenico murmured, opening to Michelangelo's long, invasive kiss. Their tongues curled around each other, Michelangelo's mouth just on the edge of rough, until Domenico broke away and sat down on the bed. "The door. No one must see."

"It's locked. But wait." Michelangelo went around the foot of the bed to the window. Without looking out, he seized the brass handle and yanked the shutter closed. "No one must hear, either." He came around to stand before Domenico's knees, rocking slightly. Then he pulled off his own shirt and trousers, undid his linen breeches, and let them fall. His excitement was obvious.

Domenico leaned back, supporting himself on his elbows, and stared at the flesh about to invade him. He shivered with anticipation. "You are the kind of man I want to belong to."

Michelangelo clambered onto the bed to kneel astride Domenico's knees. "Let me see the kind of man you are," he said, untying and then pulling away the remaining piece of linen.

Over shrunken testicles Domenico's dark phallus swelled to its full length. "Ah," Michelangelo whispered. "As much a man as I am."

Domenico pulled Michelangelo's face to his own so that they curved toward each other, one over and one under. "Tell me what you like," he whispered. "I am accustomed to obeying."

XXVI
JUNE 1510—UPON THIS ROCK

"That swine! A plague on him and his Borgia slut of a wife! I knew Alfonso would defy me, but not this far!" Pope Julius crumpled the parchment and slammed it onto his table. "To go over to the French completely, this is too much."

"Calm yourself, Holiness." Paris de Grassis set his daybook aside and poured the Pontiff a cup of wine. "What's done can be undone. Alliances are fragile things. I should think a suggestion of excommunication would sway the Duke."

"Excommunication is the least of it. This requires a hammer blow, and he will learn that I can deliver one. He thinks I need him, but he's mistaken. His cannon made a good show shooting across a river at floating Venetian galleys, but they will not stand up so well to six thousand Swiss professional soldiers streaming down a hillside."

"You are prepared to declare war, Holiness?"

"I am, Master de Grassis. On Ferrara *and* the French." He snapped his fingers. "Take notes."

The Master of Ceremonies uncorked his ink bottle and opened his daybook. Julius tapped on the still-blank page. "First, we will conscript the Cardinals. It will do them some good to exchange their white mules for war horses and to defend the Church with force instead of prayer."

De Grassis wrote as dictated. "Prayer, of course too, Holiness. We must call a special mass."

"Yes, yes. A mass. Of course. See to it. All in God's name. We will also carry the blessed host before us into battle. Always inspires the troops."

De Grassis scribbled again. "What about the French Cardinals? I rather think they are not reliable in this case."

"Arrest them if they refuse." He stared into empty air, calculating. "The best strategy would be to rally in Viterbo. I'll address the armies and then go on to Ostia, to sail north while the troops march overland. Bologna will fall like a rotten fig, as it did before, and then it's only a short march to Ferrara and Alfonso."

"You will lead them, Holiness? De Grassis stopped writing. "Wouldn't it be better left to a younger man? Your nephew, the Duke of Urbino, for example?"

"Absolutely not. I am not one of your limp prelates who twirls his rosary while his troops are in the field. What is a Pope if not a general of God's Christian soldiers?"

De Grassis resumed writing. "Yes, Holiness, although I believe the image is usually 'shepherd' rather than general. But be that as it may, there is the issue of finance. After the basilica and Belvedere projects, and the clearing of the Via Papalis, not to mention the outfitting of the Swiss troops, the treasury is in a lamentable state. I believe a large payment is also due to Signor Buonarroti."

Julius scowled. He hated it when the subject turned to money; the news was always bad. "We will have to issue another Bull of Indulgences. Surely we have Dominicans who can carry letters to the northern cities."

"Alas, Holiness. Letters of Indulgence are already circulating in Germany and as far south as Milan. Questares are collecting closer to Rome as well, but I am not sure who they are. In any case, we must be careful not to oversell indulgences, lest they be cheapened by familiarity."

Julius pressed a knuckle to his lower lip. "Infuriating, to have a war and no funds for it. We can at least postpone payment to Michelangelo. I will explain the reason to him. Would you see to it that he is summoned to me this afternoon?"

"Unfortunately, he has gone to Tivoli, Holiness. Along with Cardinal de' Medici, as guests of Lady Borgia, I believe. I will leave word for him to attend you upon his return."

"Thwarted everywhere," Julius muttered. He took a long drink of the wine that de Grassis had poured, then spoke with forced calm. "The war *will* go forward. We cannot allow Ferrara to ally with the French. You have your instructions, Master de Grassis."

"Yes, Holiness." The Master of Ceremonies made the obeisance, but while he stood in the open doorway, Julius had an afterthought.

"All events seem to conspire against me, Master de Grassis, and my head is about to explode. Please have my chapel singer sent to me. That will calm me."

De Grassis glanced away. "I'm afraid I cannot, Holiness. Domenico Raggi has requested leave to join Michelangelo and Cardinal de' Medici. Given the presence of the Cardinal, we granted, it of course," he said, as he backed out.

With sudden fury, Julius threw his goblet against the closed door. It landed with a crash, and wine dribbled in streaks down the polished wood onto the marble floor.

❖

At the foot of the path the new colonnade marked the border of the estate. Its eight fluted Corinthian columns were joined at the top by a simple curved architrave. Before them, a rectangular pool lay perpendicular to the garden path. At each corner of the pool, nymphs crouched in chitons tipping their urns, and at the center of the pool the new statue stood still concealed by a loose cloth.

Adriana walked ahead of the others and gave the signal to the gardener to draw off the cloth and open the tap. Invisible pipes rasped hollowly for a moment from several locations, as if clearing their throats. Slowly water began to trickle and then pour forth from all the stone openings and spouts.

Adriana looked back at Michelangelo, who meandered distractedly toward the fountain, and she watched with amusement as he suddenly halted. The scowl that he had held throughout breakfast opened to a grin.

"I knew you'd like it," Adriana said, walking back to him and linking her arm in his. "It's my gift to you. I hope I've got all the details right."

The five of them stood in a line before the pool. The morning light reflected off the surface of the water and shone up into their faces, dazzling them. In the center of the radiance the young Bacchus stood. The god looked over their heads toward the house, and water fell gurgling from his goblet in a twisting column into the pool. At the four corners, water also poured gently from nymph-held urns.

"I guess you have!" He patted her hand. "What a coup. You've taken a rather silly statue of mine and put him to work."

"Yes, in fact, he nourishes my entire garden. The water falls from his goblet into the pond, then passes through pipes and rivulets all the way to the house."

Kneeling, she closed her eyes against the glistening surface of the pool and let the water from the nymph's urn trickle over her fingers.

"Well done, Signora Borgia," Donato Bramante said after a moment. "A pity my daughter is not here to appreciate your stroke of genius."

"Yes, a pity." Adriana was surprised at the force of her disappointment over so small an offense. She wondered if it was a sort of revenge for the night before.

"Lady Adriana!" A young woman's voice called out, and heads turned toward the orchard. There at the center, where she had apparently watched the unveiling, Raphaela stood waving.

The company wandered toward the tree where she stood, holding a roll of sketching paper in her hand. The tree was forked and bare and with foliage only at the top. When the group arrived, she reached through the fork of the tree and handed Adriana the rolled drawing.

"Your garden has been an inspiration. I took the liberty of strolling all around it this morning. It gave me a sort of vision and, well, I drew it for you."

It was a scene sketched in charcoal. Every tree and hedge of the garden was there, and around each one wood sprites, satyrs, and pagan gods frolicked. In the foreground, Pan piped music, while in the distance, one could make out the new statue and its pool, sketched apparently in the few minutes since the unveiling. And yet it seemed the source of all the rest, as if the arrival of the "Bacchus" had caused a small pagan invasion.

Michelangelo peered over their shoulders at the drawing. "The signorina is right, Adriana. Your garden cries out for more statuary. In fact, I know an artist who could assist you. Giuliano Sangallo, a

Florentine architect who has an excellent sense of how to mix art and landscape."

Adriana stared at the drawing, speechless.

"It should be a wild place," Raphaela said. "Teeming with gods that are neither good nor evil."

❖

Donato Bramante mounted his horse with the help of a servant. "I thank you, Lady Borgia, for your hospitality, and compliment you on your new fountain." Next to him and once again in doublet and tights, Raphaela mounted and straddled her horse like a man. Like Carlo, under the chapel vault. Without further comment, father and daughter turned away and rode at a leisurely trot along the alley of cypress trees. Halfway to the juncture with the Via Tiburtina, the young woman turned in the saddle and waved.

The Cardinal's coach was brought up before the house "A final word, Signor Buonarroti," the prelate said in passing. "I foresee a time when you will assist in the work on the basilica. But not now. You must be content with that."

"I am content, Eminence."

Michelangelo made the cursory obeisance. Next to him, Domenico knelt down fully on both knees before the holy ring. The corpulent churchman made the sign of the cross over both men and swept into his coach.

As the Cardinal departed along the avenue of cypress, the grooms brought out the horses of the last two guests. Michelangelo stood for moment by his horse.

"Why don't you come back with us to Rome, Adriana? Domenico has got to report back to the choir, but I'd like to show you what we've done so far on the chapel ceiling. You can stay overnight at the Albergo dell' Orso as you used to do."

She hesitated, looking back at the house that was now quiet. The reflecting pool and statue were finished, it was too soon to plan the grape harvest, and there were only so many hours she could sit alone in her garden. There was, in fact, a sort of vacuum she did not want to face.

"I sent my housemaster early this morning to the Roman market to provision the household again. I suppose I could find him in the Piazza Navona and return with him tomorrow."

"Ah, very good." Michelangelo glanced up at the sky. "But if you're coming, you'd better hurry. The morning is far along."

Adriana turned to the groom standing by.

"Saddle the mare for me, please, with the light saddle." To Michelangelo, "Just let me change into a riding dress and inform my housekeeper."

Curiously elated, she hurried back into the house, thinking suddenly of Lucrezia. A worldliness in the air, Lucrezia had said. That glorifies nature and paganism. Something that had to do with unmarried women and disobedience.

❖

They rode without comment on the night before. Adriana knew that something had happened, but what was not named was not quite real and could be forgotten. To name the thing was to bring it to life and to stake it like a lamb before wolves.

"I have considered planting roses in the garden," she announced abruptly. "What do you think?"

"Plant white roses," Domenico responded immediately. "I remember white roses from my mother's garden. They grew up the side of the house and in summer covered it like a shawl."

"You remember flowers from your childhood?" Michelangelo sounded amazed. "I remember only fighting." He rubbed the side of his broken nose.

"The garden stays in my mind because that's where I took care of my half brothers and sisters. At least until I was sent away."

"You, caring for children? I would never have imagined it." Adriana studied him. "Forgive me. We took you from your school when you were so young. I never thought much about the family you had before that."

"Caring for those children is my best memory. I was still a child myself, but they called me 'Papito.' What a joke, huh?"

No one laughed.

They rounded a curve where the road descended sharply to the old Roman town of Tivoli. Built along the side of a hill, its streets dropped precipitously, and where the slope was steepest they became wide steps. Its alleys turned and curved back on themselves with no plan or order. A stranger would have lost his way, but during her isolation, Adriana had come to know the old town well.

"Listen. The church bells are ringing, and it's not a feast day. Something's going on. Shall we have a look?"

They entered the town, making their way in single file past a bakery and a fletchery, the clopping of the horses' hooves loud on the cobblestones. A crowd streamed alongside them on foot. Finally, at the St. Silvestro Chapel, with its crumbling Roman fountain, they came to an enormous wooden cross draped with the papal banner.

They drew up before the moss-covered basin of the Roman wall and let their horses drink. Michelangelo called to a passerby, "What celebration is this?"

The man looked up at them and snatched off his hat. "No celebration, Signore. It is the questares, with the Pope's letter. If you have sins on your head, sir."

Michelangelo glanced back at Adriana. "Indulgences. I'd like to see this."

The church was full and the smell of the tightly packed crowd was disagreeable. Adriana soon lost sight of Michelangelo, and Domenico, though tall, had moved toward the other side of the church and was also no longer visible. Left with her own curiosity, she edged forward until she had a view of the altar on one side of her and the aisle on the other.

A murmur spread like a wave through the mass as a procession came through the main entrance into the nave. At its front, altar boys carried candles and a flag with the insignia of the Church. Two Dominicans followed bearing a monstrance and a wooden chest fitted with brass. A third carried a red-velvet cushion bearing a scroll, sealed and beribboned in purple. The assembly murmured more loudly as it passed.

The monks proceeded to the narrow painted apse of the church and stood in a semicircle under the image of the Christ and two disciples. Two of the monks laid the sacred objects on the high altar, and the leader of the group, a Dominican with a ring of reddish hair around his tonsure, stepped to the center.

"Christians!" he called in a high sharp voice, and silence fell over the church. The murmuring of those outside in the square emphasized the quiet within. The Dominican raised his right hand, which held several rolls of paper. The sleeve of his robe fell back revealing a pelt of red hair on his forearm.

"Christians!" he repeated, "I have passports to lead the human soul to the joys of paradise." He pointed with his free hand toward the altar where the Papal Bull was propped up on a cushion. "This is your salvation, the remission of all your sins. This is His Holiness's tap, drawing on the vast spring of mercy granted by God to the Church of Peter. Through this spring any sin can be washed away. Anything! Sins you have committed and sins you will commit. Even sins of your departed loved ones. Some of them are writhing in purgatory right now."

He seemed to savor the word "writhing." He took a breath.

"But you can shorten their suffering, or end it, today! As soon as the coin rings in the chest, the soul for whom it is paid will fly out of purgatory and straight to heaven." He raised his hands dramatically to indicate the direction of heaven. "Have you lain with your neighbor's wife? Are you stained with adultery? Wash it away! Have you lied or violated the Sabbath or stolen? Wash it away! Even if you have stolen from a church, you can be forgiven. Even for murder. And even for buggery."

At the word "buggery," someone giggled.

"Schändung. Gotteslästerung," a man next to Adriana muttered. She glanced sideways to see a monk in the black woolen habit of an Augustinian. Though he was young, he seemed haggard, his habit soiled and torn. Most likely a pilgrim, she thought. She had seen thousands of his sort in Rome.

"Christians!" the Dominican called out again, drawing her attention back to the altar. In ringing tones he continued his enumeration of every sin Adriana could imagine and several she had not considered. When the monk finished his appeal, he called upon the faithful to sing a hymn of praise while deacons set up a table next to the altar. The wooden chest full of letters was set on it and next to it the brass-bound chest for coins.

Like thread spinning out from a ball of wool, a line formed out of the mass of worshippers and moved toward the table where the monk sat with his pile of letters. One by one the penitents crept with a lit candle up to the altar and confessed while the crowd listened in prurient fascination.

Each sin had a price: adultery and fornication cost four ducats, perjury or robbing a church nine ducats. An accountant sat at table, keeping a tally of the letters sold and at which amount. The brass-bound casket was opened, and as the letters were sold, Adriana could hear the clink of coins ringing in the chest.

"Geldwechsler im Tempel!" The monk next to her muttered again, and though she could not understand German, she shared his apparent disgust.

He glanced at her and shook his head sorrowfully, as if grasping that she sympathized, then made an about-face and elbowed his way back through the crowd. Bored with peasant confessions, Adriana followed him.

Outside the church there was still no sign of Michelangelo or Domenico, but the Augustinian stood at the fountain splashing water onto his face. "Do you speak Italian?" she asked him.

He looked up, surprised, then seemed to recognize her from the crowd. "Half Latin, half Italian, if you don't mind."

"You don't approve of that, do you?" She indicated the church with her head.

"Of granting indulgences for coin? Nowhere does Scripture tell of God's mercy being available for purchase. Buying an indulgence instead of repenting inwardly imperils the sinner's soul." He rubbed his back and pointed toward the stone steps below the fountain. "Please, let's sit down. I climbed the steps of the Lateran Church yesterday on my hands and knees, praying a *Pater noster* at each one. I'm weary from it."

She gathered her skirts and sat next to him. "It's a way for them to raise money, of course. His Holiness wants to finance a new basilica to house the saints' bones."

The monk rubbed his knees again, and she could see now that the front of his habit was worn through and spotted with blood and dirt. He winced. "I care not how he glorifies the edifice that houses the saints' relics. If holiness adheres to them, as it must, they could be revealed in a barn and still be holy. A contrite man should be able to come to them with a full heart and beg God's mercy for his guilt."

"You came to Rome looking to be free of guilt?" She added softly, "I suppose I did too, a long while ago. But I found out I wasn't guilty after all."

"We are none of us free of guilt. All of us lead lives full of sin. We are vermin-ridden with it, so many sins we don't even notice or remember them. But if we don't remember them, we can't ask forgiveness for them and they can send us to hell." There was desperation in his slightly bulging eyes.

Adriana shifted uncomfortably. "I don't know if it's that—"

"Let me tell you a story," he interrupted. "In my youth, I was caught once in a terrible storm, and I know now it was the Hand of God, testing me."

"A storm? Yes, storms can change people's lives," she ventured, but he continued without listening.

"Lightning hit a tree right in front of me and then leapt to me, knocking me unconscious. When I awoke, I felt death in the air and I called out 'Saint Anne, help me! I will become a monk!'"

"Why Saint Anne?"

"She is the mother of Mary, pure, and the kindest of women to those who are fallen and desperate. But you interrupt me, Lady. I wanted to say that God led me to the cowl, but not to tranquility. No, not at all. The contemplative life only revealed the mortal danger I was in. I fasted and kept vigils, sometimes for days on end, but it was never enough. The devil still came to me daily, nightly, in the smallest of things. Evil thoughts about the brothers, clumsy handling of the Host at mass, misspoken words in the prayers." He stopped, strain showing on his face.

"Forgive me, but I am not certain if I understand your point."

"My point is that salvation is not easily won, and certainly not bought with coin. The threat of purgatory and God's wrath hangs over us, and His devil is ever with us. Indulgences are pernicious because they cause men to avoid true contrition, true destruction of our will before His will. In short, these are empty promises and it is not God's vicar, but His devil, who tempts men with them."

"God's devil? Do you mean—"

"Ah, there you are, Adriana." Michelangelo squinted at the sky. "We probably should be going. The day is well along." Domenico was just coming behind him with their horses in hand.

Adriana stood up. "You're right, of course. I was just talking to…" She turned back to the monk. "You never said your name"

The monk stood up beside her and nodded respectfully to the two men. "Brother Martin, from Wittenberg. My family name is Luther."

❖

"It seems absurd," Adriana said, once the town was behind them. "The indulgence peddlers come from one direction, Carafa's guardians from another, and in a third place men like Brother Martin live in private terror of God. I don't know what to think."

Domenico shook his head. "God will not let us be confounded. Not on a day like today." He swept his hand in a wide arc over his head. "Look at what He gives us."

Adriana had to agree. The day was full of life. Jackdaws and thrushes swooped by overhead in pairs. In a copse of trees, a doe and her fawn browsed and leapt away lightly as they neared. Ahead of them a kestrel plummeted like a gray bolt and snatched something small from the ground. The predator rose again on powerful wings, its prey twitching helplessly in the last moments of life. All of nature seemed to play itself out before them in microcosm. But she could find no place in the stark dramas of the land for guilt and redemption.

"It's gotten hot," she said suddenly.

"My flask is empty too, but you see? God is looking after his children." Domenico pointed toward a stream that ran alongside the road. In places where the brush was sparse, sunlight caused it to sparkle. He halted and dismounted. An anomaly of black amidst the color he clambered down the bank, sending up a swarm of butterflies and insects. He knelt by the stream where it flowed over some rocks and filled his flask. Then, in returning, he snatched out flowers from the roadside, leaving their long stems.

"Our own Saint Francis of Assisi," Adriana remarked gently.

Domenico reached up his flask to Adriana and remounted his horse, one hand full of flowers. While Adriana slowly sipped the cool water, he wove a garland. When it was done, he rode alongside her and placed it on her head. "Isn't she lovely, Michelangelo? You should paint her as a saint or sibyl. Yes, that's it! The Borgia sibyl!"

Adriana laughed. "And I think you should paint Domenico as a saint."

Michelangelo looked back over his shoulder. "I had not planned on saints."

"Oh, I'd really like to be a saint, Michelo," Domenico persisted playfully. "Can't you put in just one little one?"

Michelangelo shook his head. "A saint must create a miracle. Do you think you can come up with one?"

"Why not? Adriana said. "Healing the sick with song? That would suit you."

"Well, let's see." Domenico stroked his beardless chin, miming deep thought. "If I could really choose, if an angel asked me what miraculous thing I would want to do on earth, I would say, 'Let me be a father.' That's how I'd like to please God, by founding a great lineage of people to glorify him."

"Fatherhood?" Adriana repeated, astonished. She had never discussed his castration and did not want to now, preferring to let the subject pass. "Well, if there have been miracles before on earth, there can be this one too. We'll leave it at that."

Michelangelo seemed to have no patience for their banter. "Please inform me when God has made you a father and I'll make you a saint."

XXVII

Paris de Grassis sat on his horse at the foot of the Ponte Sant' Angelo, furious that he had to wait like a knave for his chorister. He searched for a bird with which to compare the castrato and could find none. "Peacock" implied he was vain, which he was not, no more than any other young bravo. And "capon" described his condition, but said nothing of his beauty. De Grassis sighed.

Yes, he was well and truly beautiful. Everyone found him so, even those who bitterly envied him his voice. And here he was again defying the rules of the Sistine Choir. He had been granted leave to miss a day in the chapel on the understanding that he was in pious company and would return at night. He did not return, and de Grassis had the very unpleasant sense of being tricked.

He longed for the time when the only sopranos in the choir were boys, youngsters who could be controlled, even thrashed if it was necessary, though it rarely was. But this Spanish castrato was a puzzle. He seemed genuinely submissive to papal authority, but he kept stepping over the line, slipping away for… Well, it did not bear thinking for what. De Grassis's forbearance was wearing thin.

Ah, finally. There he was, approaching the bridge over the Tiber with two other people, Michelangelo and…? De Grassis felt his face warm with disgust when he recognized that the other one was Adriana Borgia.

He signaled the guard waiting with him and spurred his horse to meet the three of them at the center of the bridge. "Domenico Raggi, you have ignored the restrictions placed on you by the Curia. I am to escort you to your proper quarters to answer for it."

Adriana urged her horse forward. "Maestro de Grassis, Signor Raggi was my guest at a supper party and he performed as a musician. He has done nothing wrong."

"That will be for me to judge, Signora Borgia," he said coolly. As for you, Signor Buonarroti, His Holiness has instructed me to advise you to attend him. I suggest you take that request as urgent."

"Thank you, Maestro de Grassis," Michelangelo replied, unmoved.

Domenico looked toward his companions. "I'm sorry, Adriana, Michelo. I'll send word later." He nodded toward the Master of Ceremonies and turned his horse away from the group toward the Sistine Chapel basement.

❖

Minutes later, Michelangelo confronted the guard who barred his way to the Sistine Chapel. "What's going on here?"

The halberdier was tall, as were all the men in the new Swiss Guard, and rendered the more imposing by his Spanish helmet, topped with a high curved blade and a cockscomb of red feathers. He stood with his feet apart in a stance between attention and ease, an elaborate halberd held diagonally across his chest, the haft resting on the protruding vertical crease of his cuirass. His pose was formal and his uniform gaudy, with broad ribbons of orange and red hanging from his waist to his knee. He stared past them into the distance.

"Why is the chapel blocked?" Adriana asked.

Michelangelo poked the soldier's shiny cuirass with two fingers. "You know who I am. Get out of my way."

The guard replied emotionlessly, his Swiss accent hardening the Italian consonants. "I am sorry, Signore. The Holy Father has ordered the chapel closed to all but himself."

"His Papal Majesty seems to be put out about something," Michelangelo said to Adriana. "This is exactly the sort of crap I've been subject to for half a year. It's maddening." He rubbed the space between his eyebrows. "I'm sorry, Adriana. You've come all this way for nothing."

"Don't worry, Michelo. I have to look after my housemaster's marketing in any case. We can do this another time."

"All right. The least I can do then is accompany you to the Navona market. It's not a place for you to go wandering around alone."

"Shouldn't you obey His Holiness first?"

He took her by the arm and urged her toward the staircase again. "It can wait. I've had enough of obedience lately."

❖

Adriana had not been to the market at the Piazza Navona in years. But the confusion of sounds, of goats bleating, hawkers crying their wares, farmers loading and unloading wagons, was exactly as she remembered it. They tied their horses up at the periphery and wandered along the narrow pathways between the stalls.

There was no sign of Jacopo near the grain merchants, and Adriana resigned herself to the fact that she would have to look for him at the butchers' corner, the most disagreeable part of the market.

They made their way to the far end of the oval market, where the odors were strongest from the freshly slaughtered animals, the horse dung swept perfunctorily aside, and the ever-present urine.

There were several butcher's stalls, but clearly one family was favored, with multiple customers all trying to buy meat at the same time. An elderly couple stood at the rear tending a small stove while four young men struggled with livestock in a corral in front. Jacopo was just directing one of them who straddled a newly slaughtered ram and was handing up portions of viscera to another man to wrap. Blood still trickled from the open throat of the ram and ran in a narrow channel to the side of the piazza. The young man glanced up at Adriana and Michelangelo as he wiped a bloodstained hand on his own bare chest.

At her side, she felt Michelangelo suddenly react. He took hold of her arm and said quietly, "I've got to go. Your housemaster is here and you're safe. Good-bye, then." Without waiting for a reply, he hurried away.

"Michelo, where are you going?" she called after him, but he disappeared into the crowd without looking back.

"Ah, Madonna, it's you." Jacopo, the housemaster, turned at the sound of her voice. "Lady, you should not trouble yourself to come here. You'll only dirty your shoes. The wagon is tied up in the Corsia Agonale. Let me finish this purchase and I'll meet you there."

Adriana peered out over the market where Michelangelo had disappeared, then back at the young butcher. He scratched the side of his beardless face and Adriana saw that that half his index finger was missing. Only a stub up to the first knuckle remained.

❖

"Holiness, why am I barred from my workplace?" Michelangelo kissed the Pontiff's ring with cursory deference and rose immediately.

Julius's face darkened. "Do not pretend innocence. You left your assistants idle for two days," he growled, putting emphasis on the word "two."

"What? *That's* what provoked Your Holiness's wrath?" Michelangelo could not keep his voice from rising in pitch. "We've been working without stop for months and we're all exhausted. I simply granted us all two days' respite."

"Maestro de Grassis tells me you also took my chapel singer."

Michelangelo forced calm on himself. "He was personally invited by Lady Borgia, whose protégé he once was." He glanced, puzzled, toward Giovanni de' Medici.

Julius glowered. "Lady Borgia has become a thorn in my side, and one day she will go too far. Cardinal Carafa pleads with me daily to allow him to arrest her."

"But, Holiness, she's done nothing."

"Everyone has done something. She should take care."

Giovanni de' Medici cleared his throat. "Holiness surely has more grave concerns than this woman who has no relevance to any of the projects that are underway. She is not worth a moment's thought. What's more, I am sure that Signor Buonarroti understands his responsibilities in the chapel and in the other new works we have discussed."

Michelangelo started to speak, then grasped that the subject had changed. "May I ask what these 'other new works' might be, Holiness?"

The Pontiff allowed himself to be re-directed as well. "My tomb. I desire, as before, that it be prominent in the new basilica, but I have an idea for the sculpture."

"An idea, Holiness?" Michelangelo was guarded.

"Yes. I wish to be portrayed as King David."

Michelangelo shifted his weight nervously while he formed a reply. "I had thought a more suitable forebear was Moses."

"Moses? The stammerer?" The Pontiff scowled, threading his fingers into his beard.

De' Medici looked reproachfully at Michelangelo. Julius did not like to be contradicted. "Moses, who brought God's Commandments to the world," the Cardinal mediated. "A powerful image."

Julius reflected for a moment, then grumbled, "Perhaps."

"Very wise, Holiness," Michelangelo said softly.

Piqued at having his argument evaporate, he changed subject again. "Now, tell me about my chapel."

"The chapel. Yes. The pendentives of Goliath and Holofernes are completed, as are the Noah panels. The sibyls that run along both walls are finished, and the prophets are sketched out in cartoon. I have several new ideas."

"So have I." The Pope stared ceilingward, as though seeing the final work. "In the center panel, you must paint 'Christ in Majesty,' with the new basilica rising up behind Him."

"But Holiness, we agreed the whole ceiling would address the Old Testament. After the Great Flood, the panels will move backward in time toward Creation."

Julius threaded his fingers again into his beard and narrowed his eyes. "You contradict me too much, Michelangelo. Do not forget that you are my instrument, the hand that holds the paintbrush. That's all."

Michelangelo dropped his glance. When he replied, it was through nearly clenched teeth. "Yes, Holiness."

"See to it then," the Pope growled, dismissing him.

XXVIII

Giovanni de' Medici nuzzled the neck of his favorite courtesan, inhaling her perfume. "What a day I've had, Giselda. You have no idea how exhausting it is trying to keep peace between His Holiness and a temperamental artist."

"Do not let such cares weigh you down of an evening, Eminence. Who is it now?"

"Michelangelo. You know him, the red beard who carved the 'Pieta' in Saint Peter's. He was summoned before Julius again, to grovel, of course, but groveling is not in his character. One of these days he will find himself having to flee for his life."

She reached sideways toward a goblet of fruit wine that had obviously been waiting and handed it to him. "Not all men are as prudent as you."

He took a long drink and licked his lips. "No, they are not. But I profit from being the son of the great Lorenzo."

"Il Magnifico," she confirmed, taking the empty goblet from him and drawing him toward her bed. "Even I've heard of him, and I've never been to Florence. Tell me about it. Those must have been happy days." She sat down and patted the bed next to her.

He eased his ample bulk down beside her, caught up for a moment in memory. "Yes, they were. Though I was with my family only until I was fourteen and went away to study canon law. I remember some of the men my father kept around him—Pico della Mirandola, Marsilio Ficino. Michelangelo was there too, though much less well-behaved. He got into a fight once with one of the other boys and came out of it with a broken nose. He's changed very little."

She unbuttoned his cassock and slid her hand inside over his plump chest. "But that all ended, didn't it?" She knew, more or less, what happened. Everyone in Rome did. But she also was wise enough to know he loved to talk about himself and the Medici.

He sighed. "Savonarola happened, of course, and the French."

"Savonarola?" She knelt in front of him, undoing the rest of the buttons on his long red cassock.

He let it fall open, sending up waves of heat from his thighs. "Yes, an ascetic, Savonarola, arrived in Florence with the Medici blessings, but then he began to make prophecies. He announced that he had spoken directly to God and the saints about Judgment Day."

"And people believed him?"

"Yes, you see, the Medici were losing power in the city. The new century was approaching, and then the syphilis epidemic came. People were sure there was a connection. Savonarola convinced the rabble that the Last Days were coming and that he was sent by God to prepare us. He stirred up enough support to overthrow the Medici and for awhile got to be the new leader of the city. He liked that."

Sitting on the bed again, Giselda helped him slip off the red satin outer garment, then stroked his plump back. "A 'Christian Republic.'" He sneered. "As if all of Italy were not Christian. The first thing he did was to make sodomy a capital offense. A despicable act, to be sure, but hardly worth execution. And then it just got worse."

"Even in Rome we heard about his great bonfire." She pressed playfully against his shoulder. "Did you see it?"

"No, it was too dangerous for anyone of the family to be present. But my serving man went to the Piazza della Signoria and watched the whole thing. They burned everything of value in the city. Mirrors, cosmetics, books, sculptures, chess pieces, musical instruments, ancient poetry. The fools even destroyed paintings by Botticelli and Michelangelo."

"But he was finally overthrown, wasn't he?" Giselda sounded deeply concerned while he opened her dressing gown and exposed her splendid young breasts. He nibbled one of the soft nipples, until it became hard. "Yes. God did not seem to come to the city's aid so Florence became tired of His prophet."

"What happened?" She raised her eyebrows dramatically.

Leaning back, he allowed her to untie the cords that held

his undergarments so that they fell open. Noting with satisfaction the beginning of his tumescence, he continued. "Pope Alexander excommunicated him, then arrested him for sedition. Half a year later they burned him in the Piazza."

He laid back the sides of the courtesan's gown and exposed the full length of her fair eighteen-year-old body. "So you see," he said playfully, roaming her body with hands that had become increasingly pudgy as he ascended in rank, "that's what happens when you spark the ire of a Pope."

"Do you mean that could happen to what's-his-name? The painter?" Now she was teasing him, he knew. She liked him to talk politics while they had sex, and it did not dampen his lust in the least. Quite the opposite. Talking about his achievements in the Vatican had a direct physical effect on him. He took her hand and placed it on his member, which was rising nicely to its task.

"No. Julius tolerates arguments from artists of that caliber, and his successor will too."

Giselda's practiced hand did its work slowly and delicately, and she spoke with a velvet voice. "His successor? That will be you, won't it? Surely you are favored to be the next Pope."

He hardened suddenly both at her touch and her remark. "Ah, Giselda, naughty girl, to say that." His voice too silkened. "We must not speak of such things before their time."

"Then I will speak only of Michelangelo. Will you warn him?"

"Michelangelo will survive any Pope's anger. It is Lady Borgia who is in danger, at least until this tantrum passes. I suppose I should warn her."

He spread the courtesan's white thighs and eased his great bulk onto her, guiding himself into her welcoming wetness. "Right after this."

❖

The innkeeper in the Via Agostino fawned greatly over the Cardinal, kissing his holy ring with fervor before leading him to the room of Adriana Borgia.

She greeted him at the door, made the same perfunctory obeisance as always, then offered him wine.

De' Medici declined to sit down. "Most kind, Lady Borgia. But I will not stay long. I only want to advise you that I was party to Michelangelo's conversation yesterday evening with His Holiness."

"Ah, yes, Julius summoned him. Did it go well?"

The Cardinal chuckled. "As well as can be expected, given both their natures. But your name came up. His Holiness is somewhat put out that you invited both his painter and his best soprano to…well, to what he sees as an evening of truancy."

Adriana frowned. "I hope I haven't jeopardized them."

"That is unlikely, given their value to him. It is you, however, who are the object of his irritation."

Perturbation turned to alarm. "How great an irritation? The kind that results in imprisonment?"

"I rather doubt he had imprisonment in mind. It's simply that he views his chosen artists as, well, *his*, and does not like anyone luring them away. However, his fits of pique are short-lived, as long as you avoid offending him again. Perhaps it would be wise to leave the city for a week or ten days."

"Leave Rome? To go where?"

He shrugged amiably. "Why not a trip to Florence? Didn't you say you wanted to talk with Maestro Sangallo about your garden? The Medici still hold several houses there, not the least of which is the Villa Careggi. My cousins will be happy to accommodate you."

"I don't know. You've caught me off guard." Adriana paced the room and did not know what to do with her hands.

"I am sorry, dear Lady. It's possible I have read too much in His Holiness's remarks. He's unlikely to be looking for blood, but there are always little ways that he can punish you. Keep in mind that the Vatican has confiscated all the Borgia lands but yours, and that only because it was of no great value. If he sees the Villa Borgia as a haven for recalcitrant artists, he might seize it, and what defense would you have against a papal decree?"

"I see. Well, I suppose I could visit Maestro Sangallo as Michelangelo suggested. Only for a week or ten days, you think?"

"That should be all that's necessary. Just allow everyone to go back to work as normal for awhile, and let His Holiness lose his temper at someone else for a change. I am confident that nothing important will happen while you are away."

When he was gone, Adriana packed gloomily, her anxiety in no way assuaged by the Cardinal's assurances. Confident, he had said. She didn't like that word. She had spent far too much time at the Vatican, and then hiding from it, to be confident of anything.

XXIX

Raphaela Bramante hiked up the too-loose trousers of her disguise and climbed onto the high platform as she had nearly every day for months. She set down her paint jar and mixed water with powdered quicklime and the precious powdered cobalt glass of Florence. Soon it had the uniform consistency of cream and the color of a summer sky. She dipped a wide-bristle brush into the mix and laid it in long strokes onto the still-moist plaster overhead. When it dried, the pulverized glass would reflect light downward in such a way that it would seem to shine.

But the wonder of it was past her now. Too much had happened. She painted mechanically between the figures already there and let her attention drift inward to Adriana Borgia, the woman who had driven her mad.

First with the madness of working in the chapel in boy's clothing. Then the madness of serious disguise at Carnevale, a ruse that was, in principle, only slightly madder than the first one. If she could be a painter's boy then, anonymous in the streets, she could also be a gentleman.

At first she thought to only wander through the crowd, enjoying the wicked pleasure of a rakish new identity. She saw the women with different eyes, allowed herself to brush against them in the press of people, bowing in cavalier apology and savoring the flirtation in their responses. No drink had ever intoxicated her more. When some cheerful fellow handed her a flask of real wine, her recklessness increased tenfold. Then, in the Piazza del Popolo, among the race horses, she saw them, the Maestro, another gentleman she did not know, and Adriana Borgia.

Raphaela stayed far back at first, fearing discovery. But she was drawn irresistibly to follow the trio, and she managed to keep sight of them along the Via del Corso and even through the river of the moccoletti flames. Only when the object of her obsession turned around and seemed to recognize her had a final madness overtaken her.

It was insane, she knew, but the hours of pursuit, the river of flames, and the wine had altogether robbed her of her reason. And so she surrendered to the drunken illicit urges that had been alive in her during the months she worked in the chapel and throughout the years she painted the mysterious face.

When Adriana became separated from the men for a moment, Raphaela bolted forward, seized her, and took her to the only isolated place she could think of, a dark confessional. Of all places. In that closet of contrition, a fire swept through her as she touched the other woman's lips. Had it been a chamber rather than a confessional, she would have torn the clothing from both of them and—somehow—ravished her captive. The actual kiss, though she was gentle, was like a bolt of lightning to her soul. When she fled the church, something was destroyed in her and something else set free. Whatever line she crossed that night, she never could step back again.

Yet in the months that followed, the moment began to seem unreal. The ecstasy was so fleeting and the desire unacknowledged. Until the kiss last night in the Borgia garden, with Adriana's brief consent. Yes, it was brief. But, oh—her heart pounded at the thought—it *was* consent.

The creaking of the platform brought her back to the present, and she resumed painting the monotonous strokes of blue. The task demanded little attention and so, in sidelong glances, she watched Michelangelo work a scant two meters away. Reaching overhead he shaped the twisted, bulging musculature of a nude male, laying the tint on the intonaco in smooth, deliberate strokes. In the sweltering closeness she could hear him breathing heavily from the strain of painting so many hours with his head thrown back. He applied the color in a rhythm, never stopping, adding warmth and depth. He called them angels, though figures with such tight buttocks and bulging genitals could hardly be angelic.

She looked at the brush in her own hand, dripping the blue-white color she had painted all day, and she was sick of it. She knelt down to wash it clean. Her abrupt movement drew Michelangelo's attention, and when she stood up again clumsily, one leg still bent behind her, he stood before her without his paintbrush. Resting his elbow on one hand he rubbed his always-sore neck with the other.

"Maestro, I'm tired of background. I want to paint something living," she said, surprising herself with her impertinence. He did not reply, but still rubbed his neck and seemed to wait for her to be more specific. Fearing she had had offended him, but still determined, she clasped her hands together as if in prayer.

"Any of them. Anything with shape. Please."

"Paint the cherubs, then. Over there." He pointed to the cartoon he had transferred that morning, at the base of a painted column. A pair of naked children standing back to back. "If you do it well, I'll give you more of them."

She understood the challenge he was offering, to duplicate in miniature the sheer physicality of his figures. She would prove herself to him. The cherubs were to be paintings of statues, twice removed from flesh. But she could enliven them, as he did, with shading and expression. If he drew them plump, she would paint them voluptuous; if he gave them to her innocent, she would reveal their sensuality.

Everything around her suddenly seemed charged. The light in the clerestory windows, the shriek of the kestrels circling over the chapel, the fragrant pines in the Vatican park—every object swelled with revelation. This is what she'd waited for. As she swept her brush in little curves over rounded angel limbs and torsos, she felt as if she joined him in his creation, so that together, stroke by stroke, they covered the Sistine ceiling with new life.

XXX

Domenico knelt again on the hard floor of the confessional in Santa Maria Maggiore. "Bless me father, for I have sinned. It has been many months since my last confession and I have succumbed again to the temptation of the flesh." The ritual opening phrase of the sacrament comforted him and terrified him at the same time, for it was the first step in a change of life.

"In the name of the Father and of the Son and of the Holy Spirit," the priest intoned, and Domenico recoiled. It was Cardinal Carafa.

His hands began to tremble. Why did a priest of such high station hear ordinary confessions? A man who had already caught him in his shame and threatened him with death. How would a confession before the priest differ from an admission in a prison cell? Domenico froze.

Then, as if God knew his fear and sent an angel to speak through the Cardinal's voice, the confessor said with utmost gentleness, "Have no fear, my son. There is no sin save blasphemy, which is beyond forgiveness. Surrender your guilt to the body of Christ, which is the Church, and be at peace."

At the soothing reassurance of the priest, Domenico relaxed, and it seemed a great weight was taken from him. No, there was nothing to be afraid of. He was in the holy confessional, carrying out a sacrament, utterly protected by God. He did not kneel before a magistrate, but before an instrument of the Holy Mother Church, and here his repentance cleansed his soul. He would be sanctified and joined again with Christ. There was peace in obedience and in purity of heart, and he desperately needed peace.

"I have committed lewdness and fornication."

There was a moment of silence. Then, "Do you truly repent of this sin before God?"

"I do, Father. Now and forever, with God's help."

"If you are repentant, God forgives this sin too. If you open up your soul to receive the healing Grace, I will bear witness to your repentance, for I am the instrument of God's mercy."

"I repent. In body and soul. I prostrate myself. Only tell me my penance, Father."

"You must renounce your partner in sin, the one who tempted you."

"Renounce...yes, I do renounce them. Yet the sin is mine and I take it upon myself alone. No other souls should be tainted by it."

"Souls? Have you sinned with several partners? Have you also betrayed one for another? This too is a sin in the sight of God."

Domenico hesitated again. "Yes. I have betrayed one for another. I let another person touch me because I felt a great affection. But I repent of the act, Father. I renounce it and seek forgiveness."

"With whom have you committed this sin? This person's soul is also in mortal danger."

"I cannot tell you, Father. Each sinner must confess himself and not through another. As for me, I am weary of the iniquities of night and of secrecy."

Through the grillwork between them, Domenico could see the vague outline of the Cardinal's head nodding. Then the priest raised his stole toward him. "What the priest determines on earth, God affirms on high in Heaven. Prostrate yourself before God and mortify the flesh when it rises against you. If your penitence is sincere, God will know it. I absolve you. Go in peace."

Domenico crept out of the confessional emotionally drained, but at peace. All that remained now was to tell Michelangelo.

❖

The prisoner sat hunched in the corner of the coach, his tortured arms draped limply over his knees. He could move them again, but only feebly and painfully, for the interrogators had hung him by his wrists pulled up behind his back and dislocated his shoulders. Still, he was the lucky one, the one who had confessed and given information. The others arrested with him lay on the floor of their cells, flogged to unconsciousness.

The coach was crowded, with Cardinal, Cardinal assistant, four of the guardians of morality, and their prisoner. It rumbled without light along the sordid and pothole-strewn streets of the Trastevere.

"That's the place," the prisoner said weakly. "In the alley just behind the broken cart."

"By the lantern?" Cardinal Carafa signaled the driver to stop the coach.

"Yes," the prisoner replied. "It's the boys in the doorways near the stable."

"All right. You know what to do," the Cardinal said to the senior guardian.

The four men leapt from the coach and crept past the upturned cart and into the alley.

"You've been spared the flames this time," the Cardinal spoke to the prisoner. "Now go and sin no more."

The tortured man seemed confused by the unexpected reprieve.

"Get out," the Cardinal assistant added. "Obey God and never come to this street again."

"Thank you, your lordships." The prisoner lurched from the coach, stumbled, and cried out as he fell on an injured shoulder. He clambered awkwardly to his feet again and staggered like a drunken man along the street until he was out of sight.

"It is despicable what the Borgias let flourish in Rome," Cardinal Carafa muttered. "No matter how many of them we punish, more keep appearing, like worms from a carcass. His Holiness arms for military conquests and stares misty-eyed at foreign maps like some spice trader. And all the while this abomination dishonors the bones of Saint Peter and the Holy See."

"Some say the practice comes from the French," the Cardinal assistant replied, lighting a lantern now that the raid was underway. "Others claim it began after the knights returned from Saracen lands. Foul influences from outside infecting the Roman spirit."

"It's not just Saracens and Jews who threaten decency. Pagan voluptuousness is everywhere, painted on Roman walls and standing as statues in Roman gardens. Families like the Medici and the Piccolomini betray the old values by cultivating the wanton new fashions."

The Cardinal assistant raised the flame in the lantern, illuminating the bony skull of the Cardinal. "You're right, Eminence. In matters of virtue it seems sometimes that the barbarians are at the gates."

"They are *within* the gates. And it is not only the foreigners who have physically intruded and now poison us. Even from afar they infect the Christian soul through that most dangerous of devices, the printing press."

"Ah, yes. The heretical writings that circulate. Very dangerous."

Cardinal Carafa watched the dark street for the return of his hunters. "Dangerous indeed. Burning John Hus at the stake has not stopped his words from spreading like vermin. And more recently this Erasmus fellow plagues us from Venice. Have you seen his latest, *In Praise of Folly*? A filthy attack on the traditions of the Holy Church." He shook his head. "I tell you, Rome needs a scourge, and if God so wills, it shall be me. I am not without allies, as this Pope will discover."

The assistant lifted the curtain and peered again into the street. "They're coming back. It looks like they've got a few. Eminence has been successful tonight."

The guardians dragged three men behind them on a single rope, all battered and bleeding from various head wounds. The one in charge attached the rope to the rear of the coach.

The closest one, a well-formed lad in a red cape, lifted his hands toward the Cardinal. "Please, your lordship. I am a simple butcher, waiting for my brother to arrive this night. I have done nothing wrong." He held his hands in prayer fashion before the face of the prelate and the Cardinal saw, to his disgust, that the index finger was merely a stump.

"Shut this man up, Captain," the Cardinal said, and the officer knocked the criminal with his fist on the side of his head.

The Cardinal's coach started up again, dragging the three felons along the pitted streets of the Trastevere. All fell silent as they made their way to the Castel Sant' Angelo prison.

Satisfied, as if after a hard physical labor, Cardinal Carafa let his thoughts wander. Well done, he congratulated himself. Three sodomites caught tonight. He would catch others in the nights to come until the city was rid of them. There was plenty of crime in Rome: theft, rape, brutality, murder, as in cities elsewhere. It seemed a part of human nature. But he took it as a personal defiling of the Christ when men— virtually under the papal windows—visited their lust upon each other.

He could not imagine spending a single day in any pursuit other than service to Christ, who had suffered such agony for men. The suffering of sinners as they were made to repent, even on the rack and in the flame, was trivial before the suffering of the Son of God. As pain brought one closer to God's Grace, so voluptuousness drove one away from it. And he could not fathom a more vile pleasure of the flesh than two men copulating. He would find them, every one of them, and burn the sin out of them.

Yet there was one who eluded him, maddeningly, by his own contrition. The castrato.

A curious dilemma, to have heard the boy's confession in Church. He could scarcely arrest him after having given him absolution, and so he was torn on the question of which was more important, cleansing God's holy city or keeping the sacrament of confession. Yet it was clear, the singer had relapsed at least once and was incorrigible in his sin. A devil was in him that had to be exorcised.

It would be a sort of chess game, to isolate and catch him in his sin while he was protected. Not only by his own intermittent piety, but by the troublesome painter and the Borgia whore. Both of them caused bile to rise in him, for they were skillful at feigning piety while their contempt of him was clear.

Like a candle suddenly igniting in the darkness it came to him. His Holiness should learn of the boy's confession. Yes, Julius needed to know that his saintly singer had given himself carnally yet again and, worse, by his own admission had gone from one man's bed to another.

That would bring matters to a head.

The housekeeper touched the dozing woman lightly on her arm.

Slouched in an armchair in her chamber, Raphaela awoke with a start, dropping the sketches that had rested on her lap.

"There is a gentleman in the library, Signorina," Bruna said.

"Did you tell him that Signor Bramante was not home?"

"He wishes to speak with you, Signorina. He says he has your father's permission to visit. Very odd."

Annoyed and intrigued in equal measure, Raphaela rubbed the sore muscles in the small of her back and followed the housekeeper to the formal sitting room. Only one candelabrum was lit, and so the high-ceilinged room seemed engulfed in darkness but for the spot in the corner where a young man paced excitedly.

"Livio." Raphaela recognized her visitor with annoyance. "Well, you are persistent. I give you that." To the housekeeper she said, "It's all right, Bruna. I know him, and he will not stay long."

Reluctantly, Bruna went into the next room, though Raphaela noted that she carefully left the door ajar.

Livio Farnese was cheerful, in a nervous, tentative way. "I had to tell you the good news," he said. "I've come into money and I'll have even more soon. Now I can ask your father for your hand."

"Livio, you don't understand—"

"No, let me finish. It is a special position, a secret one, for the Curia. I already have my first assignment. The work's a little dangerous, they said, but that's why the pay's so good. In a few months I'll be able to afford you."

"Afford me?" Raphaela laughed softly. "You really don't have any idea, do you? Look, Livio. I never gave you reason to hope. It's not you, it's just that I don't wish to marry anyone."

"Don't be silly. All women marry and in the end are happy. You'll see. I've already talked to your father and he has no objection."

"Ah, that's interesting. He neglected to mention it to me."

Livio began to pace again. "It's just that, well, my current employment is secret, you see. I may have to be gone from Rome now and again, for certain periods of time. Just to let you know what you are in for."

"What I am in for?" Raphaela echoed. "I don't see how I am part of your intrigues."

He seemed not to hear her and resumed his announcement. "It's so secretive that I don't know exactly who I am dealing with. There was just a messenger sent by someone in the Curia with no other explanation. I am to do a certain job, and when it's done, I'll receive the rest of the payment."

"It sounds pretty suspicious to me. Like something you might regret when you find out what is expected."

"It can't be bad if it's for the Curia. And I told you. It's a lot of money. There's just one thing." He held out a note that Raphaela could see had been opened and then resealed with wax of another color. "It's my assignment. They told me to burn it, but I want you to keep it for me. I've resealed it because it is a secret and you shouldn't even know about it. But if something happens, you'll have it." He made the last remark with such sincerity and warmth that she almost felt sorry for him.

"I'd rather not be involved in this, you know." She sighed. "All right. If it makes you feel safer." She drew out a book from the library shelf and tucked the letter between two pages.

"I'll return in a few days, and you can give it back to me. Then we can talk some more. About the future, and us."

"Fine. Go ahead and do whatever it is they've hired you to do. Please, just don't think you're doing it for me."

"We'll see about that," he said, then leaned over and planted a quick kiss on her forehead. "Good night, my dear Raphaela. Dream about me tonight."

XXXI

Like the Villa Borgia, the Villa Medici di Careggi was a working farm. So although the fortified estate had the character of a small castle, it was not soldiers that Adriana met upon arrival, but a flock of goats.

The day was well along, but there was sufficient light for her to admire the garden from the upper-story loggia. As she gazed out over the flowering bushes, it struck her that she was staying at the villa that Silvio had talked about, where Ficino had held his Platonic academy. She found it inspiring to know she was housed where Donatello, Bruntelleschi, and Michelangelo himself had exchanged ideas under the Great Lorenzo's patronage. Did they ever quarrel? She smiled to herself. If Michelangelo was there, they probably did.

In the first days she sketched out the ground plan of her "pagan" orchard. Between walks in the garden, she refined the details and calculated the costs. Now she needed only to know what the great Sangallo would suggest to add the last refinements.

On the fifth day she rode into Florence, and as her coach rolled north from the Arno along the Via Roma she ruminated on the city itself. Having never been an imperial capital, Florence had never deteriorated from greatness as Rome had done. For all the bloodletting and the shifts of power, from Lorenzo to Savonarola to the Republic, Florence stayed the same, a prosperous city of cloth makers and bankers.

The traffic was heavy and she was anxious. It would not do to insult Giuliano da Sangallo by being late. "Try going up the Via dei Angeli," she called up to the coachman.

She had sudden misgivings about the project. Was she perhaps treading on artistic territory reserved for men, introducing whimsy where they had created law? Was Raphaela's original idea too wild, like Raphaela herself?

Raphaela, whose hands had touched her and whose mouth tasted of wine. Adriana brushed the last thought from her mind, like a strand of hair from her face, but it returned, distracting her. As a sobering antidote, she thought of Domenico, wading in a stream near Tivoli and offering her his flask. Domenico and Raphaela. How she felt torn between them. One was water, cleansing water, and the other one was wine.

Finally the coach arrived before a wooden double door with iron grillwork in its upper half and a brass plate that showed the name Sangallo. A servant opened and led her through an inner court and up a short flight of stairs into the studio. In a spacious, well-lit room were a single large table and a few chairs. On the wall behind it were shelves of leather-bound volumes and folders tied in neat bundles. On the far wall a handsome cabinet fronted with glass contained brass measuring instruments.

Giuliano Sangallo strode into the room. "Ah, Madama Borgia. A pleasure." The servant drew up chairs and the two sat down facing each other at the table. "If you don't mind, we should come directly to the matter," he began. "I'm expecting an important visitor this afternoon and am pressed for time." He held out his hand toward the roll that lay across her lap. "Let's see what you have for me."

"I appreciate how busy you are, Maestro Sangallo, and shall not take long." She handed him the scroll and clasped her hands like a child waiting for approval. Without rising from his chair, he unrolled the drawing on the table, anchoring it at the corners with the inkpots. Adriana saw it now over his shoulder with unfamiliar eyes, realizing suddenly how eccentric it was.

She had sketched out a light pencil grid of some hundred cells. At its center was the old beech tree, and radiating out from it on four transecting axes were fruit and olive trees. Four lesser axes were dotted with flowering shrubs, and between all the radii were classical statues, male and female. The grid seemed to provide an overlay of order through which the greenery and the statuary exploded in a star-shaped pattern. At the far end of the orchard a curving watercourse descended the hill and snaked among the trees. Stone nymphs interrupted its flow at intervals, causing the water to cascade around them.

The architect squinted over the draft and stroked his neck under his ear with a single fingernail. Finally he cleared his throat. "I confess, Madama, I don't know what to think. You seem rather to cross over into quite another world. May I ask what these are?"

"Nymphs and satyrs, and pagan gods. Wild things amongst the fruit trees."

"Hmm." He scratched again. "You will have peasants harvesting fruit among statues. That is putting fine art in vulgar nature. Art is not nature, but its opposite."

She did not reply.

"Let me show you what I mean, from the plan of a similar estate which I designed." Sangallo unrolled his drawing over her own and anchored it with the same inkpots. "You see? Balance and symmetry, illumination of the perfect laws of God."

The Sangallo plan began with a walled quadrant with square towers at its corners. The quadrant was exactly quartered and at its center stood a square house. The quartered land within the walls held gardens, each subdivided into squares of vegetation. She knew without asking that the number of squares counted in both directions would be the same and that the sum total would be divisible by four. The entire plan was a paean to geometric order. By comparison, her work was random and capricious. She bit her lip.

His final judgment was inevitable. "Signora Borgia, your plan has a sort of recklessness. I must tell you, on purely aesthetic grounds, I would suggest significant changes." Sangallo rolled up his drawing and retied it with its ribbon. He let a few moments pass for the lesson to take hold. "Madama—" The servant's knock interrupted him.

"What is it, Marcello?"

"Maestro Sangallo, your other visitor has arrived. He apologizes for coming so early, but his first engagement was canceled and… Well, he waits in the anteroom."

"Oh, no." Sangallo flushed with embarrassment. "Madam, I beg you excuse me. I must admit him. It is unfortunate. Very unfortunate. I do apologize, but it is necessary that I conclude our discussion."

"Of course, Maestro Sangallo." She stood up from the table where her own drawing was still unrolled, mocking her with its amateurishness. Sangallo addressed his servant. "Well, what are you waiting for? Admit him at once."

In a moment, a man in his late fifties entered. Wavy gray hair fell to his shoulders. His face, though well marked with wrinkles, was pleasing, and Adriana imagined he had been quite handsome in his youth. He wore a full-sleeved robe of dark green fabric that reached to his ankles and over it a brick red zimarra of similar length. It was well cut and of fine material but conservative of style, well suited to a man of age and dignity.

"Maestro Leonardo da Vinci, may I introduce Lady Adriana Borgia? We have been looking over her plans for a development of her orchard."

The great man turned his full attention to her in a manner both paternal and aloof. She sensed no special warmth, but a mild courtesy that sufficed in its place. "Is that so?" His voice was as smooth as the hand that took hers.

"Yes, the Signora wishes to landscape her villa, and I have shown her the ground plan for the Villa di Poggio."

"It's the fruit orchard. However, Maestro Sangallo finds my design chaotic."

"Chaotic is perhaps overstated," Sangallo cautioned.

"An artistic fruit orchard. Might I have a look at it, Madama?" Leonardo withdrew a pair of spectacles from his pocket and curled the wires over his ears. As he studied the drawing Adriana braced herself for the second humiliation of the day.

"A working orchard with statuary. Of the gods of antiquity. Intriguing idea. Your design for irrigation from a watercourse with nymphs is audacious, but it will require considerable water flow. You might need to add a reservoir here at the top of your slope."

"You mean you think that the project is artful?" she asked, confused.

He peered at her over the top of his spectacles. "You are crossing lines here, of course. When you mix genres, frivolously and without a purpose, you mark yourself as an amateur. But your plan, Madama, does not seem frivolous. I see a vision here and a vitality in your disorder."

Sangallo had taken hold of the door handle, and Adriana took it as a signal for her to exit. She rolled up her drawing, then offered her hand to both men. "I thank you for your time, and yours as well, Maestro Sangallo. I won't impose any longer."

Leonardo took the occasion to walk with her to the door and into the corridor. "I was acquainted with Cesare, you know. I was an engineer in his service in 1502, I believe. At Urbino and Pesaro."

"Yes, I remember you. It was just that one summer, wasn't it?"

"I had many irons in the fire. And other horses to shoe." He chuckled at his metaphor. "And there were more horses who wanted art than wanted war machines. A pity, though. Some were very good."

He glanced down at the garden plan that she held rolled in her hand. "Do not be dissuaded, Lady Borgia. Inviting the classical images into your industry is very much in keeping with the new ideas. Orthodoxy has its own beauty, but the time comes when one should step out of it."

Behind him in the studio, Giuliano Sangallo cleared his throat again, reminding his distinguished guest that he waited.

Adriana felt a sudden affection for the elderly artist. "A friend of mine said the same thing recently, about crossing lines."

Leonardo started toward the studio, but glanced back and smiled. "I've crossed a few in my time, in my wilder days," he said mysteriously, and waved playfully with his fingertips while Sangallo closed the studio door behind him.

❖

Adriana pulled aside the curtain as the coach halted in the piazza before the Palazzo Vecchio. In the midst of the midday noise and activity he stood there. The magnificent "David."

It pleased her to think that the beautiful boy had marble "sisters" in the Madonna and Temptress that hung around her neck.

As Michelanglo had warned, the statue was long and narrow. Rather like Domenico. Yes, though Domenico was surely less muscular, they shared the long arms and legs, the beautiful brooding face. But the sculptor was evident in the statue too. There seemed to be a strain in his deeply cut frown, like the strain that was always in Michelangelo himself. She felt a sudden melancholy and a kinship with both men.

A fine mist of rain had started to fall, and she called up to the coachman, "Drive on, please. To Careggi." As the coach rolled again over the Arno, one of Domenico's most poignant songs went through her head. *Lacrimosa dies illa*, she began to hum to herself.

XXXII

"Where were you? I've waited for hours." Michelangelo pulled Domenico into the entryway of his workshop and pushed the door closed.

"I'm sorry. You know it's always difficult to get out." Domenico looked everywhere but into Michelangelo's eyes.

"No matter. You're here finally. I've been wanting you all night, and now we've only got a few hours before dawn." Michelangelo embraced him ardently, rubbing his face against the silken hair, inhaling its scent. "You've made me love the smell of incense and candle smoke," he said, pressing his lips against hair, cheek, mouth.

Domenico yielded at first, accepting the urgent kiss. Aroused by the invasion of his mouth, he stood passive in the tight embrace and felt one hand slide down his back to his buttock. The other hand moved around to the inside of his thigh to the softness between his legs, curving around it and then squeezing gently. Heat spread through his groin and he spread his legs slightly, feeling blood rush to his sex. Memory of their last encounter stirred the urge to tear off his clothing and let himself be entered, filled, possessed.

He wrenched himself free, panting, waiting for the fever to subside. Wiping away the wetness from his mouth he pushed away the hand that held his sex. "Mother of God," he whispered.

"What's wrong?" Michelangelo asked. "You don't want me? Is that why you're late? There's someone else?"

Domenico chuckled bitterly. "Don't always be so jealous, Michelo. It's not anything like you think. There has been someone else, but in a way you would not imagine."

"What are you talking about? It's someone in the Chapel Choir, isn't it? De Grassis? Who?" Michelangelo's rough hand grasped his upper arm.

"I can't tell you. I won't tell you. It's not important any more." Domenico looked away. "I went the other day to Santa Maria del Popolo. To confess."

"Confess?" Michelangelo's hand lifted abruptly. "You've exposed us?" He took a step backward, appalled.

"No. I confessed only for myself and named no partner. Forgive me. I had to do it."

"For God's sake, why? I risked everything for you. I can't believe you would treat us so lightly."

"My risk was as great as yours. You don't know."

"Did you think confessing would take away the danger? How do you know they won't arrest you again? Or me?"

"I told you, I didn't name you. As for me, they can do with me what they want now. I renounce the physical. My place in this world was taken from me anyhow the hour I was given to the knife. I've had to live half a life, and that in darkness. Only my soul is whole and I give it to the Sistine Chapel."

"Your body is whole too, Domenico. What does it matter that you can't have children? You're as much a man as I am."

Domenico turned his head away. "I *want* children. You have no idea how much I long to have a family of my own. I'm not given to the world, like you, but to God."

"Is that what they've told you? That's how they justify what they did to you?"

Domenico's voice was tight with new conviction. "Caro, I must believe that what was done to me had a purpose—that it was for God. Otherwise I could not bear the injustice. And if it was done for God, then I must serve Him truly, in the role that He has given me." He swallowed with difficulty, as if something had lodged within his throat. "Don't you see? Either I am God's solemn servant, or I am a travesty." He pressed his lips together, holding back tears. "I'm tired of being a dirty joke of virile men."

Michelangelo's hand slid upward to the smooth, never-shaven cheek. "You're none of those things, and I'll throttle any man that says them. You're better than all of them." He exhaled slowly and his voice grew plaintive. "Please, don't go."

"God forgive me, Michelo. I love you, but I love salvation more." Domenico took the caressing hand from his face. "When you see me tomorrow in the chapel you'll understand that I belong there." As he stepped through the doorway, he lifted one hand to say farewell and Michelangelo grasped it, pressing it to his lips.

"Don't forget, you promised me a saint," Domenico said. "I shall look for him."

Michelangelo reluctantly released his hand, and rough fingers slid slowly along smooth ones until they separated. "And you promised me a miracle."

Domenico ran from the Piazza Rusticucci along the empty streets back toward the Vatican complex. In less than an hour, still well before dawn, he reached the Piazza San Pietro. In the mist, the crunch of his shoes on the gravel seemed louder than usual. He hurried to the side of the broad steps leading up to the basilica along the wall supporting them, toward the north portal. His path would take him onto the narrow street running along the Papal Palace past the Sistine Chapel and to the rooms where he housed. He hoped the gate he had left open remained undiscovered.

Just before he reached the portal he heard their voices, and then he saw them, two ominous shadows atop the wall to his left. He knew the danger at once. They had been standing under the loggia at the top of the steps, he guessed. So easy to see and hear him in the empty plaza.

He began to run and they dropped like predators from the wall directly behind him. In spite of their proximity, his long legs gave him an advantage as he ran down the narrow street adjoining the Papal Palace. He widened the distance between them and calculated whether it would give him enough time to reach gate to the courtyard and to safety.

Then he heard a third man fall in behind him on the gravel. His panic grew and he turned abruptly toward the left, down the alley to the door of the Sistine Chapel basement. Surely they would not touch him in the chapel. He threw himself against the heavy door.

Locked.

Hearing them he turned around again, panting through dry lips. Three men emerged from the mist, and two of them held cudgels. They closed in slowly, like wolves, and one of them called out in a mockery of sweetness.

"Look, boys, it's our little cocksucker." Domenico backed up, pressing himself against the indifferent wood.

The one who spoke reached him in two paces and pulled him from the doorway. The circle closed around him, and on some signal they began to kick and pummel him. He covered his face with his forearms and felt the sudden explosion of a fist in his stomach. As he dropped his hands to his pain, the wood struck him on the side of his head. The concussion made his ears ring and knocked him to his knees. Another blow to his forehead split the skin at his scalp line. Covering his head again, he felt the toe of a foot kick upward under his chest, knocking the breath from his lungs. He gasped for air. Another blow from the wood caught him at the back of the head, stunning him and erasing his vision. He mumbled, fearfully, *"Salva me, salva me."*

"What's he saying, Livio?"

"I don't know. Look, let's just get this over with, okay?"

"Some Latin shit," the third man said. "Where d'ya learn that, pervert? From sucking some priest's dick?"

The wood connected again with his unprotected face, splitting his lips and breaking his clenched teeth. Another blow shattered his nose. Gradually the pain gave way to numbness and nausea until he felt only fear and the fluid oozing in rivulets down his face. He knew then that they would kill him.

Sightless and on his hands and knees, he reached out toward the voice of his attacker. *"Agnus Dei qui tollis peccata mundi,"* he murmured.

"Sounds like he's asking to be fucked. I've got something to fuck you with, pervert." One of them danced around him holding up a stiletto.

Domenico whispered through bloody ruined lips. "I forgive you."

"Cocksucker!" A final blow to the back of his head fractured his skull, and he pitched forward onto the ground, unconscious. When the point of the stiletto was forced into his rectum, tearing clothes and flesh, he felt no pain.

Withdrawing his weapon, the leader prodded the unconscious man with his foot, turning him onto his back. He took hold of a lock of hair that had fallen over the shattered face and sliced through it with the bloody blade. "We're done here," he said, and stood up.

Bending down quickly on one knee, Livio cut the tangled purse-strings and snatched the bundle of coins before following the others.

XXXIII

"Oh, dear God!" In the early morning rain, the sacristan hurrying through the chapel court with his cowl over his face stumbled over the unconscious man. Panicked, he did an about-face and ran to summon help.

Within moments he returned with two priests, who bore the battered form of the singer into the chapel basement. "What monster would do this?" the sacristan lamented, guiding the priests to a bench against the wall where they could lay him. While they draped his limp arms across his chest, the sacristan fetched a lantern.

In the sphere of lantern light, one of the priests knelt down, making the sign of the cross. He pressed his fingers to the side of the boy's throat for a moment. "Send for the Vatican physician. It may be that he still lives." Drawing a pyx from the burse, which hung around his neck, the priest removed a tiny particle of host and touched it to the torn lips of the singer. *"Corpus Domini nostri Jesu Christi custodiat te in vitam aeternam."* He began the viaticum.

At that moment a wiry figure strode through the door and halted suddenly. Two assistants, both carrying long rolls of paper, halted with him. "What's happened?" the man asked the sacristan.

"The castrato, Maestro Buonarroti. Assaulted."

The priest droned absolution for all sins and made the sign of the cross in the air over the body. Then he opened a small vial and anointed the cold forehead and hand with drops of oil. *"Per istam unctionem liberet te Dominus ab omnibus peccatis tuis in nomine Patris et Filii et Spiritus Sancti. Amen."*

The painter stood wordlessly for a moment and then stepped into the sphere of lantern light. He stared down at the mutilated man. His face, illuminated from below, was ashen. His young assistants stepped back into the darkness, waiting for instructions. But there were none. There was only the crashing of the rain on the pavestones outside and the murmuring of the priest. When the sacrament was finished, the sacristan said, "Maestro de Grassis must be informed at once. The boy's family too."

The painter replied impassively, "He has none. Not in Italy. Only a few friends."

The priest made the sign of the cross again. *"Dominus vobiscum,"* he whispered as another man came through the door.

"The physician is here," the sacristan announced. The medicus knelt and pressed his fingers, as the priest had done, to the victim's throat, then examined the swollen face and head. Finally he undid the buttons on the front of the doublet and, pulling it open, he pressed his ear against the cold chest. "He lives, but barely."

Michelangelo knelt down next to him. "Have you no potion, Dottore, to waken him even for a moment? To let him hear my voice?"

"I fear I do not, Signore." The physician closed the singer's shirt again. "There is blood between his legs, from some internal injury, and his skull seems to be fractured. He could linger for a few hours or even for days in this way, but without a miracle he will not recover. If he has family or loved ones, they should be summoned now."

"A miracle," Michelangelo muttered, and got to his feet. He took the paper roll from the hand of one of his apprentices and tore off a corner. With a piece of charcoal from his pouch, he scribbled a note. Then he turned to the older of the two apprentices, who held his wet hat in his hand. Water still dripped from its feather. "Pierro, can I trust you to carry a letter for me all the way to Florence?"

"Of course, Maestro. You can trust me with anything."

"Take a strong horse and leave as soon as you can." Michelangelo pressed the paper into the boy's hand. "The message is for Lady Adriana Borgia. Ask at the city gate for directions to the Villa Careggi. I will pay the costs of the journey."

"Yes, Maestro. I have a good horse and can leave right now." He exchanged a few words with the younger boy and then stepped out into the rain.

❖

Pope Julius dozed fitfully at his desk until his chamberlain knocked and opened the door. "They are here, Holiness."

The Pope rose and drew on a cloak over his alb. "What time is it? Is it morning?"

"No, Holiness. It is still night. The messengers are here. Shall I let them in?"

The Pope nodded and the chamberlain signaled the door guard. As the Pontiff sat down on his high-backed chair, Gian Pietro Carafa entered with three boys. The Cardinal remained at the back of the room while the three boys came forward and knelt, forming a triangle.

"Is it done?" the Pope asked. His fingers tightened over the chair arms.

"Yes, Holiness, just a little while ago." The leader got to his feet and approached with lowered head. Without lifting his eyes from the papal slippers, he held out the dark bundle in his hand.

The Pope took the clump of hair and waved the boy back. He lifted it to his nose, held it for awhile, and nodded.

"That's all. You can go now," he said to the boys. "The Cardinal will take care of you. You know what to do, don't you, Cardinal Carafa?"

"Yes, Holiness. I know your wishes," Carafa said neutrally.

The three assailants edged out backward through the open doorway. The Cardinal followed but at the threshold looked back for a moment and stared in shock.

By the dim light of a single candelabra, Pope Julius held the lock of smoky hair to his face and wept.

XXXIV

Two days' journey, Adriana calculated, if she did not stop except to rest the horses. Could she make it to Rome in time, while he still lived? She reread the scribbled note, but it told her no more than at the first reading.

It was late afternoon. Fortunately her trunk was already packed for an early morning departure so she could leave without delay. She had perhaps four more hours of daylight left. With luck they could make it as far as the way station at Ponte Nueva before darkness. If the moon was bright, as it had been, they could continue more slowly through the night.

The messenger prepared to leave immediately on his own, and she gave him a silver coin for his trouble. Half an hour later she was on the road behind him.

She sat, biting her lip, willing the horses to go faster, willing the landscape to move by more quickly. The coach wheels jerked in and out of the ruts, throwing her from side to side.

As the hours passed and the sun dropped slowly westward, all her memories of him came back. The angelic Spanish boy who came into her life like a blessing, like the child she would never have. He sat quietly behind Juan on the horse riding from Jativa to Valencia, but brightened during the passage on the caravel *Penitentia* sailing from Valencia to Rome.

It was his first time at sea, his first time even *seeing* the sea, so it was understandable that he should be overwhelmed at first. But when he lost his fear, everything fascinated him. Everything, from the enclosed privy that hung out over the sea, to the cannons and the cargo hold and the way the sails could be raised and lowered as needed.

It had not surprised her that on the three-week journey the sailors, rough-hewn though they were, had also become smitten with him. How could they not? He was as beautiful as a girl, and they assumed he was their son, a Borgia princeling. But he also won over the sailors because he clearly was in awe of everything they did. Men who had been driven like beasts all their lives had never known admiration and, suddenly given it, they began to show off for him. They called him over while they stood their watch and told him all they knew. They explained that the square sail was for speed and the lateen for sailing into the wind, that they did not need to hug the shore, but could sail from distant landmark to landmark and by soundings from the bottom. Before a week passed, he was eating hardtack with them and learning about the main mast and the mizzen, the yardarm and the halyards. By the second week, they took him aloft with them, let him climb the rigging, and took him finally to the crow's nest.

Midway through the voyage Adriana began to wonder why their private food supply was dwindling so quickly, before she realized he had been sharing it with the seamen. It was true, the crew's single hot meal cooked on deck did seem pretty dreadful and their beer was sour, but Juan had made it clear that it was in the nature of things. Noblemen ate well and seamen did not.

They had been lucky for most of the journey; there were no serious storms. The three of them stood at the railing each morning, waiting for the navigator to consult the rudder book and the compass bearings. Domenico watched with the men for the "kennings," the mountains or capes or other landmarks, which could be seen far from shore and tell them what port they were approaching or sweeping past. First Barcelona, then Marseille, Genoa, Sienna, and finally Ostia.

When the sea became rough, just after Marseille, she found him with the men praying out loud, the sailors to Saint Elmo and Domenico to Saint Anne. She had no idea why he chose Anne. Maybe for the same reason Brother Martin did, appealing to the kindly grandmother of the divine family.

The coach halted and Adriana was roused suddenly from her reverie. Night had fallen and they'd arrived at the village way station where they would rest and water the horses. She climbed out to stretch her legs and instruct the coachman that she wanted to continue. She would pay extra for the night travel, for the hazards. Unfortunately, only one of the armed guards was willing to travel through the night. No amount of haggling could convince the other one.

She glanced overhead. The moon had risen a quarter of the way up and was nearly full. Though ragged clouds raced across it ominously, they passed quickly and the moonlight soon lit the road again. It was not very cold. Maybe she would be able to sleep a little on the way.

After an hour of rest, the team was hitched up again and Adriana climbed into the coach. She was tired now, drained of emotion, and did not want to think any longer. She wanted to be in Rome. Nothing more. Before long, swaying with the coach, she slipped into a sort of waking stupor.

They had been moving for scarcely half an hour when the moonlight faded and thick clouds rolled in. The coachman had a lantern, but if the weather became any worse, he would have to walk in front of the horses. The canopy would block direct rainfall from her, but the slightest breeze would blow it sideways through the curtains and drench her. The numb sorrow she had felt now became resentment. This on top of everything else.

The carriage stopped unexpectedly. Exasperated, she called up to the coachman.

With a strangled cry, something heavy and limp crashed through the side curtain into the coach. The escort, with a crossbow bolt through his neck, sprawled grotesquely across the seat in front of her. A moment later, an unseen hand ripped open the curtain and pulled her by the hair out of the coach.

Highwaymen.

One of them was on horseback, alongside the coach. Ragged, heavily bearded, in a leather jerkin, he held the reins of a second horse, and a shout revealed that the other one was in the coachman's seat.

In the increasing mist she could still make them out, the coachman, crouching terrified, and the other man who held a knife to his throat.

"You see, Nico?" the one on horseback said. "I told you it was worth coming out tonight. We've got ourselves booty *and* a lovely lady." He nudged his horse in front of Adriana, blocking escape.

Nico laughed in reply and sliced his knife through the coachman's throat. The dying man thrashed a little, and the robber clambered over him to get to the ground. He snatched up the lantern from its pole and leapt into the coach. Seeing Adriana's trunk, he held the light with one hand over his head while he rummaged through it. In a moment he held up the leather purse containing most of Adriana's travel money. She carried the rest, a few silver coins, in a fist-sized leather bag inside her dress. A useless precaution, since they would certainly attack her personally and find that too.

Two men dead and she was alone. She knew she would be raped and brutalized and wondered only if she would live the night.

"When you're done there, help me tie her hands," the one on horseback ordered, grabbing Adriana again by her hair.

"Why bother tying her up?" Nico said from inside the coach. "Just bring her in here and fuck her. I'll hold her down for you. Then you can do it for me."

"Don't be a donkey's ass," bearded one snarled, and dismounted. "This one's a looker. We gonna take her with us, have us a real plaything for a couple of days."

"Oh, yeah." Nico breathed with enthusiasm as he clambered out and fumbled with the rope. "Plaything. Didn't think of that."

"Hurry up, the rain's getting heavy," bearded one said. The two of them hustled her to one of the horses and forcibly swung her up in front of the saddle. Her captor mounted behind her. "Be nice, and maybe I won't cut your throat," he said, his breath foul. Then he kicked the horse away from the road into the woods. Among the trees the rain filtered down as mist, and they had to slow the horses to a walk. "Shit. It's no good. We'll be here all night," Nico said. "We're gonna have to ride along the field north of the village." He yanked his horse to the side, and in a few minutes they emerged from the woods. It was raining heavily now, and all Adriana could see was a wide gray expanse where the trees had been cleared away for pasturage.

Just as they ventured out onto the meadow, lightning crackled, a long jagged line that sparkled horizontally across the sky. A moment later, thunder crashed. Nico's horse bolted and the robber struggled to hold on as it galloped into the meadow. Adriana's horse galloped after it, slowed only by its double burden. Another bolt of lightning cut the sky in front of them. Then another thunderclap hit and the terrified beast reared up, its front legs stroking the air. The robber fell to one side and

Adriana to the other, landing on her shoulder. Stunned, she lurched to her feet. She couldn't run very well with her hands still bound in front of her and knew she had to get out of sight in the brush.

She ran full-out, swinging her clasped hands from side to side, until something caught her foot. She went down, her skirts ripping, her face scraping against the underbrush. This was her only chance, to lie flat on the ground trusting her dark dress and hair to obscure her. Only her pale face could reveal her and, holding her breath, she pressed it to the soaking ground.

She heard him cursing and knew how close he was, but he was as blind as she was. After a few moments the other man's voice called him toward the clearing, and her pursuer left. She waited, shivering in the underbrush, scarcely daring to turn her head to breathe. Finally she could stand it no longer, and she sat up. She was alone. She tugged against the ropes, but the mud had made the knots inseparable. They'd have to be cut.

Lightning flashed again, and she feared for a moment she would be seen by her attackers. But they seemed to have given up. She could just make them out in the distance, moving black spots against the gray of the field, pursuing the runaway horse.

Thunder crashed again an instant after the lightning flash, and she knew the storm was directly overhead. She would rest for a moment, just for a moment, then try to make her way back through the dark forest to the road. If the lantern light still burned in the coach, it could be her guide.

A soundless white flash blinded her. Then the crack of a tree splitting in half deafened her. In the instant she understood that lightning had hit a tree, something struck her, knocking her to the ground. She awoke only a moment later, shaken, her head ringing from where the scorched branch had struck her. The storm still raged, and something unfathomably powerful had almost killed her. She stood up again next to the smoldering tree, her hands still tied in front of her. She thought of Brother Martin crying out to St. Anne. Had she, like him, also been divinely saved?

Or cursed?

Spared death by lightning but battered by a branch. Saved by being thrown from the murderer's horse, but cursed by being abducted in the first place. It was almost as if, hands tied and helpless, she was God's plaything. Sudden rage filled her. For her abduction and the lightning bolt, for the murder of two innocent men before her eyes, and for the rainstorm—while Domenico lay dying.

She raised her rope-burned hands and shouted into the storm. "Are we all your playthings, then? All jerked around for your pleasure? What good are You?" she shrieked. Then, more quietly, her voice breaking, "A world with You or without You looks the same." She collapsed onto the ground sobbing with helpless fury. The sky answered with another clap of thunder.

Finally she gathered her strength and wandered in the direction she thought they had come. While she stumbled in the darkness, bound hands out in front of her, the storm gradually subsided. The ambient light increased and she could see the spaces between the trees now. Most importantly, she could see in the far distance the tiny speck of yellow that was the coach lantern. Numb and embittered she staggered toward the light.

XXXV

A crowd had gathered in the Piazza San Pietro at the foot of the steps leading to Saint Peter's Basilica. Among the onlookers Michelangelo stood, sunken into himself, his face concealed by a hood. He swayed slightly, not from inebriation, for he had drunk very little, but from exhaustion and lack of food. The rain had stopped but it was overcast and gray, and his cape was wet. He scarcely noticed, except to shiver occasionally.

As the cortege came down the steps, merchants in the piazza stopped their cries and the crowd parted, opening up an avenue for the procession.

The Master of Ceremonies, Paris de Grassis, was at the forefront in full ecclesiastical regalia and flanked by two acolytes. As he came close, Michelangelo pulled the hood of his cape farther over his face and stepped back behind the first line of onlookers.

Directly behind the Master of Ceremonies, the full Sistine Choir came in two lines. In contrast to their usual dress, they wore black satin cassocks and their white surplices were trimmed in lace, a dress reserved for the highest ceremonial occasions. They sang "Requiem æternam dona eis, Domine; In memoria æterna erit Justus" while a line of acolytes marched with them carrying votive candles on silver poles. Glass cones protected the flames from the cold, mist-filled wind that wafted over the square.

Giovanni de' Medici followed, accompanied by several of the Italian Cardinals. Behind him, Cardinal Carafa marched alone but for two assisting priests. There was little to be read in his face, but

Michelangelo thought he detected a certain satisfaction. A few of the Spanish Cardinals came along in a cluster, presumably out of solidarity with one of their own. Michelangelo did not know them.

Then, the bier, held aloft by four pallbearers in white, was suddenly in front of him. In the silence that fell over the people next to him, he stared at the remains of the man who had been in his arms only days before.

Domenico was clothed in the same cassock and surplice worn by his choir brothers and draped to mid-chest with an embroidered shroud. Little had been done to repair his mutilated face. His broken nose lay flat, and the open wounds at the scalp were bluish black. Though the swelling was gone, the slack mouth was distorted over broken teeth and the lips split open. Lips that had sung and prayed and kissed. Ruined. Only the eyes, somehow, had fallen slightly open, so that he seemed to look heavenward.

"Forgive me, Domenico," Michelangelo whispered, as his lips, then his whole body began to tremble. He staggered back into the crowd and watched the rest of the small cortege that passed: the dean, clerk, librarian, sacristan, and various priests who worked in the chapel. Bramante had joined too, along with his daughter. A cluster of men and women of the laity, who ought not to have even known the dead man, followed along more timidly. In their midst, striking by his height and his long hair tied behind his neck, the prison guard Claudio strode, one hand hooked into his belt.

As the last of the mourners moved out of the square, the crowd dispersed. Michelangelo remained standing in his dripping wet cape and hood, his arms hanging limply at his side.

❖

Pope Julius stood at a window in the Papal Palace and also watched the cortege leaving the Piazza St. Pietro, feeling sorry for himself. He, the Vicar of Christ, had many things on his mind: the expansion of papal territory, the defense against heresy, the renovation of the city, the construction of the new basilica, the struggle against the local barons, the French, the Venetians, the Turks. "Was it too much to ask for the occasional solace?" he murmured, entwining his fingers in his beard.

But men were not to be trusted, not even the ones who appeared the most saintly. All men were duplicitous, and most dangerous of all was the College of Cardinals. He recalled again the machinations he had to undertake to finally achieve the tiara, even going so far as to negotiate with the despised Cesare Borgia, whose soul surely roasted in hell.

Ascetic piety was for men like Savonarola and his unctuous disciple Carafa. Even Carafa had his eye on the papal throne, just like all the rest of them did. They were all hungry for power. Not just the Cardinals; the King of France, the Duke of Ferrara, the great families, the Turks were all ravening wolves. Well, they had their match in Julius.

He turned away from the window and the offending sight of the funeral cortege. Clasping his hands together behind his back, he half thought, half muttered to himself.

If Carafa thought he could sway him from his military plans he was greatly mistaken. The son of an impoverished family, Giuliano della Rovere had clawed himself up by sheer iron will from the streets of Liguria to the throne of Peter. And the same will drove him to expand and solidify the power of the Pope among the princes of Europe. Let the pallid reformers whine and scribble their laments about misbehavior in the Church or the Roman streets. The Pope was no scholar, but he knew his New Testament. God did not intend his representative on earth to be a simpering wet nurse, but a fighter. *"Non veni pacem mittere sed gladium,"* Christ had said. "I came not to send peace, but a sword."

A sword, a crossbow, a cannon, all could serve God's purpose, even against other Christians. And yet, there seemed to be no end to it. No sooner had he secured a city and defeated an enemy, when an ally betrayed him and he had to march in a new direction. He felt as if he stood on a hilltop, while armies joined him and withdrew, or fought him and withdrew, or fought each other. Through it all, he had to hold his ground to assert the throne of Peter, in the middle of a world that was turning out to be far more vast than anyone knew.

A world that belonged to God, and thus to his highest priest. It was the Book of Matthew that always lay open by his bed, for it was Matthew who told of God's promise to give Peter *"claves regni caelorum,* the keys to the kingdom of heaven." And Matthew seemed to justify Julius's own fits of rage in his parable of the wedding in which the King or God—or the Pope—cast out the unfaithful. Already as a young theology student he had memorized the command of Matthew's

God, "*Ligatis pedibus eius et manibus mittite eum in tenebras exteriores ibi erit fletus et stridor dentium.* Bind him hand and foot, and take him away, and cast him into outer darkness, where there shall be wailing and gnashing of teeth."

Julius gazed out the window again, where the funeral cortege had passed out of sight, and muttered, "Yes, the unfaithful shall be cast out."

XXXVI

Two days later, having passed through the Villa Borgia merely for a change of clothes and the escort of her housemaster, Adriana arrived in Rome. While Jacopo waited in the Piazza San Pietro, she hurried through the Sala Regia. She reached the chapel only to be confronted by the same red-headed Swiss guard who had blocked Michelangelo's way a week before.

She rubbed the side of her face, as if to waken herself. "Please inform Maestro Buonarroti that Adriana Borgia wishes to see him."

With a nod, the guard left her, closing the chapel door behind him. In a few moments he returned, the same wooden expression on his face. "Maestro Buonarroti does not wish to see anyone."

"What? You spoke to him? You told him who it was who waited?" Her voice was hoarse.

"Yes, Signora. I told him."

From the exaggerated patience in his manner, she knew he would not be persuaded to carry another message inside. She took a few defeated paces backward away from the chapel door. Exhausted and demoralized, she turned to make her way toward the stairs and nearly collided with a familiar form.

"Lady Borgia," Donato Bramante said solemnly. "My deepest regrets for the death of Signor Raggi. I know he was very close to you."

"Can you tell me where he lies?" she asked, her voice breaking. "And why Michelangelo will not see me?"

"He will see no one, Lady Borgia." Bramante drew her down onto a bench and sat down next to her, somewhat ill at ease. "He attended to all matters pertaining to the funeral, then locked himself away in the chapel. He dismissed his assistants too, including my daughter."

"What happened? To Domenico, I mean." Her throat tightened as she said his name.

Bramante shook his head. "I know only that he was attacked late at night, in the courtyard below the Pope's chapel. The Vatican has ordered an inquiry, but it's not likely to be fruitful. Murder is all too common. In fact, the bodies of three other men were taken from the Tiber the very next day. From the Farnese family. That is all I know, Lady Borgia. I'm sorry."

"Where is he now?"

"Signor Raggi? In the crypt in the city cemetery. Michelangelo arranged for him to be embalmed before the Chapel Choir held the requiem mass. And he insisted that the boy not be interred but entombed in the mausoleum. He paid the cost himself."

Terrible words: embalmed, interred, mausoleum. Adriana's eyes filled with tears and her voice became high and tight. "When I got word…" She wiped her nose. "I left as soon as I could, within the hour." She took a breath. "I didn't even let the coach stop at night." Another breath. "But the storm came." She wiped her nose again. "Robbers attacked on the road. They killed the driver and guard and abducted me." Then, as if a fragile vessel had carried all her fears and suddenly broken, she wept freely into her cloak.

Bramante's hand hovered over her, not touching. "Dear God. But you escaped."

Adriana nodded, then regained her voice. "Yes, the horse reared at a lightning flash and threw us both to the ground. I was able to run."

"It's a miracle that you were unharmed."

"A miracle?" She grimaced, bereavement giving way to anger. "For me and not for the two good men who were killed?" The more she recalled the event, the more bitter she became. "No miracle for them, was there? Why was that, I wonder? When I dragged the coach with their two corpses back to the village, I tried to hire a new driver and guards, but no one would leave in the storm. It raged two more days. And every hour that passed made it more certain that Domenico would be lost to me. No miracle for him either."

She wept again remembering the ropes that cut her wrists and the terrified horses she had to force along the deep mud with two corpses in the coach behind her—and it filled her with new rage. With tears streaming down her face, she looked at Bramante. "I cursed God that night, and I curse him still. If He's all-powerful, then He's a brute. If He's not, then He's useless."

Bramante clasped his hands helplessly in front of him. "Dear Lady. You must not let sorrow make you say such things. In time, we may come to understand His divine purpose."

She was not listening to his platitudes. Yet, having vented her fury in the outburst of blasphemy, she was suddenly calm. Letting go of the need to reconcile the tragedy with divine benevolence gave her an unmistakable relief. Nature's indifference, she found, was easier to bear than divine injustice. She cleared her throat and spoke almost normally again.

"Thank you for your comfort, Signor Bramante."

They sat in silence again until Bramante took a large breath. "I'm sorry to tell you that there have been other ominous developments while you were in Florence."

"What do you mean?" Adriana searched her memory for anything left to lose.

"Your friend Silvio Piccolomini was to be arrested. For heresy, I understand. Somehow word got out to him, though one can only guess how. A number of persons at the Vatican, including a few Cardinals, think highly of the Piccolomini family. In any case, being forewarned, he fled."

"Silvio, a heretic?" Adriana was speechless, though half a dozen of his remarks flashed through her mind, and it seemed suddenly obvious that he had always played with fire.

"So he escaped?"

"I assume so. If he were in the hands of the Church, I should think we would hear about it. By all accounts he has gone to Venice, which was a wise choice. The Venetians are resistant to papal interference and seem to have a high tolerance for heterodoxy in general, though some call it decadence."

"Then he lives," she murmured. It seemed a small comfort.

"For now," Bramante replied cryptically, then inhaled for another announcement. "His doctor, or rather his father's doctor—"

"Salomano?"

"Yes. He is also gone. He was relieved of his position with Dr.

Ligori at about the same time. Apparently also Cardinal Carafa's doing. Part of his program to, as he says, 'separate Romans from Jews.' He was not arrested, though, merely hounded from Rome. He's fled, of all places, to Constantinople. Who would have thought?"

Wiping her eyes, Adriana looked at the architect with new respect. "How do you know all these things?"

"Dear Lady, I have been puttering in and around the Vatican for over a decade, giving artistic advice to three Popes. I know a great deal of what happens and who causes it to happen. Right now, after His Holiness, it is Cardinal Carafa who is able to do that. I suggest you avoid attracting his attention."

"Unfortunately, I attracted it a long time ago. Do you think he had something to do with Domenico's murder?"

"That I cannot say, Lady Borgia. He was at the funeral and the entombment, but that says nothing."

Adriana nodded, in control of herself now. "In the crypt in the city cemetery, you say?"

"Yes, the large one, on the hill. He lies just beside the stairs on the lower level."

"Thank you, Signor Bramante. I know what I must do now. If you would be so kind to accompany me to my coach."

❖

It was sunset as Adriana's coach pulled along the gravel road into the cemetery, and mist rose from the saturated ground. Adriana drew her cloak closer around her.

A gravel path wound diagonally up a slope to a large mausoleum, one she knew was for those who could afford to pay for entombment in such an edifice, but whose families did not have their own. The temple-like structure loomed black against the last evening light.

"I'll go with you, Madama," Jacopo said. Without waiting for agreement, he unhooked the light from one of the carriage poles and helped her out of the coach.

At the foot of the hill on both sides of the path the common graves held the indigent in wicker coffins or in winding sheets alone. The lowest-lying common graves were under pools of rank water. "How awful to leave them there," Adriana said.

Jacopo shrugged. "They will all decompose, Madama, some sooner, some later. It is only the living who wish to be spared thinking about it."

She thought of her father, whom she had buried in Seville, and the remark seemed crass. "Have you ever buried anyone you loved, Jacopo?"

"Yes, Madama. Two years ago. My brother." He pointed to one of the flooded graves. "He lies there."

"I see."

They hiked up the hill, passing old graves covered with grass and newer ones still bare. Gravediggers' tools, a pick and shovel, stood near a fresh grave. One sensed them all together, the long and the recently departed, and the men who interred them, the quick and the dead. At the top of the hill, they halted before the bronze door of the crypt. Jacopo put his shoulder to it expecting resistance, but the heavy door slid open with alarming ease, as if inviting entry to the hereafter. He stepped through the doorway but Adriana held him by the arm. "No, I'm going by myself. There are things I want to say to him, alone."

Jacopo relinquished the lantern. "Very well. I'll wait here. But please don't be long. This is a haunted place."

Adriana stepped carefully on the slippery stone, her footfall hollow in the cavernous marble-walled space. On the ground level, sarcophagi lay head to foot on two levels, one on the floor and one on a shelf that ringed the chamber. A rotten, mushroom-like smell pervaded the whole place. The cadavers, she knew, were all embalmed and covered with heavy shrouds, but they decomposed nonetheless.

At the center of the mausoleum a staircase led downward to a subterranean space that was still contained within the slope and above the level of the plain. In the semi-darkness of the chamber where she stood, the pit at her feet seemed even blacker, more otherworldly. But that was where she had to go. Her fingers curved around the handle of the lantern smoldered orange red. Slowly she descended, wondering how far among the dead she would have to venture.

But she found him at the forefront. She held the lantern high over the bier and the form muted by the heavy embroidered shroud of the Papal Choir. She thought she was depleted of tears, but the sight of him struck her like a blow to the chest, and she wept again, whispering his name and recalling once again the boy she had ransomed from the choir school in Jativa and brought to the Vatican. How sweet it had been to walk with him through St. Peter's Basilica and hear him defend Rome against her accusations. Rome, which had murdered him.

Setting the lantern down on the floor she knelt by the body. It was the moment to say a prayer, but that was the last thing she felt like doing. Delicately, she lifted the head wrapped in the heavy shroud and cradled it in the crook of her elbow. Inanimate, it lolled limply away from her. Nothing of him was left. His spirit, his comforting words, his ethereal voice: all gone.

She could not bear the silence and so she spoke to him, her voice hoarse with grief. "Agnellino. I still see you on my hillside, looking up at the shafts of sunlight. As if God were somewhere in the sky. Do you stand before Him now?" She looked around at cold marble walls, streaked with black mold, and she was appalled at the thought that he might not. What did anyone know of the Hereafter?

Even with the full force of her understanding, she still could not imagine what awaited him. Or her. All of it, all the vague promises of the Catechism flew in the face of logic. How could God be merciful if his Vicar on earth was not? She trembled, recognizing her own mortality and the paucity of her faith. In all her confusion there congealed a tiny sphere of certainty, that Domenico was more precious to her than faith.

She desperately wanted something from him. Some tangible object that would forever be real while memory faded. An article of clothing, his missal, any object to show that he had been. Then she remembered. There was something precious that linked them.

❖

When she returned to the top of the stairs, it was full night. Jacopo led the way along the cemetery path, and Adriana stayed close, appreciating his avuncular strength and his simple human warmth.

"I can't bear the thought that he died for nothing."

"We all die for nothing," Jacopo said. "Early or late, struck down by sickness, accident, murder. It matters only what we *live* for. I think this young man lived well, and for something he loved." He had never before spoken to her this way, and she trusted that, once they were back home, he would not do so again. But she took no offense, for at the moment, it was a comfort to be at the side of a strong and thoughtful man.

As they retraced their steps, cicadas had taken up their soothing night sounds. At the coach, Jacopo said, "I'll take you to the Albergo now, where you can rest while I stay with the horses in the stable."

"No, there is one more place I want to go, Jacopo. Then we both can rest."

XXXVII

Adriana hurried across the Piazza San Pietro, which was emptying after the evening mass. At the top of the wide stone steps, the church doors were still open and the last of the worshippers came out, talking among themselves. She strode through the narthex and along the center aisle of the basilica, her feet tracing the same steps she and Domenico had taken together. The smell of candle wax was just as before, reminding her how he had walked at her side and now there was nothing. She made her way around the tomb of St. Peter to the apse where the high altar stood. Meter-high candles burned on massive silver stands, casting circles of trembling light on the surface of the altar.

The jewels embedded in the silver gave back the light in myriad faint glimmers. Among them, she could make out nothing that looked like a ring and so ran her palms over all four corners and slid her fingers under the altar cloth on both sides. Nothing. Desperate, she repeated the search, touching every inch of the altar surface and reaching as far under the cloth as she dared.

Gone. It was gone.

She dropped to her knees, defeated. It had been foolish to come, as foolish as the offering had been in the first place. She pressed her hands to her face.

"It's not there," a voice behind her said. Alarmed, she twisted around, still on her knees.

A figure stood a scant meter away, obscure in dark clothing, reaching out. The hand opened and in the palm something small and silver caught the feeble candlelight. "This is what you are looking for, isn't it?" Raphaela Bramante said.

"How…how did you know?"

"You told me. In your garden. Don't you remember? Then, at the funeral mass, when the priest spoke of his piety, I remembered. I couldn't be sure it was still there, but it was, so I took it for safekeeping."

Raphaela pulled Adriana to her feet and they stood face-to-face before the high altar.

"How lovely of you to remember." Adriana reached for the precious object, but Raphaela took hold of her hand and slid the ring onto her third finger.

"I've been carrying it around for days. Cardinal de' Medici said you had gone to Florence, but I didn't know when you'd return. Then this afternoon, Father said he saw you at the Sistine Chapel. So I waited here most of the evening. I'm very good at waiting."

"You've waited a long time too, haven't you?" Adriana stepped into Raphaela's embrace, an unexpected refuge.

Raphaela brought her lips to Adriana's ear. "I wish I could carry some of your grief." She slid her hands delicately along the satin-clad back.

Adriana touched her face to the warm cheek and let her lips brush once against Raphaela's cheekbone. Slowly, scarcely realizing when gratitude and comfort evolved into the amorous, she began to press soft kisses. On Raphaela's hair, her ear, then the corner of her lips. She halted for a moment, as if before a line that marked a dangerous place, then crossed it, covering the pliant mouth completely. In the chill darkness of the church, Raphaela's mouth seemed hot, at once forbidden and inviting.

Raphaela wiithdrew from the kiss for a moment, breathlessly. "This is the second time we profane a church."

"Yes, I know." Adriana laughed softly, kissing her again, feeling her respond. Her hands moved, seemingly of their own volition, exploring Raphaela's clothing, throat, hair, learning the landscape of the new body. Finally she came to her senses. "My God, what are we doing? Anyone could come in." She cupped Raphaela's cheek in the dim light, trying to see it with her fingertips. "Listen. My housemaster waits outside to take me to the Albergo dell'Orso. Come with me."

"No, it's better if I return home first and make excuses to my father. Then I can join you later this evening and stay longer. The Albergo dell' Orso? I'll come in an hour."

"I'll wait for you." Adriana caressed the warm lips with her thumb. "I think I've been waiting all along."

She hurried back through the sanctuary to the piazza, her ringed finger closed in a fist over her chest. "Forgive me, Domenico," she murmured into the air. "Tonight I choose life."

❖

Holding the candle in one hand, Adriana opened the chamber door. Raphaela swept in gracefully and sat on a wooden chair. Adriana sat across from her, on the edge of the bed, with hands clasped over her knees. Her need to rush again into Raphaela's embrace was softened by the sense that they had crossed a wide gulf that night. They were together and safe, at least for the moment. It was a time for exploration, the slow sweet discovery of each other's thoughts and ways, all while desire still grew beneath. Raphaela too seemed to understand that there was time, that she could begin with simple consolation. "Are you all right?" she asked.

"Yes. I suppose so. I've accepted that Domenico is gone. But what troubles me most is thinking I caused it to happen. I mean, did I ruin his life by returning to Rome?"

"Of course not. You had nothing to do with what happened to him."

"Oh, but I did. He had been in the Church for all those years, happily, I think. And then I arrived, cynical and embittered. I taught him doubt. Because of me he learned disobedience and left the protection of the Vatican to go into the streets."

Raphaela's face hardened. "No, it was not that way at all. It was not the streets that killed him, it was the Church."

"What do you mean?"

"Those Farnese boys, rowdies who could be gotten for any little excitement, are the ones who killed him, but someone paid them to do it and then murdered them. One of them was Livio Farnese, who was pursuing me. He must have been afraid something would go wrong because he left this with me." She drew from her bodice a tightly folded piece of paper with two different wax seals on it. "When I learned of Domenico's murder, I was suspicious, but when I heard about the Farnese boys, I knew the note would be important. Read it. It orders the boys to wait for Domenico outside the chapel to 'punish him who is an abomination and a sinner against God.'"

Adriana held the wax-soaked paper under the candle light. "It's not signed."

"No, of course not. Who would be so foolish as to sign an order for murder? But it's on the kind of linen paper that only the Vatican uses. My father gets these all the time with his commissions. It's obvious, someone high in the Curia wanted to punish him, whether for sin or jealousy, I don't know."

Adriana struggled with the irony. "He was always so keen on obedience, yet still he broke out that night. Other nights too, evidently."

"Looking for the kind of love that hides in darkness. I know this love, this smoldering that harms no one and nothing except the poor heart that burns." Raphaela fell silent and simply studied Adriana's face, weary from sorrow and the strain of travel. "You know it too, don't you?"

Adriana turned the silver ring on her finger. "Yes, I do. But I'm afraid of it, Raphaela. Not because it's a sin. I'm long past that. But because of the fury of the Church. Alexander might have looked the other way, but this Pope has Carafa and his Dominicans watching from every corner."

"I know. We're outcasts, the same as heretics. But I don't care. I renounce the Church from my side."

Adriana studied the intense young face. "You can say it just like that? It took abduction and a lightning bolt to push me that far. When did you arrive at this stunning decision?"

"When I began to love you." Raphaela came over and sat down on the bed. "When you spoke my name at Alexander's requiem mass in the Sistine Chapel. I had been watching you for months, but from that moment, I was obsessed by you. I made a myth of you in my mind."

"Yes, Europa carried off by the Borgia bull. You made me a pagan."

"That was no accident. The pagan world seemed so welcoming, so lacking in accusation. It's where I began to 'live' in my mind. I did other paintings too, of Amazons and satyrs and women like us. In a place where there's no Pope, no priests, no hateful God."

"You deny God, then?"

"It's God who denies me. And you. And people like us. Because, of course, there *are* lots of others like us. And for simply loving, the Church burns us alive and then withholds salvation." She shook her head. "I won't have it. What holiness there is, what mysteries in heaven and earth, I will look for myself."

Adriana leaned back against the headboard, breathless, as if she had been running. The two temptations at once—Raphaela declaring a forbidden love and the logic of her heresy—overwhelmed her.

"It has a daring clarity. It's what Silvio kept trying to explain, and Michelangelo kept contradicting."

"It's not so simple with Michelangelo. He has a vision all his own." Raphaela's eyes glistened. "You should have seen him after Carnevale last year. He was filled with that vision. The figures he painted—each one seemed about to explode. I was sure that he burned with the same fire as I did. Sometimes it seemed like the purest inspiration and sometimes it seemed like blasphemy." Her fingers crept forward and took hold of Adriana's hand. "And then I finally understood that they were the same thing, inspiration and blasphemy."

Adriana brought Raphaela's hand to her lips. "Oh, my soul," she whispered. "Where does that put us now?"

Raphaela curved toward her, kissing her lightly on the side of the mouth, while she still spoke. "In a wonderful new place. Don't you see? We are saved not by obedience, but by knowledge." She kissed her again, leaving moisture on both their lips.

"I want to know you, you amazing woman. I want to know all things." Then Adriana was done with talking. She drew Raphael to her and kissed her in return, ardent and unashamed.

They explored each other's mouths, little by little, each letting the other farther in until Raphaela pressed Adriana back onto the bed. Adriana recalled the delicious profanation of the confessional and the temptation in her own garden, but this time there was no wine to dull her senses. This time desire swept through her with full force.

Raphaela raised herself up on her elbow and loosened the fastening at the front of her own dress. She brought Adriana's hand to her midriff and watched as the awkward fingers finished the untying.

Adriana whispered, "Show me what to do, tell me what you want."

"This." Raphaela guided the trembling hand inside her chemise onto the swelling of her breast.

"Oh," Adriana breathed, brushing her thumb over the nipple that hardened at her touch and raising her head to press her lips where her fingers had just been. How sweet the skin of the young breast smelled and tasted. Was every woman this way, or only Raphaela?

Then her own dress was undone and Raphaela's lips were on her, hot and moist. On her breasts, her throat, finally on her mouth.

Again and again they kissed and broke away, and each time they were more insistent. Adriana opened her eyes to know every moment that it was Raphaela she was with.

How different it was from all the times with Cesare, who had fanned her lust like burning straw, and whose climax, like his invasion of her, was abrupt and violent. Now it seemed she waded slowly with another being into molten light.

"Touch me, *cara*. Do everything," she breathed, and Raphaela's hand slid under the wide folds of her skirt up between her legs. Heat spread outward from Raphaela's fingers as they slid into her, and she gasped at the delicious outrage of invasion. Brighter, ever brighter, excitement crept up along her hips and belly. She writhed, burning with it like a heretic, and the rustling of their satin skirts was like the crackling of flames.

Behind feverish eyelids she saw her own garden watercourse and the stream of glistening water flowing down the hill. At its center, Bacchus poured out dazzling droplets. Each thrust and stroke of Raphaela's relentless fingers brought another wave that bore her upward on its froth. She rose with each one, breathless, over Raphaela's hand. Incandescence spread outward through her legs as she strained toward airless heights. She climbed…and…climbed. And reached the pinnacle. Then toppled weightless into honeyed air.

She swam drowsily in the sweet euphoria.

"Raphaela, you are my temptress," Adriana whispered into the damp golden hair.

Raphaela nuzzled her back. "No, I am your deliverance."

XXXVIII
August 1510

"All the world struggles for power, after all." The brutal words seemed at odds with the baby face and effeminate manner of the young Florentine. He dipped his stylus again into the inkwell and held it in the air, poised to write. "But I never saw anyone succeed with such elegance and guile as Cesare Borgia did at Senigallia."

"You mean when he put down the rebellious *condottieri* of the Romagna?" Adriana delved into memory. "I believe Petrucci was the instigator of the conspiracy."

"Petrucci, yes." The young man wrote as he spoke. "I recall also Montefeltro, Vitelli, Bentivolio, Orsini, Baglione. It was a masterstroke to separate them from their armies, lure them into the fortress on the promise of reconciliation, and then spring the trap."

"I suppose so. But the so-called 'slaughter' of the condottieri was greatly exaggerated. I believe only Vitelli and Oliverotto were executed. The rest were brought into line through negotiation."

"Whatever the facts, that single sweep of vengeance, or the appearance of it, helped him finally reduce the whole of the Romagna to a single state. A magnificent accomplishment." Obviously pleased with his own formulations, he scribbled a few more lines.

Adriana could not sustain much interest in the subject. "I'm afraid I can't tell you any more. It seems a very long time ago, and my life has changed a great deal since then."

He took the hint and stood up, closed his notebook, and returned the stopper to his inkwell. "You have given me quite enough, dear Lady, and I will trouble you no longer."

Chatting about inconsequential things—the weather, the landscape, and the local wine—they walked together to the door and she saw him off. While she still stood in the doorway she felt a warm hand on her back and did not even need to turn around. "Good morning, you lazy wench. You missed breakfast. Will you ever learn to keep country hours?"

Raphaela embraced her, still warm from the bed. "And when will you learn there are sweeter things to do in the morning than entertain strange men. Who was he, anyhow?"

"What man?"

"Don't be coy, you heartless woman. You were talking to a man just now. I heard you as I was getting dressed."

"Oh, *that* man. Niccolò Machiavelli, a historian. He wants to write about Cesare." Adriana tilted her head back for a light morning kiss. "Come walk a bit in the garden, darling. It will wake you up."

"A biography?" Raphaela linked arms with her and they wandered along a row of hyacinth bushes.

"No, something more like a pamphlet on statecraft, I believe. In fact, that's the title he wanted to use, 'How to Successfully Rule a State.' I thought it was dreadful and suggested another."

"What's that?"

"Something with more effect, more on the line of 'The Statesman' or 'The Prince.' You know, a title that sticks in your mind."

"Was he a prince? Cesare, I mean."

Adriana broke off a blossom and tucked it into the front of Raphaela's gown. "For brief moments, but very unstable. Following him was like riding along a cliff on a racehorse, always in danger of toppling over the edge. But it was nothing like what I feel here, with you. I can't remember ever being this happy. So much so that I feel guilty."

"Guilty? You mean because of what we do?" The gardener was close by, so Raphaela kissed the flower in place of Adriana's lips.

"Oh, no. I love what we do. I thought that was obvious. No, it's just that we're the lucky ones. Domenico was killed, Silvio forced into exile, Salomano too. But somehow you and I remained unscathed. Every time a messenger arrives, I have a sudden fear that my time has come and the idyll is over."

Raphaela did not reply, but stared into the distance. "I know what you mean," she murmured.

Adriana saw where she looked. And when she could finally make out the figure that rode toward them, she knew it did not bode well.

Donato Bramante was clearly distraught and dismounted with such haste that he staggered away from his horse. He greeted his daughter perfunctorily and turned his attention to Adriana, averting his eyes as he spoke. In a man of his direct character, the gesture was ominous.

"Forgive me, Signora Borgia," he began, and Adriana felt dread erupt in the pit of her stomach. Forgive? Had he come to take Raphaela away? Her mouth dry, she said, "Please, Signore. What troubles you?"

"I was at the Vatican yesterday and speaking with Paris de Grassis. Not a warm individual, but upright. A man I trust. He was lamenting the loss of his beautiful castrato, and we fell into a conversation about the terrible death."

"Yes?" Adriana felt her heart pounding.

"He seemed so despondent that I wanted to share with him that you had mourned greatly too and that the wound was so deep that it made you momentarily curse God. I hastened to add that such anguished folly is common, and when the sorrow heals, faith is renewed. I was certain he would find the incident touching, as I did. But, alas, he did not."

"Father, please get to the point," Raphaela urged.

"The point is that Paris de Grassis said that such a remark, even in the midst of bereavement, was still a blasphemy and had to be confessed."

"Is that all? Paris de Grassis said I should go to confession?" Adrianna was less alarmed than annoyed.

Bramante looked away again. "Mastro de Grassis is not the problem. Later in the day Cardinal Carafa approached me for confirmation of the story. I did confirm it. I could not lie. But I again made the point about the effect of anguish. But he had such an expression on his face—of satisfaction, almost of victory. It looked like he had seized on something that he had been searching for and now plans to use."

Adriana's felt as if she had been struck. "Of course he will use it. He has been trying since Spain to catch me at something, and now he has evidence of blasphemy."

"I feared as much. But from what I understand, his Eminence has to check with the Holy Father before arresting certain people for crimes against the faith."

"How does that make anything better?" Raphaela fretted.

"It makes for a gain in time. His Holiness is in Ostia and not due back until tomorrow. I made inquiries and found out that Cardinal Carafa has an audience with the Pope tomorrow evening, so obviously he is in a hurry."

Bramante looked mournful. "I fear I may have endangered you, Lady Borgia. I am deeply sorry."

"I'm afraid you've endangered us both, Father. But come inside and let's try to decide what to do."

❖

Raphaela opened the window shutters wide, letting the fragrant night air of the garden waft into the bedchamber. "Did you send someone to hire the guard for you?"

Adriana threw back the bedcovers and waited for Raphaela to join her. "Jacopo has taken care of it. They'll come from Tivoli tomorrow morning."

Raphaela opened her nightgown and let it fall to the floor, then slipped into the bed. "Poor Father. I hated to let him go back to Rome knowing he was the cause of this disaster."

"Poor Father? What about poor me?" Adriana pulled herself up to a sitting position against her pillow. "Obviously I have to leave for at least a few weeks, maybe months, until His Holiness can be persuaded that I'm not a heretic—although of course I *am*. Staying in Ferrara with Lucrezia is a good temporary solution, especially now that her husband has his cannons pointed at the papal army. But I don't want to leave you. *That's* the disaster."

Raphaela placed a soft kiss on Adriana's exposed breast. "No. Not Ferrara. I've been thinking and I've got a much better idea. We can go to Venice. Together."

"Venice? Who do we know in Venice? Besides Silvio, I mean, who is probably hiding with a gang of heretic printers, reading their books as they come off the press. He can't help me."

"No, but I can. Just before I started working in the chapel, I painted a portrait of Arabella Raimondi, a courtesan of Venice. She's retired from the trade now and living rather comfortably. She gave me an open invitation, a sincere one, I'm sure, to come and stay any length of time I wanted. She even offered to connect me with people who wanted portraits. She's a little bit like you, and I know you would like each other."

"I never thought of Venice. It does have the advantage of being hostile to the Vatican. A little farther away than Ferrara from the Inquisition. But how do you know she'll welcome your arriving with no advance notice?"

"I know she will. You have to trust my taste in people." Raphaela nuzzled the warm neck next to her. "I picked you, didn't I?"

Adriana brushed her lips against the amber hair absentmindedly. "We could look for Silvio."

"I'll bet Arabella knows precisely where he is, too. She's the kind of woman who attracts artists, poets, thinkers, men like Silvio." Raphaela slid farther down on the bed so that she could comfortably press a circle of kisses around Adriana's breast. Her hand wandered, caressing first the other breast, then the smooth belly below.

Adriana let her legs fall open and threaded her fingers through Raphaela's hair. "I could be happy in Venice, with you."

"Then it's settled. We'll go tomorrow by horseback, when the escort arrives." Raphaela slid farther down on the bed so that she could rest her cheek on Adriana's belly while her fingers traced light circles over the warm mound below. "I'll tell my father that I have an engagement and that we're going for a few weeks. Jacopo can bring your trunks later with the coach." She resumed her caresses, pressing her lips where her fingers had been.

Adriana breathed a soft moan. "I'll only go if we can stay together and keep doing this."

"Of course we'll do this. And this," Raphaela said, as she slid her fingers down the moist groove that waited for her. "Do you think I want to let a single day pass without being inside you and having you inside me," she said, and entered the hot center.

"Not a single day," Adriana murmured. With tight heat rising up from between her thighs, she surrendered to the delicious torment of Raphaela's tongue.

❖

Adriana appraised the two hired escorts who had arrived shortly after dawn. In helmets and cuirasses and armed with crossbows as well as swords, they looked stalwart enough. The groom brought Adriana's two horses from the stable already saddled and with bulky saddlebags over their haunches. Jacopo was just going over a list of instructions on how to obtain funds for the maintenance of the villa during her absence. Though perplexed by her sudden departure, he could at least ensure that it was carried out with efficiency.

"Maria will see to packing your trunks. There should be nothing requiring repair in the next weeks. Since the stables are empty but for the mules, I'll put the grooms to work in the vineyard. Just send instructions when you are ready, and I'll bring everything you might need with the coach and mules."

"Yes, thank you, Jacopo," Adriana said distractedly, her attention drawn to the line of cypress trees where the dust of another rider suddenly was visible. Her heart sank. What new disaster was coming down upon them?

All eyes turned, trying to identify the unexpected visitor.

"It's Mateo, one of Michelangelo's apprentices," Raphaela said anxiously. In a moment he was in front of them. "Is everything all right with your master?"

"Yes, Lady. More than all right. He sends me to announce that the first half of the ceiling is finished and he invites you to see it. Today, before His Holiness arrives."

"I'm sorry, Mateo," Raphaela said. "Please tell him that we have urgent business that requires us to—"

"We'd be delighted," Adriana interrupted. "Come in and let Maria give you some breakfast, and then you can return ahead of us to tell him we're coming."

Raphaela was aghast. "You want ride into the mouth of the wolf? The Vatican is the very place we're running away *from*."

"I know, but your father said Cardinal Carafa would not have his audience with Julius until this evening. He won't be able to marshal his 'guardians' until tomorrow. Surely we can take an hour to see the frescoes and be far beyond Rome when the order is finally given. You know how important the chapel ceiling is to Michelangelo, to you too. Aren't you curious to see your own work now?"

Raphaela looked uncertain. "Yes, of course. But what if we've miscalculated and the Pope arrives early? God help us then."

"We don't believe in their god, remember?" Adriana whispered.

XXXIX

The two horses drew up before the Papal Palace at midday, and Adriana and Raphaela descended onto the bright light of the piazza. They entered the palace at a good pace, seeing no one, passing only the brightly costumed Swiss guard standing in front of each chamber.

Torn between the desire to see the half-finished ceiling and the urgent need to escape Rome, they hurried up the staircase that opened to the Sala Regia. Mateo met them and led them to the chapel.

Michelangelo appeared before the chapel doorway in clean clothing, unstained by plaster or pigment. And yet he looked exhausted, like a man who had not slept for days. The dark circles around his eyes and the scar on his broken nose stood out against the pale, light-starved skin of his face.

"You are the first, you know." The thumb of his right hand rubbed nervously against his fingertips, as if he constantly rubbed off paint. "Not even the Holy Father has been here. The official half-mark viewing is tomorrow."

"We're honored, Maestro," Raphaela said. "I'm only sorry I couldn't continue to assist you. We've worried about you for months."

"I've been busy," he mumbled, stating the obvious, and swung the double doors wide open to the newly painted chapel.

The effect was startling. The scaffolding had been dismantled and partly reconstructed at the far end of the chapel, reversing the pattern of the past year. Together with the adjoining walls, the dark wood of the scaffold provided a sort of framework for the newly finished work.

Contained within the outline, the explosion of color and activity drew the eye immediately upward. Brightly painted figures seemed to writhe and turn in all directions over the observer's head. It was dazzling.

"It will need some explaining," Michelangelo began. "That's the reason I—"

"Maestro Buonarroti! Signore." Mateo burst in.

"What is it?" He was obviously annoyed.

"The Holy Father is downstairs. He wants to see the ceiling."

"Christ's nails!" Michelangelo pounded his fist on the doorpost. For a moment they stood paralyzed within the entry, sensing the lupine footfall on the stairway, the ominous silken steps of the papal slipper.

"You can't let him see us," Adriana said, awakening to the danger. She took hold of his arm. "Look, Cardinal Carafa is about to meet with him to convince him to have me seized for heresy. It's a long story, but we're on our way to Venice. We thought we'd have time to see everything. But we don't. We've *got* to leave now."

"No, you *must* see it. I'll stop him." His face grew hard. "I'll tell him there's damage. I'll hold him off a day." Without waiting for their agreement, Michelangelo pushed them back into the chapel and pulled the double doors firmly shut behind him.

They looked at one another for a moment, uncertain. Then Raphaela shrugged. "We can escape through the service door, if necessary. In the meantime, let me at least show you quickly what the two of us did together."

Adriana glanced nervously toward the chapel portal. "As long as he can keep Julius away."

Raphaela stepped forward and opened both arms, encompassing the entire work. "There is a sort of framework with three layers: the actual architecture, the painted one, and then the stories. It takes a bit of staring to figure it out."

Adriana tried to focus her attention. "It doesn't take long to figure *those* out, though, all those nude men." She swept her finger in a wide circle, indicating the dozen or so nude figures in twisted poses.

Raphaela chuckled. "He calls them angels, but they look pretty earthly to me. Like real people."

"That one *is* real. I recognize him." Adriana pointed at the figure, which slouched over the northern pendentive. He turned in a graceful curve, supporting his upper body on his left arm while his right arm dangled between his open thighs. The head, haloed by reddish curls, was turned flirtatiously toward the right, and the twist of his body both exposed and delineated the fine musculature of his neck and chest.

"You're right," Raphaela agreed. "It's the halberdier who stood guard at the chapel when we were painting. He certainly looks different without his pretty pants."

"I know that one too." Adriana pointed. "The jailor's son—from the prison at Sant'Angelo. And that one on the right is sitting just as he was in the prison guardroom the night we saved Domenico." She glanced around at the others.

"That sly dog. He's painted a whole troop of naked guards."

Adriana ventured a few paces along the wall of the chapel and peered up at the ring of men and women seated on the periphery of the ceiling. "And these?"

"Prophets and sibyls."

"The sibyls look like men. Wait. I recognize them. They're from the Carnevale parade."

"He's even copied their dresses and their books." Raphaela chuckled. "I helped him paint them."

"A nice tribute to Silvio Piccolomini."

Raphaela stepped toward the southeast corner of the chapel and stared intently at the figure. Resting on his right elbow, a beardless gray-haired man peered down at a scroll outstretched between his two hands. His high forehead, hairless and smooth, gave his face a pedagogical air. The red cloak draped over his shoulders and lying across his lap was unmistakable.

"It's your father," Adriana murmured. "Incredible. Donato Bramante as the prophet Joel and sitting the same way as he did at my supper. And the scroll he's reading from is Michelangelo's note to him."

"I wonder who the others are," Raphaela said. "It's like a puzzle, isn't it?" They crossed diagonally to the second bay and studied its prophet.

The twisted posture gave it away finally, the posing of a man inclined toward drama and display. Holding his place in the great book he had been reading, he seemed about to reply to some annoying question, disdain and condescension on his face.

"It's Silvio," Adriana exclaimed. "He's put Silvio on the ceiling, clutching his Ficino translation the moment he reproached Michelangelo for not knowing Plato." She laughed out loud. "He was even wearing that exact rose tunic with the yellow sleeves. Colors no one else would wear. We teased him for it." She laughed again. "In exile, but still insulting the Pope. If we see him in Venice we'll have to tell him."

Raphaela glanced nervously toward the door. "I wish he'd hurry back so that we can *get* to Venice. Let's try to figure it out without him. It'll save time." They crossed again to the south wall. "The prophet Ezekiel," Raphaela read. "Anybody you know?"

A massive male body, his head, small by comparison, was dignified by a short white beard. A pale blue shawl covered his head and was thrown across his wide shoulders. He leaned toward the right, opening his hand as if offering a compelling new argument. The power contained in the turning of his huge shoulders suggested that the artist respected him and his argument as well.

"I can't believe he would dare to do it. It's Baldassare Salomano, the Jewish doctor who saved my life. He sat that way exactly, next to my bed, arguing with Michelangelo about God."

"Cardinal Carafa won't like that. He hounded the man from Rome."

"I imagine Julius wouldn't care for it either, if he knew."

"I'm sure Michelangelo will not tell him that his sibyls and his Hebrews are laughing at him."

Adriana shook her head. "In Spain he would burn for this!"

❖

"Then he should be thankful that he does not live in Spain," Michelangelo said from the doorway.

Adriana was relieved. "Did you get rid of him?"

"Only for an hour. So come along, there's a lot to see."

"An hour?" Adriana was all but wringing her hands. "It has to be quick, then. Listen, we've already recognized your angels and sibyls, and know that your prophets are Bramante and Salomano and Silvio. Very amusing, but we have to go."

"Amusement is not what I intended," he muttered, drawing them back to the chapel entryway. "Here is where it starts." He pointed directly overhead to the first panel, of an old man lying on the ground, with three younger ones slouching over him. It was not at all amusing. "Noah shamed by his sons," Michelangelo said.

"Very powerful, and I know where you got it, too," Adriana said. "It's the drunken King who collapsed on the Via del Corso at Carnevale. Those two are Farnese boys. You remembered the whole scene, in spite of the darkness."

They were under the next panel and Raphaela tilted her head back. "I will always think of that as 'our' Deluge, Maestro. Some of it's still under my nails."

"How many of your friends or enemies are in the flood?" Adriana interjected.

He looked up at the chaotic scene. "Too many to tell."

Adriana was already studying the third panel, of four men preparing a burnt offering. "Noah's Sacrifice," Michelangelo announced. "In case it's not evident."

Four young men were crowded into a small space struggling with animals. One of them, in a red cape, knelt over a slaughtered ram and handed some of its flesh up to another man, obviously for a burnt offering. The index finger of his left hand appeared truncated at the first joint.

"The young one, the pretty one in the cape. That's the butcher boy in the Piazza Navona, isn't it?"

"Yes, he was arrested by Carafa's guardians and brutally flogged." Michelangelo grew solemn. "This was all I could do for him."

Raphaela had hurried ahead of them, but stopped. "What…is that?"

Adriana joined her and also halted abruptly, incredulous. It was all too familiar. The rocks, the small forked tree, the leafy branch under Adam's hands. She had found the portrait that he promised her, in the Garden of Eden. "You bastard," she whispered.

A red-haired Adam, who seemed a younger, more muscular version of Michelangelo himself, grasped a tree branch, as if in shock. The disobedient Eve, bulky and nude, knelt before him with her face mere centimeters from his penis. And Eve, her head turned away, had the face of Adriana Borgia.

"You bastard," she repeated out loud. "It's your revenge, isn't it, for my refusing you that night at the Villa Borgia. You painted the exact moment when I heard Raphaela call me. Is that what you were thinking of? Us doing *that*?" She snorted and stared up at the panel again. "And why is the snake a woman? Oh, I see."

It took only a moment to recognize the face and to grasp the accusation. For it *was* an accusation, that what had turned her head from the righteous appeal of the man, tempting her with forbidden knowledge, was Raphaela. The amber-colored hair, the intelligent face, the full lips parted were unmistakable. So also was the posture in which he had painted her. He had combined their nighttime confrontation in the garden with that of the orchard the next morning, so that while Adam grasped the branch in shock, the blond temptress reached out her arm through the forked tree to drop something into the hand of Eve.

It was as if he intuited what was going on among the three of them long before she understood it herself. Her rejection of him had obviously shaken him so much that he made it the model for the world's first sin.

She stared, speechless, trying to make sense of the wide double scene, disobedience on the one side and the expulsion on the other. But God's expelling angel revolved around the same axis and had the same sensual face and outstretched arm as the snake. Thus, Adriana's Eve turned away from the man's sex toward the Raphaela-snake and then was led away from innocence by the Raphaela-angel.

"Why have you done this?" Adriana was losing patience. She was about to run for her life, and the last thing she needed to do was see insulting pictures of herself.

Michelangelo shrugged. "You asked for a portrait."

"Not *that* kind of portrait. It's filthy. And why have you made Raphaela the face of both evil and good?"

"I'm surprised you're thrown by my little ironies," he said calmly. Have you forgotten the amulet I gave you?"

"The seductress-and-saint medallion. No, I haven't forgotten it. But why Raphaela?"

"Because she *was* those things. And I created her. Which takes us to the center panel."

The same dreamy-eyed profile, the same full lips of the snake-woman and the angel, were now on the imploring face of Eve at the moment of her creation. Supported on one leg, the other one bent and caught behind her, Eve looked toward her maker. Raphaela recognized herself immediately.

"That's me, on the platform begging to paint real figures," Raphaela said. "You 'created' me and then I disappointed you? Is that how you see it? It's too bad we have no time for me to tell you I don't like it." All nerves, she shifted her weight from one foot to the other, in a sort of minute pacing, edging toward the exit.

Michelangelo shook his head. "It's not a reproach, but it's true. I brought you into the picture—my life's picture—and now all three of us are fallen. In any case, this is how I understand creation, sin, redempt—"

The chapel doors flew open with a bang and Mateo ran in again. "His Holiness is on the stairs. With Cardinal Carafa."

Adriana jumped at the name. "Carafa? They've met then." She took a step away from Michelangelo. "We have to get out of here. Right now."

"No, not yet!" Michelangelo sprinted toward the entrance. He threw the double doors closed and barred them.

"Maestro, it's His Holiness," Mateo cried. Michelangelo rushed back to where Adriana and Raphaela were halfway to the service door. He seized Adriana by the arm and pulled her back to the center of the chapel. "One more panel!" He stood behind her, holding her in place by her upper arms. "Look. You must see it before he does. Before he orders it changed."

With growing panic, Adriana forced herself to look up, and she staggered. For a moment she forgot her fear. And she forgave him.

Overhead, the virile muscular body of Adam curved languidly against the green earth. Tilting his head back, he reached out dreamily with his left hand to touch the finger of his creator. And God's first creature in His image, the father of the world, from whose loins all humankind would spring, had the face of Domenico Raggi. The thick brown hair hung back, as if he had just run his fingers through it, and the full muscle around his lips recalled the smooth skin she had caressed. That Michelangelo, of course, had caressed.

She lowered her gaze, hearing the angry pounding on the chapel door.

Michelangelo loosened his grip and stood before her, at once noble and pathetic, his face haggard, his painter's hands fallen idle to his sides. She understood him now. It was his revenge. He had cast into the images of orthodoxy the drama of his own life and populated the Pope's chapel with the faces of humanists, skeptics, and sodomites. Raphaela was right. His blasphemy was his inspiration.

The pounding was more insistent, and she retreated again. "It's God's backside, isn't it?" She could not wait for an answer. "It's magnificent," she said with utter sincerity, backing toward the escape door. "Don't let him make you change anything. Lie to him, tell him whatever you have to. Domenico must stay." Then Raphaela seized her hand and pulled her into the service corridor.

They lingered a moment behind the almost-closed door and peered through the crack as Mateo yanked up the bolt and the Pope burst in, Cardinal Carafa a step behind him. She could not see Michelangelo, but she knew he genuflected and she heard him speak.

"Holiness."

They slipped along the narrow corridor quietly and at the end, Raphaela whispered, "It's heresy, isn't it? The whole ceiling."

"The most splendid heresy in Christendom. I wonder if anyone will ever know it."

POSTSCRIPT

While the novel clearly stretches historical "facts," or what pass as facts, to suit a plot and sensibility that is LGBT, the historical context and most of the characters are authentic. Michelangelo did indeed follow a painting schedule that began in May 1508 and halted temporarily after the Creation of Adam panel, in August 1510. He resumed work some time in 1511 and completed the ceiling in 1512. Under Pope Paul III he also painted the grim "Last Judgment" on the altar wall, portraying himself as an empty skin. He completed a much-reduced version of Julius's tomb in 1545, although in San Pietro in Vincoli rather than in the basilica. As hinted by Giovanni de' Medici, Michelangelo was finally put in charge of the design of St. Peter's Basilica (after both Julius's and Bramante's death) from 1546 until the end of his life.

While there is no clear evidence that Michelangelo engaged in sex with men, there is even less evidence that he ever did so with a woman, and he lived to be eighty-eight. In any case, even the weakest "gaydar" can register signs of homoeroticism all over the Sistine Chapel ceiling. In addition, in spite of the Church's ferocious condemnation, homosexuality appears to have been widespread at the time and is often referred to in contemporaneous written accounts.

The lovely and pious Domenico is an anachronism. Although there were castrati in the Sistine Choir during the 1600s, they are recorded by name only at the end of that century. Castrated men, particularly those who performed in a secular context, are thought to have engaged sexually with both men and women, much like modern rock stars. In 1902 Pope Leo XIII signed the order banishing castrati from the choir.

Giovanni de' Medici, as he kept hinting, did succeed Julius as pope (Leo X 1513). His papacy was marked by a continuation of the Sale of Indulgences to finance St. Peter's Basilica and, later, by his bull Exsurge Domine (1521), which excommunicated Martin Luther for his 95 Theses.

Eventually, the grim ascetic Gian Pietro Carafa also became pope although, during the period of the novel, he was not yet even a cardinal. As Adriana feared, the Inquisition did indeed come to Rome and Carafa was its agent. Initially he was appointed by Pope Paul III as Head of the Holy Office charged with trying heretics. After he himself became Pope Paul IV (1555) he expanded the office to full Inquisitional force to counter the threat of Protestantism. He also ordered the segregation of Roman Jews.

Martin Luther did in fact become a monk as the result of a lightning strike. According to historical accounts, he went to Rome as a young monk where he climbed the steps of the Lateran Church on his knees, but it would be another eight years before he would nail on the Wittenberg church door his 95 theses criticizing the selling of indulgences.

God's backside is an actual biblical image (Exodus 33). And some time during 1512, Michelangelo in fact painted the Divine Derriere—provocatively attractive—in the eighth bay of the Sistine Chapel ceiling,

Silvio and his falcon are fictional, but the Piccolomini family is not. A prominent family from Sienna, they put two popes on the throne, the most famous of which was the humanist Eneas Silvio Piccolomini (Pius II 1458).

Adriana Borgia is fictional, but many Borgia men and women survived the end of the Borgia papacy, and the family line lasted until the eighteenth century.

Juan, Cesare, and Lucrezia were the three most famous of the eight known children of Rodrigo Borgia (Alexander VI). The boys came to a bad end, but Lucrezia lived and maintained a cultured court until 1519 as the Duchess of Ferrara.

Raphaela Bramante is fictional, but modeled on the extraordinary Artemesia Gentileschi (1593–1652), who resided with her father in Rome, Florence, and Genoa. Her most famous painting is *Judith Slaying Holofernes* (1614), though her sexual preference is not known.

Baldessare Salomano is fictional, but the immigrant wave that brought him to Rome in 1492 is historical. Pope Alexander VI, for all his venial sins, was wise enough to see the value of having Jewish merchants and professionals added to the Roman population.

Infrastucture, clothing, food, weaponry, politics, and plumbing are historically accurate to the degree possible for an amateur historian. While the author has tried to maintain a certain archaic flavor in the language, the use of modern American English and the desire to increase readability has allowed for certain linguistic anachronisms.

About the Author

Having traveled through much of the Arab world, Justine Saracen lost her heart early on to the desert. Together with her Egyptologist partner, she became immersed in the colorful theology of ancient Egypt, a fascination that led to the Ibis Prophecy books. The playful first novel, *The 100th Generation*, was nominated for the Ann Bannon Reader's Choice award and was a finalist in the Queerlit Competition. The sequel, *Vulture's Kiss*, focuses on the first crusade and vividly dramatizes the dangers of militant faith.

More recently, the Brussels-based author explores what religion has historically done to gay men and women. Her most daring work to date is *Sistine Heresy*, an imagined "backstory" to Michelangelo's Sistine Chapel frescoes, and a blasphemy if ever there was one.

Having had it out with the Church, Justine also faces down the devil in *Mephisto Aria* (Bold Strokes Books, forthcoming 2010), her own queer Faust story. In Berlin, staggering toward recovery after WWII, a Russian soldier passes on his brilliance, but also his mortal guilt, to his opera singer daughter.

All part of Justine's lifelong effort to "plant our flag retroactively on the literary and historical landscape." You can visit her at her Web site at http://justinesaracen.googlepages.com.

Books Available From Bold Strokes Books

Sistine Heresy by Justine Saracen. Adrianna Borgia, survivor of the Borgia court, presents Michelangelo with the greatest temptations of his life while struggling with soul-threatening desires for the painter Raphaela. (978-1-60282-051-7)

Radical Encounters by Radclyffe. An out-of-bounds, outside-the-lines collection of provocative, superheated erotica by award-winning romance and erotica author Radclyffe. (978-1-60282-050-0)

Thief of Always by Kim Baldwin & Xenia Alexiou. Stealing a diamond to save the world should be easy for Elite Operative Mishael Taylor, but she didn't figure on love getting in the way. (978-1-60282-049-4)

X by JD Glass. When X-hacker Charlie Riven is framed for a crime she didn't commit, she accepts help from an unlikely source—sexy Treasury Agent Elaine Harper. (978-1-60282-048-7)

The Middle of Somewhere by Clifford Henderson. Eadie T. Pratt sets out on a road trip in search of a new life and ends up in the middle of somewhere she never expected. (978-1-60282-047-0)

Paybacks by Gabrielle Goldsby. Cameron Howard wants to avoid her old nemesis Mackenzie Brandt but their high school reunion brings up more than just memories. (978-1-60282-046-3)

Uncross My Heart by Andrews & Austin. When a radio talk show diva sets out to interview a female priest, the two women end up at odds and neither heaven nor earth is safe from their feelings. (978-1-60282-045-6)

Fireside by Cate Culpepper. Mac, a therapist, and Abby, a nurse, fall in love against the backdrop of friendship, healing, and defending one's own within the Fireside shelter. (978-1-60282-044-9)

Green Eyed Monster by Gill McKnight. Mickey Rapowski believes her former boss has cheated her out of a small fortune, so she kidnaps the girlfriend and demands compensation—just a straightforward abduction that goes so wrong when Mickey falls for her captive. (978-1-60282-042-5)

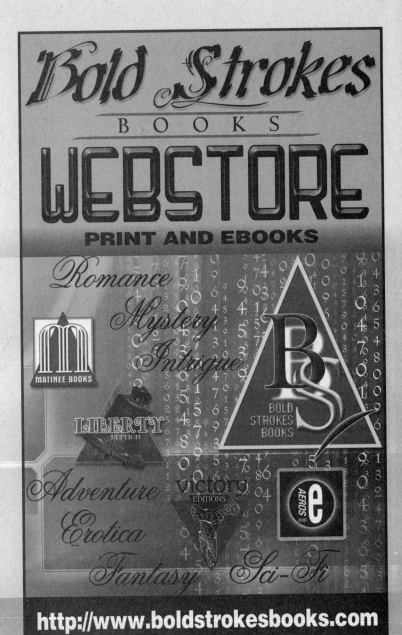